THE
ECHO
ROOM

ALSO BY PARKER PEEVYHOUSE

Where Futures End (a novella collection)

THE
ECHO
ROOM

PARKER PEEVYHOUSE

**TOR
TEEN**

A TOM DOHERTY ASSOCIATES BOOK
NEW YORK

THE ECHO ROOM

Copyright © 2018 by Parker Peevyhouse

A Tor Teen Book
Published by Tom Doherty Associates
175 Fifth Avenue
New York, NY 10010

www.tor-forge.com

Tor® is a registered trademark of Macmillan Publishing Group, LLC.

The Library of Congress Cataloging-in-Publication Data is available upon request.

ISBN 978-0-7653-9939-7 (hardcover)
ISBN 978-0-7653-9941-0 (ebook)

Our books may be purchased in bulk for promotional, educational, or business use. Please contact your local bookseller or the Macmillan Corporate and Premium Sales Department at 1-800-221-7945, extension 5442, or by email at MacmillanSpecialMarkets@macmillan.com.

First Edition: September 2018

Printed in the United States of America

0 9 8 7 6 5 4 3 2 1

for my dad, for introducing me to so many great stories

THE
ECHO
ROOM

5:37 A.M.

Someone is calling to me . . .

Rett woke to the cold press of metal beneath him and the knock of pain against the inside of his skull.

He opened his eyes. Metal room, blue with early morning light. The only window a skylight in the high ceiling.

He pushed himself upright. Diagonal yellow stripes banded the walls, constricting the room. The smell of dust and copper made the air heavy.

Where am I?

The place had an industrial feel to it: steel and dust and gloom. Cast in blue, like the prison panel he'd drawn in ballpoint pen for *Epidemic X*.

Cheerful.

His head throbbed. His skull was shrinking, or his brain was outgrowing it. He put a shaking hand to where the pain cut worst, and his fingers found the long, raised line of a scar. His stomach turned.

He got to his feet, pressed by the familiar weight of urgency that drove him from bed every morning: *Look out for yourself, watch out.*

He shouldn't be here. He should be lining up for morning

roll call with the other wards of Walling Home, wary of sharp looks cutting his way, sharper blades bristling under mattresses. Only scrap paper and a pen under his own mattress, along with the last remaining issue of his favorite comic.

Whatever this place is, I don't think I want to be here. The room was empty. Stark, barren. But a pricking sense of caution kept him on his guard. He'd known other empty places, knew how quickly they could fill with dread. Like the entryway at Walling Home, where the tick of the clock had beat like a hammer against his heart as he'd watched his mother walk out the door and leave him behind.

His attention snapped back to the present as a sound broke through his thoughts. Someone calling to him?

No—somewhere, someone was singing.

He tensed, unnerved. *What is this place?*

A wave of dizziness hit him. He leaned against the wall, which slanted oddly, tilted back as if the room knew he needed to lie down. He struggled to clear his mind, to look around for some clue as to where he was. Doorway to his left, corridor to his right. Skylight, stripes, metal floor.

A broad luminescent strip running along the wall.

He followed the glowing strip out of the room and down a short corridor to a door with a huge sliding lock.

Bolted shut.

Panic shot through him. He hefted his weight against the lock but it didn't so much as budge. He took a shaky step back to examine it. The lock was jammed, the metal bolt bent at one end. And there—on the floor: a fire extinguisher large enough to have done the damage. Rett tried to ignore the panic that flared again. *There's no way that bolt's ever coming out of its housing.*

An image glowed on the door, reflecting the dim light: overlapping, jagged lines. *Spikes of pain*, Rett thought absently while his head went on throbbing. Set above the spidery graph was a single word: SCATTER. And next to it, the number three inside a circle.

Scatter 3, Rett thought, testing the phrase for familiarity. A metallic taste filled his mouth and sent a fresh twinge of pain through his head. *Scatter 3*. Yes, there was something about those words. It would come back to him in a minute.

Or . . .

He could ask whoever possessed the eerie voice still echoing through the place. The meditative tune pulled at Rett with an almost hypnotic power. He hesitated. Tried not to imagine himself as a doomed figure in one of the comics he had drawn while he huddled in closets or underneath stairwells at the boarding facility he called home. *Boy, sixteen, ladder of bones, seen from behind as he slinks through an abandoned storage room, a warehouse for dust. Caption: He should've known he'd meet disaster . . .*

He shook away the thought.

Whoever's singing might be able to help me.

He stalked over the corridor's gritty floor, past a pair of narrow doors that he'd have to check out later, and then crossed the main room to an open doorway. Angled himself to peer through into a dim, cramped space. More luminescent strips picked up the low light and revealed a figure in a white jumpsuit like a glowing ghost. Rett's foot scraped over the dirty floor, and the singing stopped. The figure turned sharply, peeling away from the shadows. A girl who looked a few years older than he was, with short brown hair tucked behind her ears, gave him a startled stare. She was thin inside her overlarge jumpsuit, her face hollowed by shadows.

"I didn't mean to scare you," Rett said, his voice hoarse and strange to his own ears. He swallowed against the bolt of pain that shot through his head. His throat was paper-dry, his stomach unsteady. "I just— Can you tell me where I am?"

The girl stood frozen, unblinking, and Rett wondered if she, too, found the rustle of his voice misplaced in their cold-metal surroundings.

"My best guess is abandoned storage room," Rett went on, "but I'm willing to believe something as strange as experimental detention facility if you say it with enough conviction."

The girl winced. A hand went to her head.

She's hurt, same as me. "Let me look," he said. He could usually tell when a gash needed stitches and when it could be left alone—when it would leave a nice scar and when it would just go on bleeding forever. A handy skill born of experience. He'd seen scars on knuckles, good for proving readiness to fight, and gashes on arms and faces, worse for displaying the shame of failure. But head wounds bled forever if you didn't put pressure on them.

The girl hesitated and then pushed her hair aside to reveal a long raised scar above her ear. No blood—an old wound. "It . . . looks okay," Rett said, trying to keep his voice light. A mark like that was the badge of a terrible run-in. *Don't say that to her,* he thought, but he knew the expression on his face must be saying it for him. *My own head can't look much better.* "Do you know what this place is?" he asked, desperate to redirect his thoughts.

The girl shook her head, then swayed as if hit with the same dizziness that plagued Rett. He put out a hand to steady her, but she flinched away. Rett's skin went hot with embarrassment. *I wasn't going to hurt you.* He dropped his hand to his side. "What's your name?" he asked quietly, trying not to make her nervous.

"Bryn."

"I'm Rett."

Her gaze traveled to his abdomen. Rett looked down. A wide smear of red-brown stained his jumpsuit. *What—?*

"Is that—blood?" Bryn asked in a halting voice.

Rett touched his stomach. He didn't feel any pain. "Not mine," he said. He met her gaze. Alarm flashed in her eyes. He took her fear like a punch to the gut. *I swear I'm not a bad guy*, he wanted to say. Instead he wilted back, gave her some space while confusion and humiliation roiled in his already churning gut.

"I'll go look around," he finally managed to say. "There must be someone else here." He backed out of the room, muscles tight with alarm. Because he couldn't say—he had no idea—how someone else's blood had gotten onto his clothes.

5:46 A.M.

Rett stumbled through the main room, past the slanted walls striped with peeling yellow paint and dust-bathed metal. Down the short corridor that led to the bolted door. He staggered through a doorway to his right, into a narrow room so dark he could only just make out shelves stacked with white jumpsuits. He seized a jumpsuit, shuddering with relief at the sight of it. Peeled off the one he was wearing, yanked on the clean one. Stashed the bloodstained jumpsuit in a bin. Some of the red-brown had come off on his hands. The sight filled him with horror. He swiped his palms over the edge of a shelf, trying to scrape off the stain.

Blood on my clothes, on my hands. His stomach curled. *What happened? Why can't I remember?*

He tried to feel in his muscles whether he had been forced into a fight with someone. He'd once broken another boy's hand at the government-run facility he'd lived in since age ten. Garrick was taller than him by a head, meaner than him by a full set of knuckles, and the sickening crack of his bones breaking still echoed in Rett's memory.

Rett didn't like to think about that day. Fighting never ended well. *Using your head works better.*

So why is there blood on my hands?

He turned to take inventory of the changing room, as if to prove to himself that he really did know how to use his head. Beneath the shelves, a bin held thick-soled boots. At the back of the closet, a shower head angled above a stall door. Rett felt like jumping into the stall and washing away the last of the blood that stained his skin. Or better yet, the dread that seemed to coat him like the dust that sheathed every surface of this strange place. He went and turned the knob, if only so he could quench his thirst. But even when he wrenched it as hard as he could, no water flowed.

He might have lost himself in disappointment then, except that the boots in the bin reminded him of something: there were boot prints on the floor where he'd woken up. Even though he himself was barefoot, and the slight girl in the other room wouldn't have left prints so large.

Someone else is here.

He touched a hand involuntarily to the spot where blood had stained his jumpsuit.

Someone . . . He wiped his sweaty palms against the suit. *Someone I must have hurt.*

Where?

He crept out of the changing room, eyes on the floor. There they were: boot prints in the dust, smeared where Rett had walked through them barefoot. The trail led him back to the main room, where he stopped short.

One of the striped walls had been lifted into an overhead slot to reveal a room beyond like a space-age lounge. A low angled couch that had once been white but was now gray with dust ran along three walls, taking up the whole space. *I'm trapped in a creepy metal dollhouse,* Rett thought as he surveyed the cross-sectioned room. *A dollhouse with a lock.*

"Bryn?" he called, his voice creaking with uncertainty. *Did she lift the wall—or did someone else do that?* A ladder set over the couch led to an opening in the ceiling, a square of darkness that pulled at him even while it made his scalp prickle. "Bryn? Are you up there?"

No answer but the ring of his own voice against the metal walls.

Rett's heart beat faster as he stepped onto a ledge at the back of the couch and grabbed the rungs.

He eased his head up into the darkness. For a long, unnerving moment he could only blink against black nothingness. A latch clicked some distance in front of him. And then his eyes adjusted, and he could just make out a set of beds to either side of the room, and the back of Bryn's white jumpsuit against a bank of metal drawers. *What is she doing?*

Rett ducked. *She'll think I'm spying on her. I am spying on her.* He heard her coming toward the ladder, so he scrambled back toward the far end of the couch and tried to look as little as possible like the bloodstained villain she might be imagining him as. He relaxed into an easy slouch, and kept his hands where she could see them.

Bryn jumped from the ladder and snapped her attention toward him. Her hands were shoved deep into the pockets of her jumpsuit. *She took something from the drawer.*

The intensity of her gaze was more than he could bear. "Were you the one who opened the wall to this room?" he asked. "There's someone else here."

Bryn's gaze went to the phantom bloodstain on his abdomen. "Or there *was*," she said.

Rett wanted to tell her he didn't think he could have hurt anyone. But how could he explain what he couldn't remember? *If she's hiding something from me, maybe I'm better off letting her be scared of me.*

"You changed your clothes," Bryn said.

Rett looked down at his jumpsuit. The logo of overlapping lines was the same as the one on the main door, the same as the one on Bryn's jumpsuit. "There's a room full of these." He hadn't stopped thinking of what Bryn might have in her pockets. He pointed at the ladder. "Did you find anything up there?"

"No." A flat, heavy *no* that echoed off the metal walls. *She's lying.*

But she moved her hands to cross her arms, and the pockets of her jumpsuit didn't bulge at all. So maybe she really hadn't found anything.

Then again, maybe she had found something and put it in the drawer.

The thought kicked Rett's defenses into gear. Stealing, hiding—he knew how to watch out for those things. He'd had six years of practice at Walling Home.

He looked her over, head to toe, the way *she* kept examining *him*. Narrow frame, squared shoulders, hazel eyes that shone bright enough to startle as she stared back at him in unbearable scrutiny. "You don't remember . . ." He wanted to say *what happened here?* But she tensed defensively, so he said, "how you got here?"

She hesitated. "My best guess is I was drugged. But I'm willing to believe something as strange as *I sleepwalked*. If you say it with enough conviction."

Rett stared at her. *Is she joking? Or does she think I'm bullshitting her?* "The lock on the door is jammed." He didn't know what else to say.

Bryn's gaze went toward the hallway that led to the heavy door. Had she already seen the lock? He imagined her creeping toward the door to examine it while he'd been in the closet sweating out his possible guilt and certain dread.

"Your name's Rett?" Bryn gave him a look that made him feel like a dog in a kennel. She inched back like she thought he might bite. "Last name?"

Rett started to say, then corrected himself. "None, really. Ward."

"As in, ward of the state?"

He gave a small nod. It wasn't a fun thing to admit.

"Walling Home?" Bryn asked.

Rett nodded again, slowly, wondering how she had guessed which facility he belonged to.

"Me too," Bryn said, so quiet he might have imagined it.

He straightened in surprise. Everything about her took

on new meaning: her thin frame, her hard stare, the way she edged along the walls. She was like him—cautious, ready to bolt. He tried to decide if he recognized her. Yes, he'd seen her before, but the too-big jumpsuit made her look different.

He remembered something about her, a rumor . . . But it slipped out of his mind just as soon as he got hold of it.

"What's the last thing you remember?" he asked her.

Bryn's eyes fluttered closed for the briefest of moments before she locked her wary gaze back on Rett. A fine layer of dust coated her skin. Rett rubbed a hand across his own cheek and felt grit. He looked down at his feet; they were black with dirt. *I was outside,* he thought, but he couldn't remember more than the chill on his skin.

"I remember waking up in that office there, looking around," Bryn said, back pressed against the side of the couch.

"Before that?"

"Nothing." Bryn gripped her elbow, and her gaze slid away from him for the first time. "I can remember Walling Home." Her expression darkened. "I wish I couldn't."

Images flashed through Rett's mind: the dull gray of cafeteria tables, the crisscross of wire inside window glass. The other boys—lean, knobby with muscles—surging toward him in a blur of motion. Punishing him for being small, for being around when they were bored or bitter. He felt the weight of too-tight walls around him, stale air in his lungs—his worst moment at Walling, when he'd been trapped in an old firewood box. He could feel the rough lid against his fists even now, the scrape of it over his skin as he pounded . . .

He dragged in a rattling breath, trying to get his bearings. His throat was painfully dry. "I'd kill for some water right now."

Bryn's gaze flickered to his abdomen again.

Rett bit his lip. *Could have found a better way to say that.*

He turned his attention again to the chaotic pattern of heavy boot tread laid out over the floor of the main room—

And a trail of prints that disappeared under the far wall. *Someone else is here,* he thought again.

"What do you think's under that wall?" he asked Bryn as he walked slowly toward it.

"There's no latch to lift it."

Rett bent to look closer. Bryn was right—there was only a rusty plate where a latch used to be.

"I can manage it." Rett kicked at the wall with his heel until the wall bounced back enough that he could stick his foot underneath and pry it up. It lifted with a groan, and more easily than he had thought it would. Something—adrenaline, determination—was making him stronger and sturdier, if racked with pain and thirst.

Despite his newfound strength, the wall stuck halfway up. Rett turned to Bryn, checking to see if she felt any less hesitant than he did to duck blindly into the dim room beyond and find out what awaited them. He caught a flicker in her eyes that said he'd impressed her with his kick-and-lift trick. *Should I tell her how I learned to get out of tight spots?* he thought grimly.

He couldn't very well hang back now and ruin the impression he'd given her, so he steeled himself and ducked under the wall.

Three banks of cabinets greeted him and then all Rett's attention went to the floor.

"There's a bunch of supplies in here," he called.

Nylon ropes and tinted goggles and compasses spilled out

of overturned bins. Rett crouched to examine a tangle of nylon backpacks. All empty. He wondered what he should be looking for. *Anything, anything.* He grabbed at the nearest bin, suddenly seized with a familiar fear. *Just grab anything!* But this wasn't Walling Home, and he and Bryn weren't going to have to fight over the last pair of donated shoes, the last spare blanket.

No, it's worse, he thought. *Or it might be.* Trapped, and this was all they had.

The bin held ponchos folded into their hoods. Useless, unless it was going to suddenly start raining inside. Which he actually wouldn't mind, given how all he could think about was water. Rett pulled down a larger bin already sticking out from a cabinet. It held mysterious green tubes that he couldn't puzzle out. And empty water bottles—a cruel joke.

He opened another bin and cried out in surprise. The words DRINKING WATER were printed across a Mylar bag that he now realized was flat—empty. His spirits fell. He picked up the bag and was surprised to find it was wet.

Someone just *emptied this bag.*

Rett whirled around, half expecting to find another person crouching somewhere in the room with him.

He was alone. Bryn hadn't even followed him in.

In fact, her muffled voice came from behind the half-lifted wall.

Is she . . .

. . . talking to someone?

"Bryn?" he called.

She went silent.

Rett ducked back into the main room. Bryn wasn't there.

The light coming through the glass dome far overhead was

brightening. He looked into the room where he'd first found Bryn. Only a desk with a pull-out stool, and an open door that gave a view of a toilet. No Bryn.

She's hiding from me, he decided, and something hard dropped into his stomach. Then he remembered the boot prints on the floor. *Should I be hiding, too?*

He ducked back into the supply room and looked over the jumbled bins, the cabinet tops marked with boot prints . . .

A ladder set over a bank of cabinets caught his eye. It led to a dark recess. Rett's nerves tingled. *Someone climbed up there*, he thought, eyeing the boot prints at the ladder's base. The darkness grew sentient, watchful.

Rett grabbed the rungs with stiff fingers and forced himself to climb. He held his breath and eased his head through the opening in the ceiling, his heart pounding . . .

Total darkness. The smell of old dust. A distant sound of . . . something sliding nearer? He froze, strained to hear better. His skin prickled.

"Hello?" he said into the darkness, barely more than a whisper. He pulled himself up with shaking muscles and edged along the frame of a bed. "Is anyone here?" He wondered if the sound he'd heard before had been only the rasp of his own breathing.

Would I be able to sense it? If someone were crouched in an inky corner, or unconscious on the floor—would he know? He jabbed a foot into the darkness, testing for any hidden forms.

It touched something.

The something gave.

Rett yanked his foot back. His heartbeat thundered in his head.

"Hello?" he croaked.

He crept forward, reaching into the darkness.

It was just another bed, a plastic mattress on a low frame. *There's no one here.*

No sooner had he thought it than the squeal of metal on metal rent the air.

Someone was sliding a panel shut from below. The square of light that was the opening over the ladder disappeared.

Rett's heart flew into his throat. "Hey!" he called, his voice choked. He dropped to his knees and tugged on a metal handle attached to the sliding panel. The panel didn't budge. *"Hey!"*

He heaved at the handle. He was trapped inside a disused firewood box crawling with spiders. Pleading with the boy who'd shut him inside. *"Hey, let me out!"* He shrank back, caught in the cramped darkness, fearful of wasting the air he had left . . .

Stop, he told himself, his breath coming in shuddering gasps. He made his muscles go loose, slowed his breathing. Then he tried the handle again, jerking it side-to-side, wriggling the panel free from whatever held it. He marveled again at the strength he seemed to have awakened within this strange place. At Walling, he was the skinny kid with more desperation than muscle, but here—one more wrenching tug, and he forced the panel open. Something clattered to the floor.

Rett dropped onto the cabinet top and sucked in cool, dusty air. The thing that had been wedged against the panel lay on the floor: a long metal pole with a leather loop—a walking stick.

Someone tried to trap me.

Rett's heart fluttered. He jumped down from the cabinet. Bent to pick up the metal pole—then froze with his hand locked around it. A smudge of green paint glowed on the metal.

Glowing green paint. Rett's gaze traveled to the bin of plastic tubes full of green liquid. *Glow tubes?* He picked one up and bent it until it cracked and its contents glowed.

He imagined the tube breaking open, the liquid spilling, staining a pair of hands glowing green, like the branding of a comic-book villain.

A thought sparked in Rett's mind. It burned so hot he forgot to worry about who might lurk on the other side of the wall he now ducked under.

At the end of the short hallway, the fire extinguisher still lay on the floor. Rett crouched to inspect what he had seen before but hadn't registered: the extinguisher's crown was covered in smudged green handprints. With Rett huddled over it, blocking most of the light, the handprints glowed.

Rett stood and inspected the heavy bolt on the door. Red paint from the extinguisher marked its wrenched end.

His pulse throbbed in his parched throat. Whoever had tried to trap him in the upper room had also jammed the only exit. Locked him in, as good as shutting a lid and clamping it down. But with no one to let him out when the air got stale.

Or when the water ran out.

He turned slowly, his mind buzzing.

Then—a flash of white jumpsuit. Bryn darted across the main room and slipped through the open doorway at the far end of the place.

Rett's heart drummed. *What is she doing?*

He looked back at the jammed lock on the heavy door behind him. *What has she done?*

A new sound drifted out from the open doorway Bryn had gone through: the clatter of wood on metal, mixed with Bryn's grunts of effort. Rett crept slowly toward it, drawn this time not by the hypnotic fascination he'd felt at the sound of her singing, but by dark curiosity.

"Bryn," he whispered, as if he were only saying it to himself, testing the idea that she might be the one who had trapped them in this strange prison. And then louder, "Bryn?"

She appeared in the doorway, spectral in the white jumpsuit lit by the morning light.

Rett's heart stopped.

At her sides, Bryn's hands glowed green.

Rett tried to swallow the lump rising in his throat, but his mouth was too dry. His mind raced. *Why would she jam the door—why trap herself in here?*

"Did you—" Rett faltered. What had that clattering been? The sound of a door being forced open? "Did you find another way out?"

Bryn slowly shook her head. "Another room."

Framed in the doorway, she seemed so slight, hardly large enough to fill out her jumpsuit. Rett remembered how startled she'd been when he'd first seen her, how ghostly and timid.

She's just scared, he told himself. *That's why she trapped me in that room. She's not going to hurt me.*

But a long string of evidence from life in a boarding facility told him otherwise. Everyone in that place was the same— *look out for yourself, even if it means hurting someone else.*

It was what Rett had done, breaking that boy's hand.

"You found another room?" Rett could hardly grasp what she'd said. His heart was a jackhammer working on his rib cage. "Is there . . . anyone in there?"

Bryn didn't answer.

"I think there's someone else here," Rett tried again. "And . . . I heard you talking to someone a minute ago."

Bryn tensed. "Someone else *was* here. That much is obvious." Her hands curled at her sides. "What did you do to them?"

Rett flinched. "I didn't—" He'd been stupid to let her be scared of him, stupid not to try to explain that he hadn't hurt anyone.

But something didn't make sense. "Who were you talking to?" he pressed. He took a step toward her. Her eyes widened with alarm.

And then her gaze shot to the ladder in the open lounge to Rett's right.

Why?

In Rett's mind, he saw her standing in the dark room at the top of the ladder, the room that mirrored the one he'd been trapped in, and he remembered hearing the drawer *snick* shut.

"What's up there?" he asked Bryn. And then he thought of the muffled conversation he'd heard a few minutes ago, and he knew. "A phone?"

Bryn's wooden expression told him he was right.

Rett went for the ladder.

Flew up the rungs before she could make a move to stop him.

Why would she hide this from me?

Why did she trap us in here?

The room above was so dark. A bed made a vague shape against one wall, a bunk bed against the other. Rett crept toward the bank of drawers, goaded on by a faintly glowing reflective strip on the floor. Already his eyes were adjusting to the low light.

He slid open a drawer. Nothing. He felt inside to be sure.

Opened another drawer. Empty.

Maybe she didn't hide anything. Maybe she's just as harmless as I am.

He yanked open a last drawer, expecting to find nothing.

Instead: a gun.

Gray against black darkness. His mind tried to reject the sight. The tube of the barrel, the angled lines of the grip and the guard. Strange proof that Bryn wasn't harmless. He reached in to touch it, to know for sure that it was real, to calm the wild flutter in his chest—

A voice ruptured the silence: *"Rett."* Bryn's voice—so sharp, so close behind him it pierced his skull and sent his mind spinning into blackness.

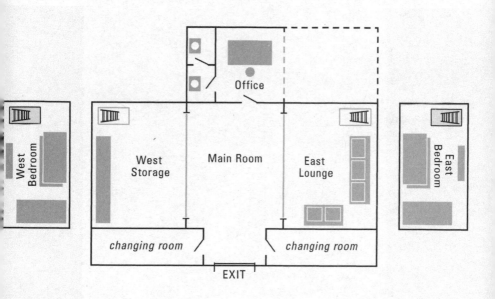

West Bedroom

West Storage

Main Room

Office

East Lounge

East Bedroom

changing room

changing room

EXIT

5:37 A.M.

Someone is calling to me . . .

Rett heard the voice now, calling his name. The boy who had him trapped in a wooden box. *Rett . . . Rett . . .* He heard jeering laughter as the boy sat on the lid. Rett couldn't get out, no matter how hard he pounded—

He woke with a gasp. His skull shrank around his throbbing brain. His eyes snapped open to find the rough walls of a firewood box replaced by scuffed metal glowing faintly in the morning light.

Where am I? What happened to my head? A fog had settled over his brain.

For a moment, he felt trapped inside his own comic-book creation, *Epidemic X.* He imagined the panel: *Boy, seen from above through a skylight, curled on the floor of a metal room, blue with cold or early morning light. Alone.*

The grit on Rett's skin told him he'd been outside. He stood, slowly. The pain only worsened, but he felt safer on his feet. *I'm not alone,* he thought, before he realized how he knew: in the next room, someone was singing.

For a moment, it was his mother's voice bringing him out of the fog of sleep, like when he was little and she'd sing about the trees outside the window, or the birds or the people passing, so that he'd finally get out of bed just to see what she saw.

But of course it wasn't his mother singing. The song was strange, eerie in this unfamiliar place:

> *"One lonely lighthouse*
> *Two in a boat*
> *Three gulls circle*
> *Four clouds float . . ."*

Rett was sure he knew the song. *Some playground rhyme the little kids at Walling sing?* But there was only an empty space in his mind where the next line should have been, same as when he tried to remember what it felt like to be safe and warm in a place he could call home.

The teasing familiarity of the song drew him toward an open doorway. Something told him the song was important, that he must listen to it. *Two in a boat . . .* he thought.

Two in a boat, and one of them is hiding something.

Ice slid down his spine. Where had that thought come from?

> *"One lonely lighthouse*
> *Two in a boat—"*

The singing stopped.

From where Rett leaned into the open doorway of a small office, he could make out the back of a figure in a white jumpsuit standing near a desk. For a moment it felt as if he were keeping an appointment with a ghost. He turned sideways to let in more of the faint light, and the figure turned. It wasn't a ghost but a girl with short brown hair tucked behind her ears. At her feet was a gray shape, angular, a piece of discarded metal.

"Who are you?" the girl asked sharply.

Rett took half a step back. His head rang. He put a hand against the doorframe to steady himself and was surprised to find it lined with heavy rubber. "Do you know— What is this place?" he asked.

"I don't know. I woke up and I was here. Although, I'm not actually convinced I'm awake." The girl took an uncertain step toward him, closer to the light so that Rett could see pain etched on her face. "I'm Bryn. And now I feel like I've just introduced myself to a phantom in my own dream."

"I'm Rett. And I'll take the role if you promise to wake up so we can get out of this." He felt a twinge of concern at her pained movements. *If her head hurts anywhere near as bad as mine does . . .*

Her gaze traveled to his abdomen. Rett looked down to see a wide smear of red-brown staining his jumpsuit.

"Is that—blood?"

5:45 A.M.

Rett trembled in the cool darkness of what he guessed was a closet or a changing room and tried to fill the gaps in his memory. He'd been at Walling Home—*where else?*—and now he was here. It didn't make any sense.

He dumped his stained jumpsuit into a bin and kicked the bin out of sight. Blood. Someone else's blood on his clothes. Not even *his* clothes, but the clothes he'd been wearing. His legs shook as he turned toward the doorway.

He moved to where he could take another look at the heavy

door just outside the closet. At the bolt jammed into the housing like it'd never come free again. At that weird logo painted onto the metal. *Scatter 3. I'm in Scatter 3, whatever that means.* He stood for a minute with his eyes closed, willing himself to remember what had happened.

He hadn't left the boarding facility in six years, since his mother had dropped him off with the hollow promise to return. *Not her fault,* he always told himself. *She didn't know how bad things would get.*

They'd watched the images together on the news, years ago: stunted stalks of wheat, shrunken ears of corn. Farmland in the heart of the country plagued by droughts and heat waves in turn.

And then Rett's mother had gotten sick, and she'd had to choose between doctors and food. Neither of which they could afford. Rett tried to be content with less to eat, tried not to notice his mother growing thinner, tried not to look at the images on TV of farm animals acting strangely, their eyes rolling as they twitched in their pens.

And then it all got worse.

Rett could still picture the moment his mother had told him she couldn't take care of him anymore. They'd sat by the window near the trees she'd once sung about in early mornings to wake him, trees that had now gone black and stopped putting out leaves. She'd given him the last piece of bread for his toast and hadn't eaten anything herself. When he finished, she'd said, *For a little while, I need to go away to see the doctor.* The clouds moved outside the window. Shadows passed over her blue dress and over her eyes, and he reached for her because he was afraid he was sinking into lightless ocean depths. It was his fault, he'd done something wrong, had somehow made her sick, made her want to leave him. He wanted to tell her that he'd do better, but she said it for him: *Soon everything will be better.* And he vowed it would be, in his childish thoughts. Now he understood that *better* wasn't something anyone could promise.

His mother had gotten treatment at one of the government clinics, and the cancer had gone into remission. But she couldn't come for him—she had no money left to take care of him. So she'd moved on to a government-funded workhouse. Same as so many other parents who'd gotten sick or gone hungry and had to send their kids off to places like Walling Home with false promises to return.

Rett was still waiting.

Because the cancer had returned—his mother needed more treatment.

Needed it soon, and didn't have the money to pay for it.

She was sinking into ocean depths again, and the light grew dimmer every day.

Rett wiped his sweaty palms on his new jumpsuit. *Don't think like that.* He had a plan—he was going to help her.

He just needed to figure out how to get out of here.

Maybe there's another door, or a phone, or—

He licked his dry lips. *I wish I had some water.*

First things first: he'd look around, figure out what this place was and if there was another way out.

He went back to the main room. One of the striped walls had been lifted away to reveal a lounge filled by a sectional couch. The lounge was the last thing Rett had expected to see, unless he counted the terrified girl who'd come out of hiding and was now trying to pry up the wall at the other edge of the main room. "Here," Rett said, moving to help her. "I use this trick to get into the shed after-hours, when my arms are full of food from the kitchen."

He popped the wall up with a kick and smiled at her, but she slinked away.

"Maybe that's why I'm here," he said. "Punishment for nicking food." The phrase *experimental detention facility* floated into his mind.

"Are you some kind of thief?" she asked.

"Only when I need to be."

He thought of other tight spots he'd gotten out of, into. Thought of things he'd stolen from closets, pantries, lockers: blankets, bread, clothes.

Was that why he was here? Was this some kind of punishment?

"You steal food?" she asked.

"Food, blankets, shoes. I used to trade my comic books for what I needed, but those ran out a long time ago."

She narrowed her eyes, intrigued or concerned. Either way, guilt settled over Rett.

"Mostly I just steal stuff back from whoever stole it from me in the first place," he said. And he didn't do it just for himself. He stole back stuff for the smaller kids, too. *Soon everything will be better*, he'd promised them.

Her stony gaze told him she wasn't buying the innocent act from the boy who'd introduced himself to her covered in blood.

He hefted the wall up now, ready to drop the subject. Bryn only stood there, eyeing him and making no move to explore the room beyond.

I guess she needs proof I'm not actually into attacking people.

Rett backed away, turning so she wouldn't see the humiliation on his face. "You check in there. I'm going to look around the rest of the place. See if there's some way out of here." He skulked toward the lounge, where a ladder led up from a ledge behind the couch.

Behind him, he heard Bryn duck under the wall, eager to get away from him. *Can you blame her?* he asked himself, and felt anew the horror of that dark stain he'd found on his clothes. He paused halfway up the ladder, stunned by the traces of blood on his hands. *I did something bad,* he thought. *I might have done something bad. I wish I could remember.*

He thought of Walling Home, stolen beers pressed into his hands, nicked food smuggled under his shirt. A hundred other things that might have landed him here, in this strange prison. The wrench he'd hidden in the yard. Garrick's broken knuckles. *I didn't want to do any of those things.*

Above the ladder: a dark space. A room someone might be sent to as punishment. Rett's muscles tightened at the memory of another dark space—a box he'd climbed into, on the edge of Walling's property, clutching his last issue of *Shine Fall.* He'd lain inside the open firewood box, hoping to catch sight of a meteor shower promised on the news, a hundred shooting stars. But Garrick had found him. He'd closed the lid and trapped Rett inside to punish him for escaping a beating in the yard the day before—the day Rett had defended himself by bringing a wrench down on Garrick's knuckles.

Rett had tried to tell him about the meteor shower: *I need to see it.* Like Hikaru in *Shine Fall,* who'd wished his way home on a shooting star. But Garrick knew. Knew Rett loved that two-page, star-spangled spread in *Shine Fall.* Knew Rett hoped in the magic of wishing. Garrick picked that night to get his revenge, to shut Rett in the box so he couldn't see the shooting stars . . .

After that night, Rett started drawing his own comics. Scrap-paper issues, filled with magical artifacts—amulets, wands, keys—found just when they were needed most. *There's always something that can help. There has to be.*

He groped along the wall for a light switch, unnerved by the darkness. His hand came upon something else instead: a lever. *There's always something.* But the lever didn't want to budge. He pulled harder, finding within himself a spring of frustration left over from that memory of the dark box, from the image of Bryn's frightened eyes, from the thought of *I did something bad.*

Some machinery shifted behind the wall as the lever came down, but nothing else happened.

"What's up with this place?" he mumbled. "Is everything broken?"

Rett's eyes were adjusting to the dim light coming from below, but he still couldn't make out much more than a few beds and a wall of drawers. No doors, no window. No way out, other than the hatch in the floor. No sign of water, either.

Then it occurred to him: maybe the lever didn't work because the power wasn't on. Maybe if he could find a way to get the electricity going, the lever would activate . . . *something.* He just had to find a main switch, probably somewhere on the ground floor.

He slipped back down the ladder. Quick and quiet, so Bryn wouldn't know he'd been up in that room. He paused, confused, feet on the last rung. *Why do I care if Bryn knows I was up there?*

He didn't know her. Didn't trust her. Except—she did seem familiar. Her hair? Her eyes?

Her voice. That song.

He turned from the ladder to find her standing there. His heart lurched. "Bryn."

Her jumpsuit glowed in the brightening light from the window in the high ceiling. "Find anything up there?" Her voice was strained, but at least she was talking to him. *We could help each other, you know,* he told her silently. *I promise I've had practice at it. More than fighting or stealing.* Would she believe him if he told her?

"I found a lever," he said. "But I don't think it works without—"

"Did you look in the drawers?" she interrupted.

How did she know there were drawers? *She's already been up there.*

Rett shook his head. "There isn't any light up there. You haven't seen a way to turn on the power, have you?"

"No, but I saw some power cords in there." She nodded toward the room she'd just come out of. "Look around for yourself."

Rett hesitated. But his curiosity got the better of him. He ducked under the wall.

The room was a mess.

Tangled power cords, first-aid kits, empty canvas bags, sets of tinted goggles like strap-on sunglasses, coils of rope and nests of carabiners, a box of compasses. All jumbled on the floor. Rett bent and slipped a compass into the pocket of his jumpsuit without really thinking. He pulled a pair of goggles down around his neck. It was all he could do not to stuff his pockets full of carabiners. *Old habits . . .* he thought. He sneaked a glance at the opening behind him, suddenly embarrassed at the thought of Bryn coming into the room and seeing him hoarding junk.

The power switch, he reminded himself. But he couldn't find anything like that along the walls or inside the cabinets.

He surveyed the mess again. Why did everything come in sets of six? Six water bottles, six first-aid kits, six pairs of goggles.

. . . Five backpacks.

He untangled the nylon sacks and counted again: five.

A half-opened box tipping out of a cabinet held a couple dozen tubes of mysterious green goo. He took one with him to search elsewhere for a way to turn on the power.

He discovered Bryn leaning against the couch in the lounge, arms crossed, like an unassuming security guard. *Or a villain born of desperation, ready to strike.*

But she didn't make any sudden moves, so he asked, "Any idea what this is?" and held up the green tube.

Bryn's arms flexed as she pressed herself farther back against the couch's edge. "A light stick? Try bending it."

Rett followed her advice. It made a cracking noise and the green goo began to glow. He beamed at Bryn. Surprise flickered across her face at his smile, and for a moment Rett thought he might finally win her over.

"You're a genius," he said.

"Maybe I just wanted to hear something crack."

Rett's smile faltered at the aggression she loaded into the

word *crack*. He quickly composed himself. "Should we take a better look at that lever up there?" He pointed his glowing tube at the ladder behind her.

Bryn just stood with her arms folded, blocking his path to the ladder. *Guarding it?* Rett thought. *Why?*

So much for winning her over.

"I thought you were looking for a way to turn on the power," she said at last.

Rett didn't think he could bear to see her flinch away from him again, so he dropped the idea of climbing the ladder. "Maybe I should check the other rooms for breaker switches." He waited a beat for an answer that didn't come. Then he ducked through the open doorway, into the office where he'd first found her. *Maybe there's a circuit breaker in here.*

A desk and a pull-out stool took up most of the small space. A narrow door stood to the left. Rett opened it to find a toilet and sink. He tried the taps. Nothing. He swallowed against the scratchy feeling in his throat, but it gave him no relief. He opened the toilet in a sudden burst of desperation. Dry as the sink.

The back wall of the bathroom was really another narrow door, which slid aside to reveal an identical bathroom. A mark on the second bathroom's far wall caught the light from Rett's glow tube. He froze. For a moment, he saw the emblem from the cover of his *Shine Fall* comic—the last of any issue in his collection, the one he refused to trade away. It was his only physical connection to his mother, who had spent their hard-saved money to buy him all six issues in the limited-run series the day he'd come home early from school because he'd made himself sick worrying about her.

But as Rett lifted his glow tube, he saw it wasn't an image

of a shooting star glowing before him. It was a triangle enclosing a lightning bolt.

And just to the side of it jutted a handle.

The wall was a door.

It felt like a wish come true. And even before Rett popped the door open, he knew what he would find behind it.

A power supply.

I guess this place is too small to stick the door somewhere easier to get to. He crept through, into the cramped space beyond. The green glow from his plastic tube hit on a bank of switches, a row of metal cylinders. "We have power!" he called as he threw the breakers and the cylinders hummed to life.

Now let's see what that lever in the top room is good for. He turned, and his foot sent something clattering over the metal floor.

The light from his glow tube glinted off the object: a small rock, as shiny as if it were made of metal. "Where did you come from?" Its smooth surface glinted in the green glow from the light stick. Rett slipped the rock into the pocket of his jumpsuit with the compass, another artifact he couldn't help hoarding.

A strange noise greeted him as he stepped back into the office: wood clattering against metal.

Bryn was tugging aside an accordion-fold partition he hadn't noticed before, forcing the wood-and-metal slats with a long metal pole. All thoughts of the lever in the upper room left Rett's mind for the moment.

There's another room here, Rett realized just as Bryn managed to finally shove the folding slats aside.

Rett's pulse pounded as he took in the details of the newly revealed room: stark white sheets on a narrow bed, pill bottles in glass-front cabinets, splints scattered over wall-mounted shelves. Things he would expect to find in a hospital.

He shrank back with dread. Everything was sterile and neutral and blank.

Just an empty room, he told himself. *Nothing to be afraid of.*

And then, as if to prove him wrong, blood bloomed in Bryn's palm. Rett stared in shock.

Then he realized—

She must have cut herself on the slats.

Without a word, he flew from the room, ducked into the supply room where he'd searched the cabinets, and yanked out a bin he had found earlier. Reached inside and then ducked back under the wall—

He stopped short.

Bryn stood an arm's length from him, wielding the metal pole like a baseball bat, her face a mask of fear and resolve.

Rett's muscles locked. He waited for the blow.

Waited a moment longer, his lungs heavy as stone.

The blow didn't come.

Bryn's gaze had gone to the object Rett held out to her: a roll of gauze.

She looked from it to the blood dripping from her hand and then to Rett's expression. He'd never meant to scare her. Could she see that? Did she know what he knew, what he'd known since the first moment he'd met her and seen her face shadowed with pain?

They were the same.

They both desperately needed things to be better.

Bryn lowered the pole. "There was someone else here," she said, as if it were a reasonable explanation for why she had almost bashed Rett's head in.

"I know." Rett's breath came fast in his tight lungs. *She's not swinging.* "But I swear I didn't hurt them."

"Then how did you get blood on your clothes?"

Something cold trickled down Rett's spine. "I . . . I don't know." He watched the pole in her hand, pretending that if he kept his eyes on it, she wouldn't raise it again. "Let me help you with your hand."

He reached out, but she took the gauze from him instead, her fingers grazing his palm, and drew back out of his reach.

"Fine," Rett said. "It's fine. To be honest, I could use a little personal space."

6:06 A.M.

"What's inside the pack?"

Rett stood leaning in the far corner of the main room, keeping his distance while Bryn sat in the lounge, wrapping her wounded hand. He'd thought she might need help with the gauze, but she clearly didn't.

In response to his question, she reached into the half-open pack balanced on her lap and brought out several Mylar pouches.

"Is that—?" Rett took a few steps closer. The labels on the pouches read DRINKING WATER.

Rett couldn't help himself. He darted forward and seized one of the pouches from the seat next to Bryn, barely registering that she flinched away from him as he did so. His throat constricted as he tore away the Mylar tab. Then water was pouring into his mouth and he was almost choking with relief. *Finally.*

Bryn just watched him while he reached for another one and drained it as quickly as he had the first.

"You've had these the whole time?" he asked her.

She was leaning away from him, her bandaged hand cradled to her chest. He took a few steps back, feeling guilty for having made her nervous again.

"I just found them a minute ago," she said. "The backpack was on the floor behind that folding partition."

She hadn't opened a pouch for herself.

"It's not poisoned or anything," he assured her. "Or anyway, I haven't keeled over yet, and that's got to be a good sign." He gave her a brief smile that she didn't return.

She examined a pouch, as carefully as if it were a piece of evidence in a murder trial—*one unit of poisoned water, which the male victim swallowed without urging.* Then she finally pulled the tab and drank.

Rett was about to reach for another one when it occurred to him that there might not be any other water except what was in that backpack. And the door out of this place was jammed shut, and there didn't seem to be anyone else around. There was still that lever in the upper room to check, but unless it opened a hidden exit—which Rett highly doubted—they were stuck here for who knew how long.

Bryn seemed to read his thoughts. "Should we save some of these?"

"Yeah." Rett tried to make it sound casual, but his voice came out a little too high-pitched. "I think we should check that lever in the room up there. It's the only idea I have right now."

He pointed at the ladder, but Bryn just rummaged in the pack like she hadn't heard him.

Rett fidgeted. "Unless you have a better one?" He sat on the couch, careful to leave some distance between them.

Not enough, apparently—Bryn pulled down a hinged table that was bracketed to the wall so it could serve as a barrier between them.

"I'm willing to go along with whatever plan you have, at this point," Rett said, eyeing the table like it was a door she'd just slammed in his face.

He looked up to find her gazing into her open backpack. Even relieved of its water pouches, it bulged like a big, black grub.

"We could charge these up." Bryn pulled several small black devices out of the pack and arranged them along the edge of the table. "So we can turn them on," she added, and prodded the buttons on one to prove they had no charge.

"What are they? Phones?"

"We'll find out when we turn them on." She watched him for a moment longer, her hazel eyes liked chilled honey, and then she asked, "You don't remember . . . anything?"

The way she said it made Rett uneasy. "Do *you*?"

Bryn leveled her cool gaze at him. She looked away and shook her head.

I wish I could tell if you were lying, Rett thought. He was no good at reading her. One minute he thought she might let him help her—and the next, she'd come at him ready to introduce the inside of his skull to a metal pole.

Like my head doesn't hurt enough already. He skimmed a

hand over it, grimacing at the dull ache that still pushed back at his touch. At least the water had helped a little.

"Are you always this guarded?" Rett asked her. "Or just when you're trapped in a weird place with a stranger?"

Bryn examined her bandaged hand. "You forgot *bloodstained*. A *bloodstained* stranger."

Rett cleared his throat. *I did change my clothes.* ". . . Who's really good at checkers. And at doing funny voices, but please don't ask me to perform right now because I'll feel like an idiot impersonating SpongeBob in a bomb shelter."

"This isn't a fallout shelter." She pointed at the skylight—a fragile barrier to an atomic blast. "And I'd prefer political impressions over cartoons, if you're taking requests." One corner of her mouth lifted, almost a smile.

Warmth spread through Rett's chest. "What, like the president?"

"Say 'extreme weather patterns' and I'll laugh my head off."

"What's that supposed to mean?"

"That everything he says is bullshit," Bryn said evenly. "That droughts and heat waves don't cause cancer."

Rett sat back. *Cancer.* "My mom . . ." Did Bryn already know his mom was sick? What did she mean about cancer?

"You grew up in a boarding facility," she said.

Rett felt a twinge in his gut. "How did you know that?"

"Walling Home."

Another twinge.

"I finally remembered your face a few minutes ago," Bryn said. "You look different, though. Kind of . . . ragged."

Rett's face flushed. He pulled at the front his jumpsuit, as if straightening his clothes would help.

"I'm from there, too," Bryn said.

Rett's bewilderment vanished. Yes, he'd seen her there. That's why he'd thought he recognized her earlier. She looked different, too. It might have been the way the dim light shadowed the hollows of her face.

Or maybe barely contained panic just takes a toll, he thought wryly.

"A lot of parents who left their kids at Walling had cancer," Bryn said. "Strange coincidence, right?"

"Not exactly. If they weren't sick, they wouldn't have had to leave their kids there."

Bryn shrugged. "Anyway. Looks like we're out of there now."

"It's not that I'm not happy about that," Rett said, looking around at the metal walls, "but this isn't exactly better."

He took her silence as agreement.

"Do you think they kicked us out?" he asked. *For being too willing to swing poles at people's heads? For being terrible at remembering bloody run-ins?*

She jerked back, as if struck with some sudden thought. "How old are you?"

"Sixteen."

"Too young to graduate out."

"Yeah, but . . ." *Could that be what had happened?* "I requested to leave early. Because my mom is sick." *So I left Walling for good? And . . . I came here?* "How old are *you*?"

"Sixteen. But . . ." She clutched the backpack to her stomach. "My boyfriend's eighteen. I asked to be allowed to graduate out early with him."

"So we both graduated out." Rett let the idea hang in the air, waited to see if it sounded wrong. "But how did we get here? This isn't exactly what I planned to do with my freedom."

Bryn gripped the pack harder. "Freedom's a funny way to describe this situation."

"I'm supposed to find my mom. She's been living in a workhouse," Rett said. "One of those government places on the East Coast? They take people in out of guilt for not knowing how to stop the center of the country going to crap. 'Sorry for your trouble, how'd you like to perform hard labor to earn medical treatment?' Typical first-world stuff." Crowded dormitories and bad food and long days on a manufacturing line. How much money had his mother saved there? Not enough. How much more would they need for her new round of treatment? Too much.

"They're closing all of the workhouses," Bryn said, narrowing her eyes as if she suspected he were lying. "No more funding."

Rett tugged at the collar of his jumpsuit, even though it was already loose on him. "I know."

He looked around. At scuffed metal walls and a mess of dirty footprints on the floor. He felt ten years old again—shut in the box, no way out, Garrick sitting on the lid. Air so hot and stale, Rett could hardly breathe. He'd missed the meteor shower, missed his chance at a wish for his mother to get well . . .

He slumped against the table, thinking about the pouches of water and longing to drink another one. *There's always something that can help*, he told himself, but in that moment, he wasn't sure he believed it.

"I remember you now," Bryn said in a low voice, and Rett

jerked upright. She looked at him with dark fascination. "I remember . . . you're the one who broke Garrick's hand."

The blood drained from Rett's head. "That wasn't my fault." But the words sounded unconvincing in his thin, defensive voice. "He . . . It wasn't a fair fight." That didn't sound much better. Why couldn't he explain it? *Garrick's bigger than me. Stronger. Dumber, too, so I had to use that to my advantage— had to hide a weapon in the yard, where he always came after me.*

He stayed quiet. *Probably not a great idea to use the word* weapon *right now.*

Rett trained his gaze on the pack, avoiding Bryn's stare. He suddenly resented her—she'd been unfair to him yet again.

And worse, she'd found some hidden cache of guilt he hadn't known he had.

Why does it always turn out that way—why do I always have to hurt people to protect myself?

Silence stretched between them, thick with tension. Bryn started pushing the devices back into the open backpack, probably planning to get away from him, to hide again. One of the pack's straps was wound around her hand. *Like it's hers*, Rett thought, annoyed.

The thought unlocked a memory, something so startling he blurted it without thinking: "You're the girl who steals."

Bryn's chin snapped up. Her eyes flashed with anger or alarm.

"I mean, from the staff," Rett said. *Impressive, really. How does she even manage it?*

Bryn glared at him. "And look at me, back to my old ways." Then she went on loading the devices into the pack.

One of the devices clattered to the floor, and Rett leaned to pick it up. Bryn lunged for it, too. In that moment, a small plastic case tumbled out of the pack and clattered onto the floor. Rett got to it first and opened it, one more obligatory investigation to undertake in a place that hadn't yet turned up any answers.

Inside was a block of foam with a cavity cut into it. Rett looked up at Bryn. She went rigid, her arm still extended toward the floor.

The cavity was cut into the shape of a handgun.

Rett eyed the backpack, his heart banging like a prisoner on the door of his sternum. He felt the room receding from him, as if he were floating away. He fought to stay grounded. "Is the gun in there, too?" He said it lightly, trying to make it sound almost like a joke.

The blood drained from Bryn's face.

For a moment neither of them moved while Rett's heart kept trying to break free of his chest. The strange floating feeling passed. Rett reached out and took the backpack from Bryn—snatched it, almost. She didn't say anything. He carefully sorted through the contents: the electronic devices, the pouches of water, a stash of foil antiseptic packets.

No gun.

He breathed.

"All right." He handed the pack over. "Guess not." He gave a strangled laugh.

Bryn settled the pack in front of her like a shield. "The blood . . . on your jumpsuit earlier."

Rett's skin went hot. "I didn't shoot anybody." *I wouldn't. I would never do that.* "I don't have a gun. There isn't one."

She seemed to consider his words for a moment. Then she ran a hand over her head, a pained look on her face. She looked suddenly exhausted, like all her adrenaline had finally evaporated. Rett shared the feeling. "Okay, never mind," she said. "I just want more water. If these pouches are all we have left . . ."

"The sink and toilet in the other room are both dry," Rett said. The thought made his stomach seize. Now that he knew they'd searched the whole place and found only a handful of water pouches, he was just about ready to give in to panic. "The shower in the changing room wouldn't turn on. But I guess it wouldn't hurt to try the shower in the other changing room."

Bryn pressed her eyes shut. The lines in her face smoothed, and Rett took it for relief. "Okay," she said, opening her eyes. "Will you? I promise not to steal anything while you're gone. Couch cushions and wall-mounted tables included." She gave him a small smile that he didn't know how to read.

I guess thirst overrides suspicion? At least we're working together now. The thought gave him new energy, if only a little. "So if I leave the dust with you, it's still going to be here when I get back?" *Look at me, joking like a pro in the face of dread and danger.*

"Promise."

He slid off the couch and went into the changing room across from the one where he'd found the clean jumpsuit. Tried the shower. No luck. *The plumbing must be switched off.* They needed to find a way to turn it on. A knob or . . .

He spun toward the doorway. *That's what the lever in the upper room is for. It turns on the plumbing.*

He shot out of the changing room, his mind on the ladder near where he'd left Bryn. He only made it a few steps. Just outside the narrow doorway, something cracked under the weight of his heel—a glow tube, leaking green goo on the floor. No longer glowing now that the lights were on.

A thought tickled at the back of Rett's mind. *Glowing green . . .*

He leaned to pick up the fire extinguisher that still lay near the bolted door. Its shiny paint reflected the light. Something about it unsettled him but he couldn't place it. He set it down and continued on.

Bryn no longer sat on the couch where he'd left her. And the wall to his left, the one he'd lifted to find the supply room full of cabinets, was closed again.

She sent me off on an errand she knew was pointless and then closed herself away from me. His jaw tightened. He shouldn't have said that thing about her stealing. Didn't everyone at Walling steal? Didn't they have to, just to get by? Practically everything he called his own was stolen from someone who'd stolen it from someone . . .

Bryn's voice floated through the wall, a quiet murmur Rett could hardly make out. He stepped closer to the striped metal. Was she talking to someone?

No, she was reciting something, almost chanting.

"One lonely lighthouse, two in a boat . . ." The words to the song he'd heard her singing earlier.

"Bryn?"

"Three gulls circle, four clouds float . . ."

"Bryn, open the wall, will you? Please? I'm sorry for . . ." *For everything. For being stuck here, for scaring you, for being just as afraid of you as you are of me.* "The shower didn't work, but I think I know how to turn on the water."

The singing stopped. Rett waited, but the wall didn't budge.

Frustration welled inside him. She was afraid of him, and there was no way he could convince her not to be. It was the blood on his other jumpsuit. If only he'd changed before she had first seen him. Then she might actually believe he didn't want to hurt her, that he only wanted answers. They could work together.

The song went through his head. *One lonely lighthouse . . .*

An account of his misery—trapped, alone.

Although if I'm listing complaints, waking up in a bloody jumpsuit goes right at the top. "One, bloody jumpsuit," he said wryly. He lifted his face to the skylight and bathed in the blue glow from above. "Two, parched throat."

He went for the ladder set over the couch, singing absently, "One, bloody jumpsuit . . ." *I think I'm losing it.*

At the top, he found the lever again. He heaved it up and heard that familiar clunk behind the wall. Did it work like a pump? Some hidden reserve of strength powered his effort to move the lever down and up and down again. *Is it working?* He stopped to lean against the wall and catch his breath.

The bank of drawers at the far end of the room caught his eye. Something Bryn had said came back to him, something that had been bothering him this whole time: *Did you look in the drawers?*

Did she *look in the drawers? Did she find something?*

Realization hit him: *That's why she asked me—not because she wanted me to look. She was making sure I* hadn't *looked.*

He slipped a hand into his pocket and found the glow tube he'd used to explore the power supply. An image flickered through his mind: the plastic case with the foam cut in the shape of a gun.

His breathing sped up.

He went to the bank of drawers, wielding the glow tube like an eerie wand. He grabbed a handle, yanked open a drawer—

Empty.

Why did he have a feeling there should be something in this drawer? Why did he hear the *snick* of it closing even before he pushed it shut?

He tried a couple more. Empty and empty.

Okay, so I was wrong, he thought. *She isn't hiding anything up here. She probably isn't hiding anything but herself, and I can't exactly blame her. I'd hide from a guy in a bloody jumpsuit, too.*

He turned back to the ladder, defeated again.

And then stopped to gape at what was on the wall above it.

His glow tube revealed markings above the lever he had pulled: a cloud and several water drops, outlined in silvery stuff that shone in the light like magic.

Water. His throat felt choked with the dust that covered the floor, his hands. He'd been right about the lever—it must have turned on the water! With a start, he saw that he hadn't pulled the lever down all the way. He yanked on it again, then leaned his full weight down on top of it. Something on the roof went *clunk,* and the lever slid to the bottom of its housing.

Rett listened for the sound of water running somewhere but heard only his ragged, desperate breathing. Still, it must have worked. He'd go back down and try the showers.

"Bryn, I think I did it," he called as he climbed down the ladder. "I think I turned on the water."

He hadn't expected an answer—but he also hadn't expected to find the far wall open again. He ducked underneath it. The black devices were lined up on top of the supply cabinets, looking like strange mice trailing power-cord tails. He picked one up and jabbed at its buttons.

Nothing. It needed more time to charge.

"Bryn?" *Where did she go?*

A light tapping answered him. A familiar sound, more welcome now than it had ever been in his whole life—

Rett stood in the main room, gazing upward in longing. Rain fell on the skylight. It speckled the glass, a mesmerizing sight. "Bryn, it's raining." How nice it would be to open the skylight and feel the water on his face . . .

A slap of footfalls in the hallway. Rett whirled around.

"Bryn?" He crept down the empty hallway.

The sight of the fire extinguisher lying on the floor, of the damaged bolt on the door, unsettled him. *I'm missing something . . .*

He stopped. He'd heard that scrape of feet over dirty metal again, coming from the closet. *Bryn.*

But he'd also seen something on the floor that he'd been ignoring: boot prints.

Someone else was here.

What happened to them?

They couldn't still be here. He and Bryn had searched the whole place. Hadn't they?

Still, he crept more cautiously toward the closet. *It's just Bryn. It's Bryn.*

Why doesn't that thought make me any less freaked out?

The fire extinguisher caught his attention again, and the green liquid from the glow tube that he'd trailed out from the closet.

He stood there trying to puzzle it out. Then, without warning—

Bam bam bam. A sharp banging sounded on the other side of the heavy door, the sound of someone knocking.

At the same moment, Bryn appeared in the closet doorway, the gun in her hand.

Rett's heart jolted and blackness swept over him.

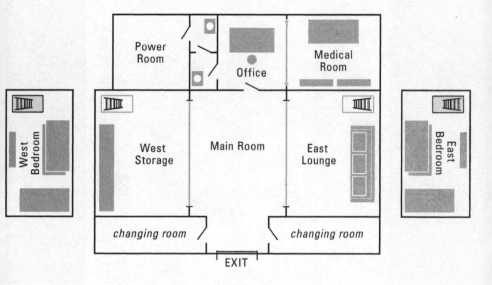

Power
Room

Office

Medical
Room

West
Bedroom

West
Storage

Main Room

East
Lounge

East
Bedroom

changing room

changing room

EXIT

4:38 A.M.

Rett gasped in the cold air. He spun, taut with alarm. But he was alone on a barren slope under a starry sky, with only a solitary boulder interrupting the hilly landscape.

But Bryn—the gun—

She was nowhere in sight. He stood alone in a dark hollow. The ground rose on all sides, vacant and rocky. His mind reeled. He had just been inside and now he was out here, in the cold—

Cold and quiet.

He looked up—and caught his breath. The sky seemed so close, he swore he could hear the stars. The faint crackle of distant life.

He felt ten years old again, lying in an open box, staring up at the night sky. Waiting to catch a glimpse of shooting stars so he could wish his mother well. So they could be together.

A sound brought him back to the present: the scrape of shifting rocks. Of footfalls on gravel?

He tried to think clearly but fear smothered all thought. At the top of the rise before him was a humped building: Scatter 3. Rett scrambled up the slope. He had to get inside. Before anything else, he had to get inside *fast*. There was something out here. His skin prickled with fear.

At the edge of his vision, a dark shape scuttled.

Get inside, Rett told himself.

5:37 A.M.

Someone is calling to me . . .

Rett woke to the eerie sound of a distant voice. And to the ghost of a vanished dream, a nightmare about . . .

But he couldn't remember.

He touched his fingers to his throbbing head. *Someone gave me a good crack. One of these days I'm going to stop volunteering to be the smallest guy in my dorm.*

He looked around, his heart beating fast: scuffed metal walls tinged with blue morning light. *Something familiar about this.* The place felt disused, abandoned. But not empty—from somewhere close by came the sound of singing: "*One lonely lighthouse, two in a boat . . .*"

Rett wished the lilting song brought him comfort, but it only unsettled him further. He could swear he knew the song, but from where? Something his mother had sung to him? He closed his eyes and saw his mother's face floating over him like a second sun, still lined with sleep but glowing in the morning light, with happiness to be near him.

But the song filling up the cold-metal place wasn't from his childhood. He'd learned it more recently. *One lonely lighthouse . . .*

For some reason, Rett pictured a tattered flag atop a lighthouse, like a scene from a dreamscape. *Or the perfect detail for an apocalyptic comic. Did I draw something like that for*

Epidemic X? In his groggy state, he looked up, half expecting to see a flag flying over him. But there was only a skylight set into a metal roof. And high up on the wall, a chalky white line. *What is that?*

The song started again, eerie, haunting. And again the image came to mind of a lighthouse topped by a flag.

Except that it wasn't a flag—it was a jumpsuit.

What?

Another set of words popped into Rett's head: *One, bloody jumpsuit.*

Rett looked down at his clothing, a white jumpsuit that wasn't at all familiar. *This isn't mine . . . Why does it feel so stiff?* He shifted, and recoiled in horror when he saw a red-brown stain covering his abdomen.

Blood.

He touched a trembling hand to the spot. It was mostly dry. He didn't feel any pain. *It's not mine, at least.* That was a new development—someone *else's* blood on his clothes. He'd used the sight of his own blood as motivation to get better at hiding from the older boys. But someone *else's* blood?

How did this happen?

The strange singing got louder, and Rett felt a stab of panic. *How do I explain this? I don't even know how I got here. I don't know what happened.*

He shot to his feet. Too fast—he steadied himself against the wall while his head pounded and his stomach reeled.

He had to hide. A luminescent stripe pointed him away from the direction of the voice, down a short corridor to a bolted door. Rett gave the bolt only a cursory glance before he ducked into a dark side room.

A minute later, he had pulled on a clean jumpsuit and

stashed the soiled one in a bin. *One, bloody jumpsuit. Two, parched throat.* He had no idea where the words had come from. *What am I doing here?*

He'd been outside—that much was obvious from the dirt on his feet and the grit that wouldn't come off his face. Outside in the cold. His skin was still clammy. He remembered darkness, panic. *What happened? Where am I?*

It was a dream, or some cruel prank, one Garrick had set up. *He lured me here somehow, pulled that let's-be-friends-after-all bullshit that I fall for way too often.* It had been Garrick's favorite trick to play ever since the disastrous day Rett had tried to be kind to him. He'd overheard the director say that Garrick's mother had died, so Rett had given Garrick a Milky Way he'd snatched from a charity package. A foolish thing to try on a guy like Garrick, who hated pity more than anything else. Garrick had split it between them, waited until Rett had started chewing, and then said, "*Your* mom's not coming back, either, you know. None of them are."

Rett had been left to shut out the dark thought with better ones: the sun on the pond near his home, the smell of paper and ink in the comic store, the magic of Times Square lit up at night.

The trip to New York—buildings so tall and spangled they seemed made of starlight. At the door to Walling, his mother had asked him to remember that trip, her lips trembling at the corners of her smile. *"All the lights, and the Statue of Liberty out on the water. We'll go again when I come back."*

She wasn't coming back—but Rett had a plan to go where she was, the workhouses. He'd finally get what he'd tried to wish for years ago, under shooting stars.

But first, I have to get out of here.

He bolted out of the closet and almost tripped over a fire extinguisher lying on the floor. Completely out of place in front of the heavy door with the massive sliding lock. And why was the lock bent like that? He tugged at it. *Jammed.*

Sweat broke out on the back of his neck. *This isn't a prank.*

The singing had stopped. The place was too quiet now. Rett crept down the hallway feeling like the bait in some great metal trap.

He gaped at what he found: one of the striped walls had been lifted away to reveal a room taken up by a long sectional couch. And kneeling on the couch, looking at a ladder overhead, was a girl with short brown hair tucked behind her ears.

She caught sight of Rett and whipped around to face him, so fast that Rett shrank back. But then she winced and put a hand to her head, her fierce expression both fragile and sharp, like broken glass.

Rett's hand went to the scar over his ear, so that he was a mirror of the girl. The sharpness went out of her as she met his gaze and they exchanged looks of pained sympathy.

"Do you know—?" Rett peered around at the scuffed metal walls. "What is this place?" *A warehouse for odd happenings,* he answered himself.

"I don't know." In her baggy white jumpsuit, with her hand lifted and her shoulders squared, she looked like a bird readying for flight. Like she could break her way out of their strange cage at any moment.

The thought dazzled Rett. *She could help me get out of here. If I don't mess this up.*

"I think someone mixed up my reservation," Rett joked. "I booked the Industrial *Plus* room."

"And I made the mistake of assuming the Quarantine Suite would be private." The corners of her mouth twitched.

"Quarantine? Is that what's happening?" Rett ran through the list of his body's current complaints: nausea, dizziness, headache. Gnawing anxiety.

"I'll admit I've felt better." The girl moved her fingers through her hair and grimaced with fresh pain.

"Are you okay?" Rett almost moved closer to help, but he didn't want to spook her. And anyway, with her cut-glass expression, she seemed strong enough to help herself. To help him, too, maybe.

She softened a little at whatever look he was giving her. Something pitiable, he guessed, based on how his head throbbed. "Are *you*?" She looked him over as if to check for further injury. Rett tensed under her scrutiny, remembering the bloodstain on the jumpsuit he'd stashed in the bin. *Whose blood?* he wondered again. And then thought, *Good thing I changed.*

Rett realized he still had his hand to his head in some salute to pain. He put it down. "I can pretend if you can." He smiled weakly and gave her the same look he used on new kids at Walling Home, the one that said he wasn't looking for a fight, that they could watch out for each other. "I'm Rett."

"Bryn." Her eyes were honey under glass, hard but warming. She moved her liquid gaze to an open doorway, and the honey went molten with dread.

"What's wrong?" Rett asked.

"Do you ever see something and think, *'If this were a movie it'd be no big deal. I'd just go with it'*?"

Rett held his breath. *What is she talking about?*

"There's a gun," Bryn explained. "On the floor in there."

5:52 A.M.

The gun: a menacing gleam of metal against the darker floor. It didn't look like Rett thought it should. He'd never seen a real gun in person, but he'd seen them on TV and on the internet, and inked in the comic book pages kids drew and passed around Walling. The barrel of the gun on the floor in front of them was a tube that might detach in your hand, like something added as an afterthought. The grip was a grooved rectangle. It looked like someone's idea of a space-age gun. "What should we do with it?"

Behind him, Bryn said, "Put it in the desk?"

Rett hesitated. *How would other guys act in this situation? Excited? Tough?* Guys like Garrick, who came after you in the yard, trapped you in small spaces until you bribed them to let you out. Made you drink beer with them in the shed, *let's be friends now*—and then hid the empty bottles in your drawer so you got in trouble. *Yeah, he'd love this*, Rett thought.

He leaned down and picked up the gun with his fingertips, trying to touch as little of it as possible. Its grip was rough and scarred from use, and the gleam of the metal was marred by scratches. He opened a desk drawer and laid the gun inside. It occurred to him that he should take the bullets out, but he had no idea how to do that. He closed the drawer and immediately felt relieved that the gun was out of sight.

"Wish we had some light in here," Bryn said, her soft voice brushing away Rett's gloomy thoughts. "I feel like I'm breaking and entering somewhere I don't even want to be."

Rett felt along the wall until he discovered a switch. Flipped it up and down.

"Oh, is *that* how people turn on lights—with *switches*?" Annoyance edged Bryn's voice. "I already tried that."

"Right." Rett's face flushed. "Here's another one. Or a button, anyway." It was marked with a painted symbol, a row of three overlapping circles. Rett squinted at the strange, segmented blob and then gave the button a jab.

Nothing.

"Guess the power's out," Bryn said.

"What's this for?" Rett prodded the heavy rubber that lined the doorway. He moved to examine the doorway from the other side—partly for the chance to pass close enough to Bryn to test whether she really gave off electricity, or if that was just the way she made him feel.

He thought he felt a current, but it was just the brush of her sleeve. *Focus,* he told himself. *Got to figure out what happened in this place.* "There are scratches on the wall out here."

Bryn came to look over his shoulder. Her gaze followed the scratches downward. "All over the floor, too."

Rett looked down at the strange array of gouges—

And at the half-smeared trails of boot prints.

Boots. Someone else was here. Might be here still.

Rett touched the place on his jumpsuit where that someone's blood had been smeared just minutes ago.

What did I do?

What will Bryn *think I did?*

Bryn knelt to look closer at the floor, and Rett's heart stopped. Her fingers trailed over long gouges. "How do you think this happened?"

"I—" All Rett could think about were the prints. Had she noticed them?

She squinted at the skylight overhead. "Could be someone set up a ladder to get to the skylight and it scratched the floor."

When he didn't respond, she said, "I also happen to know from experience that this is what a floor looks like after you play indoor field hockey on it."

Rett tried to laugh, but he was all nerves. "I would have expected more broken teeth."

"You're thinking *ice* hockey. Field hockey is more about breaking shins."

"Uh." His shins suddenly itched.

"Don't worry." She gave him a wry smile. "I don't have much practice at it."

He looked around, desperate for something else to distract her from the prints. "What do you think is behind *there*?"

He pointed at the striped wall opposite the room with the couch.

"No handle," Bryn said, squinting at a rusty plate on the wall.

"Hang on." Rett went over and kicked at the wall so that it bounced up and he could get his fingers under it. He turned, hoping to catch a look of approval from her, but she was frowning at how the wall had stuck halfway open.

"This place looks like it's seen better days," she said before she ducked into the room beyond.

Quick, Rett told himself. *The boot prints.*

He swiped his bare foot through the tell-tale prints, but there were so many, tracked all over the floor of the main room in a dizzying pattern.

She'll think I'm bad, that I did something bad. He couldn't bear the thought. Because it wasn't fair. Even though he'd always had to fend for himself, he'd tried not to be like the others, like Garrick, who hunted people and hurt them and humiliated them.

And because . . .

He couldn't explain the blood.

Or the sinking feeling that he really might have done something terrible.

He got down on his knees and used his sleeves to wipe away as much of the dirt as he could, even while he thought, *This is crazy, what am I doing, this is—*

"Rett? What're you doing?"

Rett bolted upright. The half-lifted wall between him and Bryn shuddered. *She's coming back.* And most of the floor was still covered in boot prints while he knelt there obviously trying to get rid of them.

In an instant, he was on his feet, bolting down the hallway to the closet where he'd found the clean jumpsuit. He yanked a bin out from under the shelf. The sight of the bloodstained suit stashed inside sent a sharp pain through his gut.

"Rett?"

Bryn appeared in the closet doorway, rigid with suspicion. She looked down at the boots Rett had yanked onto his feet a moment earlier, and then at the bin he was shoving back under the shelf. *Now if she sees boot prints on the floor, maybe she'll think* I'm *the one who left them,* Rett thought. *No need to explain that someone else has been here, that whoever it was must be sporting an unpleasant injury that I might have given them . . .*

"Where did you get those boots?" Bryn asked.

Rett cleared his throat, and the sound was dry as a death rattle. "They were here." He glanced at the bin and then quickly away. "In the bin."

Bryn made a movement as if to look in the bin herself, so Rett quickly added, "This was the only pair."

Bryn pulled back stiffly. She looked at Rett for a moment, unease showing in the flat line of her mouth. A wild thought crossed Rett's mind: *I wish I knew a joke that would make her laugh. Knock, knock . . .*

"What's in your hand?" Rett asked, eager to shift her attention.

She held up a tube full of green liquid.

"Emergency smoothie?" Rett tried.

Bryn's eyes flashed, but her stony expression didn't crack. "It's a light stick." She pulled another out of her pocket and handed it to him, stretching her arm out so she wouldn't have to step any closer. "It'll glow if you bend it."

Rett tried not to take offense at the distance she kept between them. *I'm messing this up.* "What else did you find? Any water?"

Bryn's gaze went to something over his shoulder and he turned to see a showerhead over a stall door. He must have seen it earlier but it hadn't registered. "Try the knobs," Bryn said, her words coming out in a rush.

Rett lunged toward the stall and fumbled with a knob on the wall. "Nothing." Disappointment settled over him like cold fog.

"There's got to be some way to make it work."

"Maybe we need to turn the water on at the source?" he said.

"Which is where, usually?" Bryn asked.

"Where are the water controls in an experimental detention facility? I don't know."

"You think this is a prison? I thought those were supposed

to be locked from the outside." She gestured at the mangled bolt barring the exit door behind her.

"Whatever this place is, there should be a way to get the water going. A knob . . . or a lever." As soon as he said it, an image popped into his head of a lever mounted on a wall. Where had he seen that?

Bryn leaned against the doorway. "Clearly something is wrong here."

The back of Rett's neck prickled. He couldn't help glancing again at the bin that held the bloodstained jumpsuit. *What went wrong? What happened?*

I swear I didn't do it.

Did I?

"Neither of us feels great," Bryn explained. "What if this really is a quarantine situation?"

Panels Rett had drawn for *Epidemic X* flashed through his mind: biohazard suits looming over sickbeds, patients staggering through hallways, zombies breaking through windows.

Rett pressed a testing hand to his forehead. Sweaty, but not feverish. Without thinking about it he reached for Bryn's. His fingers brushed her skin, but he couldn't say whether she felt warm, because a tingling sensation now traveled up his arm. "You feel . . ." He cleared his throat again. ". . . okay." He took a hasty step backward, a little fevered now.

Bryn didn't seem to notice. "It's just . . . you know how all those kids have to live in boarding facilities because their parents are sick?"

Rett's stomach clenched. "I live in one of those facilities."

"So do I." Bryn's gaze was probing. "Walling Home."

"Walling Home?" Rett's head buzzed. *We're both from Walling Home?* "Same here."

"This might sound stupid," Bryn said, "but do you remember that comic that someone drew on scrap paper? And people passed it around and added their own pages?"

Rett nodded. *Epidemic X.*

"There was this one big panel that showed a guy infected by a zombie plague and locked in someone's basement. It wasn't even a great drawing, but I can't stop thinking about it."

Rett swiped a hand over his heated face. "I drew that panel."

Bryn's mouth twisted. "Oh."

"I mean, you're right, I've never been great at drawing."

"I can't draw at all, if it helps." Bryn fidgeted. "I just meant that I keep wondering if that's what happened to us, if we got sick and so they left us here alone?"

Rett looked at the boot prints on the floor between them. *We aren't alone.*

"I know there's no such thing as a zombie plague," Bryn went on. "Although, honestly, I've spent a whole lot of time listening to my boyfriend argue decently plausible zombie outbreak theories . . ."

Rett felt a strange pang in his chest at the word *boyfriend.*

"But what if it's something *like* that," Bryn went on. "Everyone at Walling has parents too sick to take care of them. It's strange, isn't it? Why are so many people sick?"

"I guess when you live in a place for kids whose parents are sick, then of course it seems like *everyone's* parents are sick. Right?"

Bryn shrugged. "There's a conspiracy theory website, Dark Window, that says it's the government's fault that people are getting sick. That there was this big experiment to make crops more resistant to pests and drought, and it went wrong, and the corn and wheat and everything made people sick."

"I'd believe that if there were enough corn and wheat and everything to go around."

"Dark Window says that's the government's fault, too," Bryn said. "Another outcome of their failed experiment."

"Do you believe that?"

She shrugged again. "My stepdad used to say the internet's really only good for checking the point spread before a Buckeyes game."

"And what do you think?"

"I think the Buckeyes have a bad habit of choking when it matters most." Her gaze went to the floor, and Rett wondered if she noticed the boot prints, if she thought it strange that they stretched out into the hallway even though Rett had only just put on the boots. He startled when she spoke again. "And I think this place feels like an isolation cell. Like if we could get that door open, we'd find ourselves in a forgotten section of some kind of medical complex. Probably yet another place the government decided to pull funding from because public health is such a frivolous cause."

Images flashed through Rett's mind: a hospital bed, a bank of bright lights, a huddle of white lab coats—

"I . . . I think you might be right," he said weakly.

Bryn swiped her fingers over a dust-coated wall. "Do you think anyone knows we're here? Do you think they've forgotten us?"

"We could bang on the door, if you feel like that would help."

"Would anyone hear us? What if we're in some abandoned part of the city that everyone's steering clear of because they know there's an outbreak situation?"

Rett moved around her to the heavy door and pounded his

fists on it. "Hey! Hey, is anyone out there?" His voice echoed off the metal walls.

"Rett," Bryn said.

Rett beat his fists some more, unloading his frustration on the door.

"Rett, I don't think we should do that." Bryn pulled at his sleeve. "I have a bad feeling . . ."

Rett turned and collapsed against the door, panting, thirstier than ever.

"I don't think anyone's going to come help us," Bryn said, her shoulders tense.

Rett reached to touch her arm, trying to comfort her. "At least we're not alone."

She leaned back, just out of his reach. *Why is she staring at my boots?* Rett wondered. He looked down and was stuck by how clean and white they were. No trace of dirt on them. His gaze moved to the prints on the floor between them, and the trail leading down the hallway. *She figured it out. She knows I didn't leave those prints.*

"I'm going to look for a way to turn on the water, like you said," Bryn mumbled, and backed out of the space.

Rett's heart thudded. His own words echoed in his head: *At least we're not alone.*

He watched her walk to the other end of the depot and disappear through a doorway.

She doesn't trust me. I'm in this alone.

His heart squeezed. *No one's coming to help us, and Bryn doesn't trust me. I have to figure this out myself.*

The muffled thud of his boots echoed in his ears as he walked back to the main room. The scratches on the floor caught his eye again. He remembered what Bryn had said about using a ladder to get up to the skylight. And *there*, next to the glass dome brightening overhead—was that a handle?

The skylight opens.

A ladder—he needed a ladder.

The one set over the couch to his right was too short, and anyway, it was mounted to the wall. He ducked under the half-lifted wall to his left to see if he might find a better ladder in the room beyond.

Junk spilled out of cabinets and over the floor: backpacks and first-aid kits and coils of rope. On top of a cabinet was another short ladder, bolted to the wall. Useless. Maybe he'd have more luck in the room above?

He climbed the rungs, trying not feel uneasy about entering the dark opening overhead. At the top, he fumbled for the glow tube in his pocket, then bent the plastic like Bryn had told him to so it cracked and glowed with green light.

The room held only a few beds and a bank of drawers.

No ladder. He let out a sigh of frustration.

He was about to head back down to the supply room and come up with another idea when the light from his glow tube hit on something on a top bunk. He climbed up to find an object half-tucked under the pillow: a long black talon.

He turned it over in his hands. It reminded him of a set of fake dinosaur fossils he'd had as a kid, before Walling Home. His mother had found them under a layer of dust on the grocery store shelf, next to dented cans of beets that were the only thing left to buy when they finally got to the front of the line. She walked Rett to the park and cleared away some of the garbage that people had taken to dumping there when the trucks had stopped coming into their neighborhood to pick it up, and then she hid the fossils in the sand for Rett to dig up. Rett marveled at the process of lifting them out and fitting them into their proper shapes. He heard his mother's voice clearly in his mind even now, listing the names of the bones: *tibia, vertebrae, scapula.* Magical words, the way she said them; and magic, how they all fit together. The world outside their dig site had faded, the rotting garbage, the roaming dogs, the blackening trees . . .

But the talon in his hand now wasn't plastic, wasn't fake.

So many strange pieces to this odd place. He just had to fit the puzzle together.

He ran a finger along the grooved side of the talon, tested the point. A spot of blood welled on his fingertip. The sight of it awakened a sense of foreboding.

He slipped it back under the pillow, feeling oddly guilty for having moved it. A sudden urge to get away from it overtook him, but as he shifted to jump down from the bed, he spotted letters scratched into the metal wall: *G. W. was here.* And underneath, a string of numbers. At first he thought the numbers were a date, but the last digits were too high to be the year.

"Maybe it's the number of days the last guy was trapped in here," he mumbled to himself, and then wished he hadn't thought of that.

The next moment, as if by magic, a humming and a sudden spill of light came from the opening in the floor. Rett slid down from the bed to investigate and discovered that the overhead lights in the supply room had come on. Bryn must have found a way to turn the power on.

That's one piece of the puzzle solved. He climbed down the ladder and ducked into the main room, where he discovered more lights adding to the glow from the skylight.

"Bryn?"

A strange sound of metal clattering against wood answered him. It came from the room where he and Bryn had found the gun. Rett followed it.

Bryn stood next to a folded partition, staring at what looked like a hospital bed surrounded by glass cabinets. She turned to Rett, horror in her eyes. "Something happened here, didn't it?" She put a hand to her head. "Do you remember?"

Rett touched his own head, probed along his skull until he found what he knew he would find: the raised line of a long scar.

A flurry of images passed through his mind: needles and flashing metal and an angular face set with grim determination.

He saw the face before him now, and a white lab coat—a woman turning from the bed to tell him something. She opened her mouth, but no words came out, just the buzz of a drill or a saw—

It's not real, Rett told himself, clenching his eyes shut. *It's just me and Bryn here, no one else.*

He opened his eyes to find the visions gone. He touched Bryn's shoulder, trying to anchor himself. She flinched away.

Blood dripped from her fist onto the floor.

"Bryn, you're bleeding." He reached for her hand, but she jerked back.

"I can take care of myself," she barked, and bolted from the room.

Rett lingered, rooted by anxiety. Over the blood on Bryn's hand, and the way she had recoiled from him. Over the sight of the hospital bed.

He turned back toward it, wondering if he really had lain there or if the images passing through his mind again were memories of some other place. A shape on the floor caught his eye: a nylon backpack. He'd seen identical packs in the jumble of supplies in the other room. *How did you get in here?* Unease settled over him. *The same way those boots prints got all over the floor: someone was here.*

His glow stick reflected on something inside the open pack. He jerked at the zipper. The words DRINKING WATER met his sight.

In a moment, water was from pouring from a Mylar pouch down his parched throat. He reached for another—

But a thought popped into his head: *Water. A water line. That's what that chalky mark was.*

He hauled the pack with him into the main room. Bryn was nowhere in sight. She must have gone into the supply room again, probably making use of the first-aid kits Rett had seen in there earlier. He wanted to tell her about the water pouches he'd found, but first he looked up at what he had seen when he'd first awakened: a chalky mark up near the top of the wall. A water line.

The place had filled with water once.

Could he make it fill up again?

He eyed the handle next to the skylight. If the place filled with water, he could float up to the skylight, open the glass . . .

And they'd be free.

He took in the evidence around him with new eyes. The doorway to the office was lined with rubber. Now that he looked at the walls to the lounge and the supply room, he saw that they, too, were lined to keep out water. And down at the base of the walls . . . Rett crouched to prod at a tiny panel. Out popped a small metal nozzle.

I'm right. This room was made to flood.

I just have to figure out how to get the water going.

A familiar phrase popped into his head: *One, bloody jumpsuit. Two, parched throat.* And then: the image of a lever mounted to a wall. *Where?*

The ladder in the lounge pulled at his attention. *The lever.* He dropped the pack and started climbing.

The room at the top was dark. *Guess no one left the light switch on in here.* But Rett still had his glow tube. He held it up to the wall, and there it was: a lever, labeled with what looked like a rain cloud. It yielded when he pushed down on it, but only a little. He leaned all his weight on it. Something moved behind the wall and a *clunk* came from the roof.

"What, that's it?" he asked the empty room. He swept the light tube along the wall, and at the same time ran his hands over the cool metal, searching.

His fingers brushed something: a button. Just like the one downstairs: marked with a row of three overlapping circles . . .

. . . and a wavy line.

Rett's finger hovered over the button. The one downstairs hadn't worked. But then, neither had the lights. Now that the power was on—

He pushed the button.

An alarm echoed through the matrix of rooms, a throaty bleat that made Rett duck in panic.

What did I do? He flew down the ladder. The lounge's huge wall was swinging down to seal off the room. Rett caught a flash of something white on its underside—*gouges in the metal?* The sight only made him move faster, jolted him to launch himself under the wall just before it slid home.

The alarm still blared, and to his right, the office door slid shut. Clunking noises from the corridor to his left told him the changing rooms were also sealing themselves off. *I did it—the room is going to flood.*

"What's happening?" Bryn shouted over the ringing alarm. Behind her, the supply room wall was doing its best to close as the lounge wall had. But it seemed to be stuck in its half-open position.

"I pushed a button," Rett shouted back to Bryn. Her frown dampened his excitement. *Maybe I should have thought this through a little longer.*

The sound of rushing water interrupted his thoughts. A milky-white wave swept over the floor. High up on the wall, near the ceiling, a panel lit up, showing a warning sign:

Do not drink, Rett thought.

The water lapped over his feet, cold and stinking of minerals.

"How do we make it stop?" Bryn shouted.

"We don't." Rett pointed up at the skylight. "We float up there and open this place up."

"*What?*" The pitch of her voice suddenly filled him with doubt. She craned her neck while he sweated over whether he'd done something clever or incredibly stupid. His head spun. The sharp smell of sulfur made him want to gag.

"There's a ledge up there," Bryn announced, her voice wavering like she still didn't trust his plan. "People-sized."

Rett had missed it, but Bryn was right: a long shelf hung just under the glass and off to one side. "We can get on there and open the skylight! Can you swim?"

"So glad you asked *after* pushing the swim-or-die button."

Guilt stabbed at Rett. "Please say yes."

"Yes, but this water smells terrible."

The water had now reached their knees and was still rising. The alarm bleated on, sending waves of pain through Rett's head.

"What's that?" Bryn shouted over the alarm.

Rett followed her gaze to the backpack he had left on the floor. Bryn rushed to pick it up. Water dripped from the open flap.

"I found it in the other room." Rett jerked his head at the door that now sealed the office.

Bryn rummaged in the pack. She brought out a small device, slick with water.

A phone? Rett felt sick. Whatever it was, it was ruined.

"Why did you leave the pack on the floor?" Bryn demanded, her expression a mixture of confusion and alarm.

"I didn't know there were phones in there." *Idiot*, Rett scolded himself. *Why didn't you look through the pack earlier?* But he'd been so eager to find that lever, to turn on the water and get out of this place. "It doesn't matter anyway. We're getting out of here. We don't need phones. Or whatever they are." *This nightmare's almost over.*

The water sloshed at their waists, rose to their necks. They pumped their arms and legs, working to stay afloat as the water level climbed over the slide-away wall of the lounge. Rett kept his eyes on the shelf overhead, trying to make sense of the marking.

Bryn spotted it, too. "What is that?"

Two painted wavy lines marked the underside of the ledge, along with a familiar symbol: a row of three overlapping circles. Almost the same as the symbol that marked the buttons now submerged in the rooms below. Except these circles weren't quite round, and the uneven way they overlapped made Rett think of the segmented body of . . . some sort of creature? Rett thought of the talon he'd found in one of the sleeping rooms. Dread mixed with the panic still bubbling in his stomach. *Was this some kind of joke?*

The alarm silenced. Rett thought the water might have stopped rising, too. He reached for the shelf, but he could barely get his fingers over the edge. "Not high enough."

"The other wall never closed," Bryn said, her voice quiet now above the slap of water against the walls. "That room must be full of water by now."

Rett kicked hard, willing himself to rise higher in the water. His legs felt oddly strong and powerful, almost as if they belonged to someone else, someone who hadn't always been small for his age and prone to spending all his time sitting around drawing comics. *Must be my steely resolve not to die.* He managed to get a hand over the ledge and then swing the other one over and pull himself up to safety.

He reached down for Bryn. She went on treading water, making no move to accept his help. Rett couldn't tell if she didn't notice his hand or if she preferred staying in the putrid water to making physical contact with him. Finally, she gave him a wary glance, then gripped his wrist. A memory surfaced: her palm sliding to fit against his, a trail of freckles across the back of her hand. But then he was pulling her up onto the ledge next to him, and in a moment she slid her fingers out of his grip.

They lay on the shelf, panting. Rett rolled over to look through the skylight. Raindrops dotted the glass, and beyond them—gray sky, up and up forever.

"The handle," Bryn said.

Rett reached a stiff arm for the crank next to the skylight. "If you want to go your separate way after this, I won't blame you. But I swear I didn't ruin those phones on purpose."

"I'm not going back to Walling." Bryn coughed, desperate for the clean air they were moments from breathing. "I've already missed out on the big-screen experience for too many new Star Wars movies."

She offered him a smile that felt like an uneasy truce.

Rett went on cranking. "Lightsaber duels weren't meant for shoddy internet connections."

The skylight lifted with a *pop*.

6:27 A.M.

Rett kept cranking until the glass dome had lifted away. He struggled to pull himself up into the cool open air, feet planted on the ledge.

Finally, fresh air. The pain and fear and thirst pounding in his head gave way to relief. Rain fell on his face, and the chill cleared away the mineral stench lingering in his nose. It took a moment for his eyes to adjust to the faraway sight before him so that he could make sense of where he was.

And then his panic returned.

He wasn't in a medical center. Wasn't even in a city.

He was in a wasteland.

The ruts and spines of crumbling buttes stretched in every direction. He could find no glimpse of green, no sign of life for miles all around. Only the striations on the faces of canyons and cliffs offered any variation to the landscape. It was like looking out at a stone sea. Wave after petrified wave.

No.

This can't be happening.

Bryn drew up next to him. She turned to take in the full view of stark ridges and pale rock. A strangled noise sounded in her throat. "Where are we?"

Rett shook his head. He couldn't speak. His gaze swept over the bleached hollows, the grooved and weathered rock sloping down into sandy crevices. He felt as if he were looking at the world dissolving.

He seemed to be dissolving himself, his insides crumbling. "I have to get to my mom. I—" Panic choked his voice.

"What are we doing here?" Bryn asked the wasteland before her.

Rett scanned the rocky shelves, but there were no signs of roads, no break in the buttes, which stretched to the horizon.

They were alone in the middle of a wasteland.

"I can't be here," he said. "This can't be real."

The rain fell harder. It drummed on the metal roof. Bryn stood still as a statue, water running off her jumpsuit in rivulets. Rett wondered if she could see something out in the wasteland that he couldn't. She seemed to be noting every spire and ridge.

He slowly turned as he looked out over the horizon. "Bryn, look."

Bryn turned to see what he pointed at: a river. "Water," she croaked.

But how do we get down from here? Rett turned and inspected the outer shell of their odd prison. Solar panels covered a sloping section of the roof. A strange construction of metal flaps sat opposite, looking like a flower open to the sun. And starting just inches from Rett's fingers was a series of rungs leading over the rounded edge of the building. "We could climb down," he said. "It's not far. We could walk there easily."

Bryn gazed into the distance, her eyes fogged. Rett touched her hand, trying to call her back. "Something's out there," Bryn said. "Do you feel it?"

Rett tried to open himself to whatever she was sensing. He smelled sulfur and rust and the mineral smell of fresh rain on dirt. He thought he could hear a clicking or pattering from somewhere below—the rain, falling on rock and metal.

He glanced back inside and saw with a start that the water level had gone down a couple of feet. "Bryn." Now he could hear the distant suck of water in pipes. "The water's going down."

Bryn snapped her head around to look.

"We have to jump back in before it gets any lower," Rett said. He nodded at the rungs set into the side of the building. "Unless you'd rather take the ladder?"

Bryn considered for a moment while Rett watched the water line fall and tried to come to his own decision. "The river might be the only drinking water we find," Bryn said. "But if we climb down now, we'll never be able to get back inside the shelter without the water to break our fall."

Rett agonized: *Clean drinking water, or shelter and supplies?* "Wait—there's rope in the room with all the supplies. What if one of us waits up here, and the other goes down to get the rope? We throw the rope up here, tie it off, and then we can go down to the river and still have a way to climb back into the shelter."

Bryn squinted at the falling water level and then at the rungs, calculating. "Fine." She eased herself down onto the ledge inside the shelter.

Rett stiffened. He'd been planning to be the one to go back into the shelter. He didn't like the idea of being stuck up here with no way to get back inside. What if Bryn didn't come back with a rope?

But Bryn jumped down into the water before he could protest. He had a feeling she knew what he was thinking and didn't want to wait to argue it out with him.

"You'll get the rope?" he called down after she surfaced.

She swiped water off her face. After a moment in which Rett wondered if she'd heard him, she finally nodded.

Rett watched the water line sink lower. *Can I really trust her?*

He thought of how she edged away from him every time he came near. How the only emotion she didn't bother masking from him was suspicion.

He shivered in the cold rain. The pale wasteland stretched out in all directions, a graveyard of dust.

How am I supposed to trust someone who doesn't trust me?

His wet boots squelched as he scrambled down onto the ledge, and before he could think better of it, he slid into the water.

Bryn gave him her hollow stare when he surfaced. He looked away, and they tread water in silence.

When the water had gotten down to just a few feet, Bryn wasted no time in finding the pack.

"The drinking water's still okay, at least," Rett said. "But there's only a few pouches of it."

Bryn didn't seem interested in the Mylar pouches. She fished out one of the waterlogged phones and turned without a word to dive under the half-lifted wall into the supply room.

"What're you doing?" Rett followed her. When he came up, she was considering plugging a power cord into a wall socket. "Are you crazy?" He grabbed the cord out of her hand. "That phone won't work anyway. It's not worth getting fried."

She spun to face him. "You don't *want* them to work. You ruined them on purpose and now there's no way to call for help."

Rett gaped at her. "Why would I do that? I don't want to be stuck here any more than you do."

The water had vanished through drains along the baseboards. Rett felt he'd never get the stink of sulfur out of his nose. The taste of it lingered in his mouth.

"I swear, Bryn. I didn't do it on purpose. I'm not trying to keep us trapped here."

Bryn slumped against the cabinet. The sound of rain hitting the metal floor of the main area filled up the room. Rett hunched over the cabinet, listening. It could have been the sound of his nerves drumming.

"You don't remember anything?" Bryn asked. "About how we got here?"

Rett was about to say no. But then the strangest thing happened. He *did* remember something.

He remembered Bryn.

Sunlight behind her, his name on her lips. Something spilling out of her pockets. Daisies?

He remembered holding her hand.

Impossible. They'd been at Walling together, but they hadn't been friends, hadn't really known each other.

And yet he remembered the feel of her palm against his. A line of freckles along the back of her hand like a dusting of cinnamon.

He reached for her hand now, to see if the memory could be true, if he would find a familiar speckling across her skin.

He saw only the bandage she had used to bind her cut palm.

She pulled her hand out of his grip, frowning in confusion.

"I . . . I don't remember anything," Rett said, and hoped she didn't take his strained voice as evidence that he was lying.

Bryn's gaze went to the scar over his ear. She reached as if to touch it, but her fingers only brushed his hair. "Would you tell me if you *did* remember?" she asked him.

Rett's scalp tingled. He could think only of Bryn's hand hovering near his ear, and then she stepped away. "Yes," he said. "I'd tell you."

Bryn's arm twitched like she might reach for him again. But she turned away instead.

"Would *you* tell *me*?" Rett asked.

She kept her back to him. A coldness settled around Rett's spine. "We have to help each other. We're all alone out here."

"Is that why you didn't wait up on the roof for me to get the rope?" Bryn spun to face him, eyes flashing. "Is that why you've been hiding something from me since we woke up in this place?"

Rett's mouth went dry. He looked down at his sodden boots.

"Whose boots are those?" Bryn asked. "Who did you take them from?"

His thoughts raced. He tried to think of some way to explain it all to her. But he could only think of how she was inching away from him even now, ready to bolt. Ready to believe he had done something terrible and would again. "They were in the closet. I swear. I didn't take them from anyone." It wasn't a lie, at least. "There's no one else here." His throat tightened at that last bit. Did she hear it in his voice?

They stood for a long moment, considering each other.

And then: a sound like thunder.

Someone was banging on the door.

6:51 A.M.

Rett stood frozen, his heart hammering. The room swayed. His vision narrowed . . .

"What's that?" Bryn asked, calling Rett back to the moment.

The banging came again. *Bam-bam-bam. Bam. Bam. Bam.* Someone was pounding on the main door.

"Someone else *is* here," Bryn said in a low voice. She ducked out of the supply room.

"*Wait,* Bryn." Rett tried not to slip on the wet floor as he followed her out.

The banging had stopped. But fearful thoughts lingered in Rett's mind: blood on his clothes, and someone waiting outside with a plot for retribution.

Bryn crept toward the bolted door.

"Bryn . . ." Rett whispered.

"It could be someone here to help us."

All of Rett's muscles were tight with alarm. "I don't think it is."

She went to the door, and Rett told himself, *It's not going to open anyway.*

He was right. Bryn tugged at the bolt, but it seemed as stuck as ever.

Bam-bam-bam.

Bryn jumped back from the door as the banging sounded again. "Someone wants in here," she said to Rett.

Rett glanced up at the skylight. They had left it open. Rain fell in to patter on the wet floor. He thought of those rungs bolted to the side of the building.

Bryn seemed to read his mind. She came to stand under the skylight, lifted her face to the rain. "We're in here!" she shouted.

"Bryn, no!" Rett pulled at her arm, but she jerked away.

"Come up to the roof!" she called.

Rett backed away on shaking legs, gaze trained on the skylight. He tried to reassure himself: *Whoever's out there can get in, but they can't get down.* It was a long drop without any water to break the fall.

Still, they might have some rope. Like the coils of it stashed in the storage room.

Or a gun. Rett turned toward the office.

"Where are you going?" Bryn asked.

Rett slipped through the doorway and went to the desk. *Just in case,* he told himself as he pulled open the drawer where he'd left the gun.

The drawer was empty.

He pulled open the other drawer. Empty.

He turned slowly toward the main room. "Where's the gun, Bryn?"

The banging on the bolted door stopped abruptly. From outside came a scream that shattered Rett's nerves.

Bryn whirled to face the door. Rett turned into stone. Fear coursed through him as he strained to hear what was going on outside.

Then, a curious noise: a tapping on the walls. *Scritch scratch* . . . Something scraped over the building's metal shell. Rett looked up to the open skylight. *The rungs,* he thought. *Someone's climbing them.*

"Bryn, move!" he shouted.

A black shadow bloomed into sight, blocking the light from above. It squirmed through the opening, a huge glistening bulb bristling with antennae. Rett could hardly make sense of what he saw: the swing of a jointed leg, the swipe of a claw. The creature shrieked—

No, it was Bryn, screaming as the writhing creature pulled its segmented body through the skylight and crashed onto the wet floor between her and Rett.

"Bryn!" Rett screamed, hot panic coursing through his veins.

The creature lurched to its feet, an impossibly enormous insect with long serrated mandibles the length of Rett's arm. It swiped at the slippery floor with black talons and lunged for Bryn.

Something inside of Rett flailed for escape. His mind seemed to be reaching, *reaching* for invisible rescue. And then, before Rett could make sense of it, he was pulled into blackness.

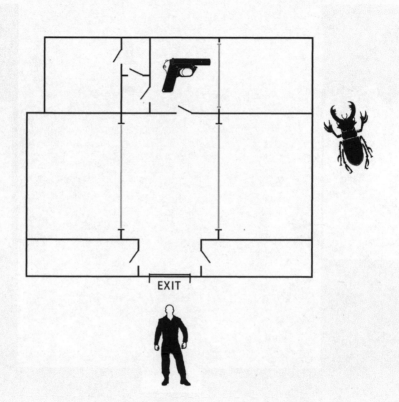

EXIT

4:38 A.M.

Rett stumbled forward and fell to his knees in cold dirt. A strangled noise escaped from his throat. *Bryn—*

He scrambled to his feet. He was alone in a dark hollow. Above him in the sky a green flame flexed.

Bryn—

The green light shimmered over the dark angles of buttes and canyons. All was silent.

But Rett remembered: he and Bryn had been inside a shelter, and something had come down through the skylight. Rett still heard in his mind the sound of its scythe-like feet scratching over the metal floor, Bryn screaming.

The humped silhouette of the metal shelter loomed at the top of a slope. Rett hurried toward it, picturing Bryn on the rain-slicked floor, the creature over her . . .

Rett stopped. Something didn't make sense. *Why is it so dark out here?* It had been morning. Now it was night. *What happened to my boots?* Grit clung to his bare feet.

He peered up at the shelter again. *Scatter 3*, he thought, remembering the marking he'd found on the inside of the door. *Is Bryn really in there?*

Then he remembered something else: while he and Bryn

had been inside, someone had been outside, pounding on the door. Rett whipped around, but there was only a lonely boulder interrupting the empty landscape. Still, someone might be out there, at the edge of the darkness.

Get inside, he told himself. He turned back for Scatter 3.

5:37 A.M.

Someone is calling to me . . .
 Someone is . . .
 Screaming.
Rett woke to a crushing headache and a strange string of thoughts. He had the faint impression he had been outside— his hands were cold and grimy. But he couldn't remember much beyond that except . . . *Someone was screaming.*

A swell of fear overtook him and he scrambled to his feet. For a moment, the room before him was slick with rain, and a dark form fell from the ceiling—

He looked up. Blue morning light filtered in through a skylight.

A nightmare, he decided. *That was just a nightmare.*

The metal room glowed faintly in the morning light, underwater-blue. From another room came the sound of singing. Rett closed his eyes, drinking in the hypnotic tune. The words brought a strange scene to mind: a lighthouse topped by a tattered flag, a piece of metal hidden in a boat, fleshy black bulbs circling overhead . . .

Whatever you do, don't open that skylight, Rett told himself. He shook away the nightmare images.

Then he looked down and saw the blood on his clothes.

5:47 A.M.

He emerged from a changing room, dressed in a clean jump-suit and a pair of boots, shaking with nerves and thirst and pain. *What am I doing here?* He glanced again at the bolted door. *Locked, trapped.* The logo on the door caught his eye. Jagged strokes like an uneven skyline. He had a sudden vision of ragged cliffs raked over by the massive hand of weather. *Where?* A place seen in a dream—no place he had been.

He turned back to the room he had first awakened in and was surprised to find a wall had been lifted away. And sitting on a long couch, like a figure in a diorama, was a girl. Slender frame inside a baggy jumpsuit, large hazel eyes bright against a dirt-streaked face. She folded herself even smaller in the tight space. Rett agreed with the sentiment. "It's not safe here," he said, his voice an unfamiliar croak. "We need to get out."

She nodded slowly and moved from the couch to the middle of the main room. Blue light from above tinted her suit, her skin, so that she seemed to be surfacing from a darker place. Rett thought, *Take me with you.*

The girl dragged her gaze to the glowing skylight overhead. "Something's coming for us."

Rett tensed as he pictured again a black, fleshy form falling from above. "Do you know what it is—what's out there?"

"No." The girl moved her gaze to an open doorway. "But there's a gun."

Rett's scalp prickled. "A gun?"

He crept to the doorway. The gun lay on the floor, a faint gleam of gray in the dim light. Rett regarded it for a long moment, thinking he was the wrong person to be here, to be expected to do anything like shoot a gun. But the girl was right—something was coming for them. He picked up the gun. It was cold against his palm and not as reassuring as he needed it to be. "We might need this later," he said as she came into the room behind him. He spotted a desk against the wall and shut the gun in a drawer.

As the drawer slid shut, he realized something: he had known about the gun even before he had seen it, even before the girl had told him. *A lighthouse topped by a tattered flag, a piece of metal hidden in a boat . . .*

"What's wrong?" the girl asked, her voice echoing faintly in the small space so that the question seemed to reverberate in Rett's head. *What's wrong, what's wrong?*

Something's very wrong here, Rett thought.

He turned to study her, still frowning in thought. He'd known about the gun because of the song she'd been singing. *One lonely lighthouse, two in a boat . . .*

A memory tickled at the back of his mind. "I know you from somewhere," he said to the girl. "What's your name?"

She tipped her head to one side, curious, or trying to take him in from a new angle to study him better.

And what do you see? Rett asked silently. *Someone familiar? Or just a scrawny stranger trying not to shake with fear at the visions in his head?*

Finally she said, "I'm Bryn."

"Bryn . . . ?"

"Bryn Ward," she said quietly.

"Are you a ward at Walling Home?"

Surprise flickered in her eyes. "Is that a lucky guess, or have we met before?"

"I'm . . . not sure. I'm from Walling, too. We must have been sent here together." It wasn't exactly comforting to know she was from Walling. *Some* of the boarders helped each other—played lookout, warned each other about moldy food and the moods of the staff. But sometimes, perfectly nice kids ratted you out for skipping chore rotation, or cleared out your stash of pilfered food. And the not-so-nice ones, the ones you thought might be useful to have around, decided your face was the perfect canvas for their sudden, violent art.

Rett had figured it out a long time ago: you couldn't really know who to trust. He'd learned that at age ten, when an older boy, Garrick, told him about a disused firewood box on the edge of Walling's property that made the perfect place to watch shooting stars in secret. And then Garrick had come along and shut the lid with Rett inside. The stars had trailed above, unseen, while Rett imagined them behind his eyelids and tried not to waste his breath on pleading.

You choose who to trust. And sometimes you choose wrong.

What if I choose wrong again?

"Do you think . . ." Bryn frowned in thought. "I asked to leave Walling early. I think I might have graduated out."

In his mind, Rett heard the click of the director's door shutting, the wheeze of the man's impatient sigh, the uneven scratch of his own broken voice: *She's sick, I need to go to her.* "I think I did, too—graduated out."

They turned to look around at the scuffed metal walls, the dour gray gleam of the place. "Congratulations," Bryn said wryly.

This can't be right, Rett thought. *I'm not supposed to be here.* His mother needed him. Without treatment she couldn't hope for more than a few months. *And how long ago was that?* Rett wondered, eyeing the thick layer of dust coating the walls. *How long have I been here?*

"You don't know what this place is?" he asked Bryn, trying to keep desperation out of his voice.

"I don't even know how I got here."

Rett cataloged the details around him: scratched metal, dirty footprints, a ladder mounted over a couch, a wall with a rusty plate where a handle should have been. "Do you feel like—somehow, this has happened before?"

Bryn looked from the ladder to the rusty plate, like Rett had done.

"This place feels familiar, this situation," Rett said. "And . . . you. You seem familiar."

"I don't even know your name."

Her words stabbed at him in a way he didn't understand. "It's Rett."

"Rett . . ." Bryn seemed to be testing the name for familiarity. "You recognized me from Walling Home?"

"I guess, but—somewhere else, too." Rett pictured her suit sun-dappled instead of tinted by muted morning light. He imagined a long stalk of grass twined through her fingers. "I knew you somewhere else."

Bryn's wondering gaze swept over him. It made Rett feel more vulnerable than any piercing stare ever could.

"Can you sing that song again?" he asked her. "Maybe it will help me remember."

"What song?"

"The one you were singing a few minutes ago." Rett moved to the wall that wanted lifting and kicked at the rusty plate.

"Was I singing? That's a weird thing to do in a quarantine tank."

"You were singing about a lighthouse," Rett said, turning as he lifted the wall. "A boat . . ."

A haze passed over Bryn's expression. She put a hand to her head. Rett's fingers went automatically to a scar under his short hair. *How did I get this?*

Bryn swayed, and Rett moved to steady her. She grimaced with the same pain that knocked against his skull.

"Never mind," he said. "Let's just sit down."

"I'm thirsty."

He helped her over to the couch. "Sit here and I'll look for some water." He glanced at the ladder again. *There's water up there. I know it.*

5:59 A.M.

In the room atop the ladder, Rett found a lever in the dark. He leaned his weight down on it until something moved behind the wall and a *clunk* came from the roof. He waited for something more to happen.

A line from Bryn's song went through his mind: *Three gulls circle, four clouds float.*

He lifted a hand to the wall, slow as a sleepwalker, and traced the outline of what he knew was painted there in the dark: a cloud and scattered raindrops. The paint was smooth under his finger. *How did I know?* he wondered. *How did I know something was painted here?*

A chill went down the back of his neck. *I've done this before.* The thought nagged at him as he climbed back down the ladder.

"Sorry, no luck," he called.

Bryn was nowhere in sight, but it was easy to guess she had disappeared behind the half-lifted wall opposite. Rett ducked under the wall to find her rummaging through some cabinets.

"You don't waste time, do you?" Rett said, looking around at the equipment strewn over the floor.

Bryn glanced back at him before returning to her work, a shadow of resentment lingering in her gaze. "It was like that when I came in here."

"Okay," he said, a little defensively. "I promise I wasn't angling to stake my claim to rain ponchos."

She pushed the bin of ponchos toward him without comment and went on searching the cabinets. He blinked down at her offering and couldn't decide whether he owed her a *thank you* or a *sorry*.

"So," he tried, "you didn't feel like sticking around Walling until you were eighteen and a proper adult?"

"Does taking health and safety matters into your own hands make you a proper adult? Because I think I might already be one." She pulled a long metal pole out of the cabinet and hefted it to check its weight, preparing herself for whatever danger might await them.

"Now I'm changing my mind," Rett said, watching her slow-swing the pole in practice. "I think I prefer a sheltered childhood after all."

Bryn leaned back to scour the metal room with her gaze. "Depends on the shelter."

"Good point." Rett swallowed against the sticky pain in his throat. "At least Walling had water."

"Why'd you ask to leave early? You had someone's couch in mind, or where were you going to live?"

"I'm supposed to be on the East Coast. My mom's at a work-house, or anyway, she will be until they close them." *Or have the workhouses already closed? How long have we been here?* He massaged a sudden ache in his chest. "She . . . she's sick. I'm going to go take care of her."

A barrage of questions went through his head. He waited for Bryn to ask them: *What will you do if she's already gone?* Or: *What if you can't do anything to help?* Questions Rett couldn't answer. Because his mother hadn't told him what her plans were. Because . . .

Because . . .

Some vague feeling of anger passed through him, like the ghost of it. He'd written those emails, before she'd gotten sick again. Written things he shouldn't have said: *You never came back . . . I'm better off without you anyway . . . I don't need you . . .*

Only one of those things was true.

He waited for Bryn to say something.

Her amber eyes warmed. "I'm sorry," she said.

Rett felt like he'd been walking down a narrow stair and had missed a step. He turned, freeing himself from Bryn's magnetic gaze. "What about you? Did you leave Walling so you could start a new life in a metal dungeon?"

"I'm planning to meet up with my boyfriend. He's two years older than I am, so he was already getting the boot."

Rett tried to make sense of the disappointment suddenly washing over him. *What do I care if she has a boyfriend?*

"He's one of the biggest reasons I survived five years in Walling," Bryn went on. "He has a really great talent for find-ing bizarre alien movies online. Any time we felt sorry for ourselves, we'd watch Ripley get covered in alien saliva-slime."

She gave Rett a wry smile that sent electricity through his heart.

"But where will you go? I mean, the two of you. Without any money."

She tensed.

"Sorry, it's none of my business," Rett said quickly. *Like she doesn't have enough to worry about right now.*

But she didn't even seem to hear his apology. Her eyes had gone hazy with some thought. "I wasn't going to leave empty-handed. I wouldn't have done that. I had a plan . . ."

"Was this your plan?" Rett asked with a glum smile.

Bryn went on ignoring him. "You need money for your mom, right? To help her get better. And I wouldn't have left unless I had some way to help me and my boyfriend get by."

Rett felt another stab in his gut at the word *boyfriend*. "So we both need money. Is that why we're here? What, there's something . . . valuable here that we came to find?" The moment he said the word *find*, he knew there was something to the idea. *Yes, yes! I'm supposed to find something!*

Judging by the way Bryn's gaze snapped to his, she felt the same way.

All at once, they launched themselves at the junk spilling out of the cabinets. They yanked out coils of rope and tangled power cords and slippery plastic sheets as if they were disemboweling a compliant creature. They turned over bins and pawed through empty backpacks and boxes of compasses and worthless empty water bottles. Rett even slid his hands all over the insides of the cabinets in case they had missed a hidden drawer or shelf. The most he discovered was an itemized list of the supplies they'd already found. He ran an eye over it: *12 feet of rope, 9×9 plastic drop cloth, 6 nylon backpacks,*

6 pairs of binoculars, 6 shovels . . . It finally registered that the cabinets held only supplies they didn't need, nothing valuable, not even water—which Rett would have happily accepted over anything worth actual money.

But Bryn didn't seem fazed. She shot to her feet, a glowing green tube in her hand, and announced, "I'm going to search the rest of this place." She ducked out of the room without waiting for his reply.

The metal pole she'd found lay among the scattered debris. Rett lifted it by its leather strap and wondered why it gave him an uneasy feeling.

We need to get out of this place.

But how? Door's jammed shut.

A thought came to him that made his stomach shrink: *What about the skylight?*

He hefted the metal pole, a decent weapon. He had the feeling there was something out there, something bad.

But the skylight might be their only way out.

If it even opened.

He suddenly remembered the itemized list he'd found. Hadn't he seen something on it about binoculars?

He hunted through the debris until he found a bin full of them—real binoculars with metal casings and leather straps.

Back in the main room, he lifted the binoculars to inspect the skylight overhead. The glass was dotted with rain, reminding Rett again how thirsty he was. Just underneath the skylight, off to one side, a narrow ledge was marked by odd symbols: two wavy lines and a row of overlapping circles. *Strange,* Rett thought. He moved the binoculars and found something else: a small crank that likely opened the glass dome. *But I already knew I'd find that. I already knew the skylight opened.* He moved to the edge of the room, haunted by the impression that something might come through the glass at any moment.

Something about the symbol on the underside of the ledge tickled at the back of his mind. He used the binoculars to inspect it again. Then he saw on the wall near it a chalky white line, stark against the dusty metal.

A wavy symbol, a chalky water line . . .

But why would the place fill with water?

He tried to understand what the segmented blob was trying to tell him. "Something's going to break into pieces?" But the symbol wasn't just a blob. When he focused the binoculars, the blob sprouted a pair of—

Antennae?

"The water gets rid of bugs," he murmured.

A sound from the open doorway to his left interrupted his thoughts: the *click* of a drawer shutting.

Rett stepped into the doorway to see what Bryn might have found during her search.

She quickly turned from the desk. "Nothing in there."

"Well." Rett frowned. "Except the gun, you mean."

"Right," she said quickly. "I meant nothing new. Nothing we hadn't seen."

Rett watched her toy with the ends of her sleeves. *What is she so nervous about?*

Bryn nodded toward a narrow door to one side of the room. "Should we check in there?"

"Go ahead. Looks like there's only room for one."

The door opened with a *pop*. "Just a bathroom," Bryn reported, "but it looks like there's another door through here. Maybe just a closet . . ."

Something in Bryn's stiff posture made Rett worry. *If she finds something, will she tell me about it?*

A feverish need to search the place for himself sent Rett out of the dark office. He darted back to the lounge area and slid his palms over the wall, feeling for any hidden switches or—

There! A panel slid away, revealing a blue spigot. *Water!* Rett slapped at the spigot. Nothing came out. *Damn.*

The couch cushion he knelt on shifted under him. He yanked off the cushion to discover Mylar-wrapped bars wedged into the hollow seat. Each was marked RATION BAR.

Rett yanked one out. Underneath the lettering was some kind of serial number and an expiration date. "Still good for another decade," he mumbled to himself. "Let's hope we're not stuck here that long." He pocketed the bar, too thirsty and queasy to consider eating it, and then pocketed a few more.

What next? He'd already searched the room at the top of the ladder. Could there be anything else here he'd missed? *What's that white stuff?* A smear of white chalk marked the edge of the wall that had been lifted into a slot over the room. Rett reached up to touch it, and the white stuff came away on his fingertips. He lifted his hand again to pull down the wall and examine it.

But just then, a light came on overhead. "How did I do that?" Rett wondered aloud.

"You didn't," Bryn called from the office. "*I* did. I found a fuse box . . . And what's this?"

The clack of wood on metal echoed through the small space. Rett darted to the office just in time to see Bryn tug aside a partition they'd both missed earlier.

Another room lay beyond. The bed and the sharp smell of

cleaner and medicine were enough to tell him it was some kind of medical area.

Bryn slumped against the wall, one hand clutching her head.

"Bryn?

"Something happened here," she rasped. "Do you feel it?"

Rett scanned the room again and a memory flashed through his mind: a hospital room, a bank of bright lights. "Not here. Somewhere else. Some place bigger than this."

Bryn blinked up at the overhead lights. A faraway look came into her eyes. "They put something in our heads." She touched the scar that Rett knew must lie along her scalp.

Rett touched his own scar. A surge of remembered pain overtook him. He clenched his eyes shut and saw a face, a white lab coat. Heard a voice: *If you ever find yourself in danger, remember the song. It signals the mechanism.* The *woman in the lab coat touched his head, carefully, near where the mechanism had been inserted into his brain* . . .

Rett willed the pain away and the memory vanished with it. Bryn stood staring at him, still touching her head, grimacing with fear. Rett reached and moved her hand away. "Don't think about it," he said. His stomach churned, threatening to revolt. *What did I let them do to me?*

Don't think about it, he told himself as he pushed away the memory of pain splitting his skull.

But his nightmare thoughts came to life: Blood bloomed on his fingertips.

Rett gaped at the sight. *How* . . . ?

A vision of a black talon surfaced in his mind.

Then he realized where the blood had really come from:

Bryn's palm welled with it, so much that it dripped onto the floor.

"*Bryn.*" Rett took her hand in his again and led her out to the main room while she stared at her injured palm in shock. "Wait here."

Rett ducked into the supply room. When he came back with a roll of gauze, she was gone.

"Bryn?"

Only spatters of blood on the floor where she had stood moments ago.

Then, her voice: "Look, Rett."

Rett jerked back in surprise. *Why am I so jumpy? It's just Bryn.*

She sat curled on the couch, cradling her injured palm in her good hand, a nylon backpack hooked over her arm. She gave him a weak smile and gestured at the Mylar pouches spilled along the seat next to her. "I found water."

6:20 A.M.

"You remembered something."

Rett held Bryn's hand in his, palm up, as he finished wrapping the gauze and tucked in the loose end. "Yes," he answered slowly. "I remembered . . ." Rett wasn't sure if the reason his mind was buzzing was that he was still holding Bryn's wrist or if the memory had left him shaken. "I remember someone saying that if I ever find myself in danger, I should use the song you were singing earlier to signal the—the thing in our—" A fresh bolt of pain went through his head.

"Here." Bryn took her hand from his to offer him one of

the water pouches between them on the couch seat. "We'll think about everything else later."

Rett pulled the tab almost mindlessly, but then thought better of drinking the water himself. "You first."

Bryn lifted her eyebrows as she took the pouch. " 'Women and children first'? Very chivalrous."

His face heated. "*Injured* first, I was thinking. And I'm pretty sure I'm younger than you, so if anyone's the child here . . ." His hands were already fumbling to open another pouch. "Anyway, cheers."

They drained their pouches and then Bryn said, "I could swear you're older than I am. Maybe your wisdom just shows better on your face."

"I can honestly say this is the first time anyone's ever accused me of being wise."

"You know how to wrap an injury." Bryn held up her hand, which was wrapped with so much gauze, anyone might think she'd put on a mitten.

"That's just me showing off my skills at winding things. I'm pretty good with yo-yos and electrical cords, too."

"Electrical cords? You wind a lot of those?"

"If you wind them up and keep them out of sight, people are less likely to hurt you with them."

They both fell silent. *Great conversation skills*, Rett told himself. *Really cheerful topic.*

Bryn didn't take her gaze off him, but her eyes turned murky, almost gray. "You broke that guy's hand. Garrick."

Rett hid a jolt of surprise. "Garrick was the kind of guy I hid electrical cords from."

Bryn scrutinized him for a moment longer, her expression unreadable but her uninjured hand moving closer to his on the seat. She slowly nodded. "I guess we do all kinds of things to survive."

Rett knew he should take comfort in her sympathy. But her stony voice made him wonder exactly what kinds of things she meant. He saw her in his mind, hunting desperately through the supply cabinets in the other room. The image unlocked a memory of her from Walling Home. *Best not to bring that up*, he thought, noting her dejected slouch.

"Anyway, I could have really impressed you with my yo-yo skills," Rett said. "Too bad there aren't any of those around."

She gave him a small smile. "Isn't that convenient."

"And checkers. I would destroy you in checkers."

"Anything else?"

"I could draw you a terrible comic if we had some paper."

"Only a terrible one?"

"My skills are . . . still sharpening. I only started drawing my own comics because I traded away all the issues I brought with me to Walling. Except for the last issue of *Shine Fall*. You ever heard of it? It's for younger kids but . . ." He shrugged. For a moment, he was eight years old, marveling over illustrations of Hikaru's daring adventures while his mother read the captions aloud, her voice a promise of warmth and safety.

"I only ever liked the scary comics," Bryn said. "The kind you read by flashlight on camping trips until your stepdad complains the light is keeping him up."

Rett grimaced at the scratched walls. "I'm pretty sure I have plenty of inspiration for *scary*."

Bryn brought something out of the pack Rett hadn't noticed she was rummaging in. She pushed the notebook toward him and said, "Give me your scariest."

"Really?" He unclipped the pen from the cover and flipped through the blank pages. "I'm warning you, I'm not great at this."

She watched him sketch. His skin warmed under her gaze. "What did you mean about using a song to . . . ?" Her voice trailed off.

"Someone told me that song you were singing is supposed to help us," Rett said as he sketched. He paused. "That means someone knew we would end up here."

"There must have been a plan, then, and we just can't remember it. Why don't we remember anything?"

"Except the song," Rett said. "You remembered that."

"Music's easier to remember than other things."

Rett got a flash of his mother's face glowing in the morning light while she sang, heard a broken phrase from the song she played on repeat when they most needed to forget the things they'd heard on the news. *Yes, music's easier to remember.*

"Do you think if you sing the song, something will happen?" Rett asked.

"Nothing happened earlier. Not that I could tell."

"Try again. Please?"

Bryn shifted in her seat. For a moment, Rett thought she was going to refuse him, or tell him she didn't remember the song. But then the familiar tune came in Bryn's quiet, clear voice. It echoed in the small space like a spell:

> *"One lonely lighthouse*
> *Two in a boat . . ."*

That's us, Rett thought, *trying to get through this together.*

*"Three gulls circle
Four clouds float."*

Even though they were sitting under the overhang of the upper room, Rett could swear he felt a shadow pass overhead as Bryn sang the last lines. He shivered.

"Nothing happened," Bryn said. "Maybe we both have to sing it?"

Rett hunkered over his drawing. "My singing could only ever make things worse, not better."

"I'm not asking you to romance me. Just get the words out."

Rett kept his face lowered. "Well, that's a relief. I'm pretty sure I wouldn't know how to romance anyone."

"Seriously, whatever you've got is fine." Bryn touched his hand and he almost jumped in surprise. "Okay?"

"Sure, yeah." *Just let me move my hand first so I can think straight.*

She started singing, and he managed to join in. *"One lonely lighthouse . . ."*

Her voice was like water pouring over him. It cooled the hot pain that throbbed deep in his skull, in his chest. *It's not so lonely in here, actually. In our bizarre lighthouse.*

The song ended, and then the echo of it did. The only change Rett could see was that the light bathing the main area of the shelter had brightened a little, but he attributed that to the sun rising. And while he was ready to believe that Bryn's singing could command all celestial bodies, he was convinced his own tuneless voice would cancel out any magic she might wield.

"You're right," Bryn said. "We're probably better off if you don't sing." She cracked a smile, and Rett thought, *A smile looks good on you.*

"Too late for refunds now," he said.

She nodded at the notebook under his hand. "You going to show me?"

It almost startled Rett to see the pen poised over the paper. He looked down at what he had sketched.

"What's wrong?" Bryn asked. She pulled the notebook out from under his shaking hand.

The open page showed a jointed creature emerging from shadow, bristling with antennae, its jagged mandibles shaded so they threatened to strike from the page.

The notebook slipped from Bryn's hands. "I thought you said you weren't any good at drawing," she mumbled. The color had drained from her face. "Guess you've practiced this one."

Rett clutched the edge of the table. "No . . . I saw it in a dream or something. I don't know how I . . ." It was the best thing he'd ever drawn. Well, the most horrifying, but the most skillfully rendered. If he hadn't seen that very image in his head when he'd first awakened here, he would almost suspect someone else had drawn this picture and slipped it under his hand.

Bryn started to say something, but it seemed that the last of her strength had drained out of her. She pressed her eyes shut. Her skin looked gray.

Rett glanced at her injured hand and pressed another pouch of water on her. "Drink this. You need it."

She shook her head. "We don't have much. Better save it." Her voice trembled.

Rett yanked open the backpack sitting on the seat between them. No shine of foil inside—not a single water pouch. The six pouches on the couch were all they had. "Drink it anyway. We'll find more."

She relented. Rett pulled the pack open again and squinted at its jumbled contents. He pulled out a black device to inspect it. Swiped at the screen, jabbed at the buttons along the side. *Battery must be dead.*

Didn't I see some power cords in the supply room?

His heart sped up. The devices didn't look quite like phones. A two-way radio, maybe? *Something.*

"Wait here," he told Bryn.

"I'm going to look around a little more," she said. But her eyes were closed, her head tipped back against the couch.

"It's okay. Just rest for a minute."

Rett scooped the rest of the devices out of the pack and took them to the supply room. He went to work plugging in power cords from the cabinet, and then it was just a matter of waiting for the devices to charge.

A metal clang sounded in the other room. "Bryn?" *What is she doing?*

He turned to duck under the wall, but before he could, a button set over the cabinet caught his attention. A familiar set of symbols marked it, a segmented blob under a wavy line.

The water drowns the bugs if they get in. Could that be right?

"But I don't need to get rid of bugs," Rett told the empty room.

He abandoned the mystery and ducked back into the main room.

Bryn no longer sat in the lounge. *That's weird. Why is that* panel shut over the ladder? "Bryn, are you up there?" *And why did you shut me out?* "Bryn?"

No answer.

A dark thought came over Rett. It made him tremble, made his mouth go dry.

She said she was going to look around. He bolted for the changing room where he'd stashed the bloody jumpsuit. *Did she come this way—did she see it?*

He reached down to yank out the bin under the shelf.

But he didn't need to. The stained jumpsuit hung half out of the bin.

Oh no oh no. Rett raked his fingers over his scalp. *She found it and now she thinks—*

What does she think? That I've been hiding something all this time? Something terrible?

Another thought crept into his mind: *What if I did* do *something terrible?*

No no no.

His feet took him back toward the lounge, but he could only stare up at the panel shut tight over the ladder. He imagined her huddled in the dark room, listening for the sound of his feet on the ladder rungs.

Listening . . .

He whirled toward the open doorway that led into the office. Remembered the *click* of a drawer closing . . .

He crept through the doorway, going hot all over.

Opened the drawer where he'd left the gun.

Empty.

He stumbled back and caught himself against the door-frame. *Bryn has the gun. And she thinks I'm dangerous.*

And then another thought occurred to him. *What if she's*

not up in that room? What if she hid somewhere else, but she closed that panel just to make me think she's up there?

The air around him went electric. *What do I do?* Rett gripped the doorway. It yielded strangely—it was lined with heavy rubber strips.

What—?

Images flashed through his mind: the ledge under the skylight, the button with its mysterious symbol, the chalky white water line up near the ceiling, the rubbery strips along the doorway and—yes, under the half-lifted wall to the supply room.

In an instant, it came to him: *The button makes the place fill with water.*

It seals off the doors and floods the middle area.

Before he realized what he was doing, he found himself in the supply room, ripping the devices from their power cords, wrapping them in a plastic sheet, stuffing them in another backpack along with everything else close at hand—binoculars and rope and a first-aid kit. *For what?* He didn't know, didn't care, just couldn't stop the impulse. He reached for the button set over the counter.

Wait. Am I really going to do this? Fill the place with water to keep myself safe from Bryn?

He remembered her electric smile, her hand reaching for his.

But the thought of her hiding—with a *gun*—panicked and weak and afraid—shouldered out all other thoughts.

He slammed his fist onto the button.

An alarm blared through the complex, throaty and insistent. Rett watched milky water pour under the half-lifted wall. *I was right.* The thought held him in thrall for a moment, and then he threw himself back into action.

He made to duck back under the jammed wall into the main room but stopped to grab the metal pole from the floor. *I might need this.*

In the main room, the wall had swung down to seal off the lounge. Water flowed over the floor while Rett watched in shock. *This is happening. The room's going to fill up.*

The wall over the lounge shuddered.

Bryn. She was pounding on the wall from the other side. *So she really was hiding in that upper room.*

And now she was sealed away in the lounge.

What did I do?

The water had crept up to his ankles.

She has a gun, he reminded himself.

The water rose over his knees.

He looked up. *Is something out there, waiting for me?* He peered at the skylight, looking for any sign of movement beyond the glass. But there were only raindrops reflecting light.

The alarm went on blaring while Rett focused on holding the metal pole over his head and treading water with the backpack weighing him down. Finally, the water rose high enough to where Rett could toss the pole onto the ledge and then pull himself up.

He lay for a moment with his quads and shoulders aching. Then the alarm quieted. He watched the water for a long moment and decided it had stopped rising.

Now what? He turned over on his back to look up through the skylight. But a matrix of raindrops blocked any view through the glass. *Raindrops . . . water . . .* His throat was still dry, his head tight with the effect of thirst. If only he could collect the water from the glass, could let the rain fall into his mouth . . .

The crank he had spotted earlier was inches from his head. Just a few turns of the crank would open the glass. The rain would fall cold onto his face. Fresh air would drive away the stench of minerals and whatever else tainted the water so it wasn't safe for drinking. And he could look outside and know, finally, exactly where he was.

He reached, tentatively. He tried to sense whether anything was out there, waiting for a chance to get inside. The only sound was of rain drumming on the metal roof, a maddening sound that chased away all thought except that of fresh water. Rett turned the crank. In his other hand, he readied the metal pole.

Pop. The glass lifted half an inch. A gust of wet air blew in and made Rett hungry for more. He went on cranking until the glass lifted away to reveal luminous gray clouds.

He pulled himself up through the opening.

A wall of black met him.

Rett gasped. A gleaming orb of an eye, the serrated edge of a long mandible. He ducked back down, heart hammering. *What the hell?* Clawed feet scraped over the metal roof. Rett crouched, frozen. *This can't be happening.*

The long hook of the mandible shot through the opening. Rett couldn't move, couldn't think. His vision narrowed. He felt a strange pull on his consciousness, but the next moment a voice in his head cried, *Fight!*

He snapped back into the moment and hefted the metal pole. His hands were wet and shaking.

The pole slipped.

It fell into the water.

No! Rett watched it vanish, his only weapon gone.

His attention snapped back to the jagged mandible angling closer. *What do I do?*

There's always something, he told himself.

He scrambled to slide off his backpack. It was heavy with the weight of the devices, the binoculars. *Heavy enough to do damage.*

He swung it as hard as he could.

Crack. It made contact.

Then—scratching and scrabbling as the creature retreated beyond his sight.

Rett's heart shook violently as he pushed himself up through the skylight again and swung the backpack harder than he thought he had it in him to swing. This time something crunched. The creature fell away from the side of the building. Rett leaned out as far as he could, but the edge of the building cut off his view of the fallen creature. Still, it was gone. His heart went on trying to escape his chest. He gulped cool air. *It's gone,* he told himself, and lifted his face to let the rain fall into his mouth.

He looked out over his surroundings. The landscape was nothing but towering folds of barren rock as far as the eye could see. *No,* he thought. *This can't be right.*

He couldn't have done this to himself. Couldn't have gotten himself stranded out in the middle of a wasteland. Especially when he needed so badly to get to the workhouse that might be closing even at this moment. To get to his mother before it was too late to help her.

What am I doing here? How did I get here?

His hand went automatically to the scar over his ear. *They put something in our heads.*

A memory hurtled out from some locked-tight place: *A room, a medical lab. A woman with a determined grimace. Bryn stirred on a white-sheeted bed nearby. Rett fingered the* scar along his bare scalp, listening to a lilting song playing from a scratchy record.

And then another memory: *Rett touching the scar under his cropped hair. The woman's hard voice: "If you haven't managed it yet, you never will. There's only one way left to do this. You'll have to find it . . ."*

Rett's heart beat fast. *She brought us out here. The woman in the lab coat. Why?*

The peaks of spires and buttes rose in waves all around. *What am I supposed to do?*

He remembered the devices in his pack and scrambled to pull out the plastic-wrapped packet he'd enclosed them in. Maybe they could help him—if they had enough charge to turn on. Maybe he could use them to call for help.

He wrestled one out of the packet and punched his finger at a button.

The screen bloomed to life.

It displayed a jumble of icons that made Rett's heart race even though he couldn't decipher them. He jabbed at one of them, which only opened up another screen of cryptic symbols. "What is this thing?" he wondered aloud. *Not a phone, not a walkie-talkie. What good is it?*

He tapped another icon and the screen displayed a prompt: ENTER COORDINATES.

Rett blinked at it. *Coordinates.*

This thing has GPS.

"What coordinates?" he asked the device.

He shook his head in confusion. *I can't get out of here if I don't even know where I am.* He'd been so sure he was supposed to find something, but the best thing the shelter had to offer were GPS units he didn't know how to use.

Isn't that what GPS is for? Finding things?

A wave of horror slowly washed over him as he took in the endless wasteland with new eyes. *The thing we need to find isn't inside the shelter.*

It's out here.

Out in the bone-colored canyons unspooling in every direction. Out in the lifeless wastes.

"No. No, I can't do this," he mumbled.

A series of rungs led down over the sloped edge of the building. Down to rocky canyon floors where he could wander forever with no hope of being found.

And the creature had fallen down there. Rett thought it might be dead—there had been that loud *crack* when he'd hit it with the backpack. And it was a long fall.

But he had no desire to go down there and find out if the creature was alive.

What am I supposed to do? I don't even know what I'm looking for.

Inside the building, the milky water was gently sloshing against the metal walls. Rett noticed with alarm that the level had gone down several feet. There was no other choice—he'd have to jump in or be stuck out here.

He turned to take in the full scope of the white-gray vista. In the distance, a foamy line could only be a river. He could hike to it—it wasn't far. Get more water. And then . . .

Head out into a wasteland. To search for who knew what.

He turned back to the opening that led into the shelter. The alternative was to go back inside and face Bryn.

Bryn and her gun.

The screen on the device in his hand still waited for him

TO ENTER COORDINATES. *I don't have any coordinates. I don't know where I'm going.*

"To the river," he told himself. He'd go there first, drink his fill, and then . . .

Then he'd figure out what to do next. At least he didn't need to know any coordinates to get to the river.

He let the rain fall on his face while he waited a moment for another option to present itself. None did. He started down the rain-slicked rungs.

I'm leaving Bryn trapped, he thought while he descended. *Even when she gets out of the lounge once the water level goes down, she won't be able to get up to the skylight. There might not be enough of that water to fill the place twice.*

He stopped, clinging to the wet rungs. He'd closed the lid on her.

Just like the time Garrick had convinced him to crawl into that firewood box. "No one will know you're here," he'd told Rett. "I'll put your pillow under your blanket. Nobody's going to miss you at bed check. Go see your meteor shower."

And then Garrick had closed him in the box.

Trapped him, same as Rett had trapped Bryn.

But I have *to get away from Bryn. She has a gun.*

Guilt twisted in his gut. *Is that why I'm leaving her?* he asked himself. *Or is it because she knows now that I must have done something bad?*

He ignored the thought. Jumped down from the last rung and landed in ashy dirt. No sign of the creature he'd encountered earlier.

Didn't it fall this direction? It should be here . . .

He crept around the back of the shelter.

Not a single mandible in sight.

Just go, he told himself. *Go fast and hope it crawled away to die.*

He gripped the straps of his backpack and picked up his pace, angling toward the river. The ground sloped so that Rett half ran, half slid down it, rocks trickling down after him like tiny scuttling creatures. *What about the person whose blood was on my clothes—what happened to them? Are they out here somewhere? Inside the shelter with Bryn?*

Before him, scattered boulders lay like the heads of petrified giants, watching his progress toward the river, toward relief from the painful thirst that intensified with every step now that water was in sight.

Some nagging thought pulled at him while he hiked, but he refused to listen to it. He already had the missing creature to think of, and his overwhelming thirst, not to mention the guilt that came over him when he thought of Bryn's electric smile, her hand grazing his . . .

Then he finally had to admit it to himself: the smell of sulfur that lingered in his nose was not a ghostly impression of the water he'd floated in inside the shelter. The smell had been getting stronger for the past ten minutes now.

It was the smell of the river.

The water that had filled the shelter must have been from the river. And if he couldn't drink the water in the shelter . . .

He couldn't drink the water in the river.

What's more, the rocks he heard trickling down the slope behind him were not still falling from when he had skidded down—

No, something was coming up behind him.

"Rett."

He whirled to face her—Bryn, her jumpsuit still wet, her hair damp from the rain.

Her hand at her side curled around the gun.

"What did you do?" she asked.

Rett's heart jumped into his throat. "Wait, Bryn."

"What did you do?" she asked again.

"I—I don't know." Did she mean pushing the button, flooding the place? Heading out without her? Or was she talking about the blood on the jumpsuit he'd hidden from her, the one he'd found dragged from its hiding place? His answer was the same either way. "I didn't mean to hurt anyone."

The rain pattered against the dirt. Otherwise—silence.

"Please, Bryn. We've got bigger things to spend bullets on. There's something out here, something—"

"Rett." She raised the gun to aim at his forehead.

Rett froze, every muscle taut with fear. "Bryn, listen . . ." His voice was hoarse, completely lost in the rain. For a moment, neither of them moved. *I was right to try to get away*, Rett thought, grimacing with fear and regret. *I wish I'd been wrong*.

Behind him, the rain tapped an uneven rhythm on the rocks.

It's not the rain, Rett realized.

Tap tap tap-tap-tap.

Rett knew that sound.

He dove to the ground just as an earth-shattering *crack* sounded above his head. The sound rippled outward before it was covered by the pop and sizzle of something burning.

Rett dared to lift his head and found Bryn, a statue, arm outstretched, gun smoking in the rain. He whipped his head around in time to see the segmented body of a monstrous insect crumple to the dirt, squirming in agony against a burning mass of blinding red. *A flare*, Rett realized. *Bryn's gun is a flare gun.*

He managed to breathe, though he shook so hard the rocks clattered in the dirt around him. "Thanks," he said to Bryn.

His voice seemed to snap her out of some spell. She lowered the flare gun. With the sunlit clouds behind her, she made a dark sentinel. "You're welcome."

7:54 A.M.

"Why is there blood on a dirty jumpsuit in the closet back there?" Bryn demanded, her hand still clenched around the gun. "Why are you wearing a clean jumpsuit?"

Rett had gotten to his feet, and now he looked down at the dirt that clung to the front of his jumpsuit.

"You know what I mean," Bryn said.

"I woke up. There was blood on my clothes. I don't know why—I swear I wouldn't hurt anyone."

"Unless."

"Unless . . ." Her cold stare unnerved him. "Unless they were trying to hurt me. Okay? Yes, I would defend myself." In his head, he heard knuckles breaking under a wrench. His stomach clenched.

Bryn's gaze didn't waver. "That makes two of us."

Rett wiped his sweaty palms on his jumpsuit. *I believe it—I believe you'd defend yourself.*

"That picture you drew back in the shelter," Bryn said. "How did you know about the . . . ?"

"Six-foot-long killer insect?" Disgust pulsed in Rett's stomach at the thought of the monster behind him. "I can't explain that, either. I saw it in a dream. Or I think I did."

He had that premonition again, the feeling he'd gone through all this before. He looked back at the black mass still smoking in the rain. It smelled of rust and rot. Near the creature's ruined head lay the charred stub of the flare Bryn had shot.

"Was that the only flare?" Rett asked Bryn, wrinkling his nose at the terrible smell that lingered in the air.

"I don't know." Bryn slipped off her backpack. "There's a case in my pack but—" She jerked open the zipper. A red case tumbled out, and Rett retrieved it from the dirt.

His heart drummed in his chest. "If there's another flare in here we could—" He wrenched open the case. Inside lay a block of foam cut into the shape of the flare gun. And underneath the foam lay one unspent flare. "—signal for help," he finished breathlessly.

Bryn looked around at the endless stretch of bleached dirt and rocks, the silent boulders, the shadowed canyons. "Do you think anyone would see a flare if we shot one up? Would we just be giving ourselves a nice light show?"

Rett squinted against the glare of the slopes shining in the humid air. Every part of the landscape seemed to be set against them—the wet crumbling ground, the snarled canyon paths. The stony emptiness, on and on for miles around.

"No other buildings anywhere," he said, "no helicopter, no radio tower."

"If we shoot the flare into the sky and no one comes to help us, we're stuck with no way to fight off any more monsters."

"I had the metal pole, but I dropped it in the shelter. You didn't bring it?"

"Does it look like I'm carrying a giant metal pole?"

"We could shoot the flare and get back into the shelter to

wait for help." It occurred to Rett that they were making the decision together, that Bryn no longer gripped the empty gun like she wished another flare were loaded into it.

"Door's locked, remember?" Bryn said. "And the water will have drained away, and I'm too fond of my ankles to make a two-story jump. Maybe we could . . ."

There it is again, that "we."

Does she believe me, then—that I don't mean to hurt anyone?

Or should I keep holding on to this last flare in its case?

"What is it?" Rett asked. A maze of lines had appeared on Bryn's face.

"We said earlier that we thought we were here to find something."

"Yeah . . . but I don't think that something is inside the shelter. I think it's out in this wasteland."

Bryn nodded, and Rett had a terrible feeling she was agreeing to a plan he hadn't meant to propose. "So," she said, "we head out and try to find it."

Rett gaped at her. Was she joking? Hadn't she just watched an oversized bug monster try to attack him? "And how are we going to do that?"

Bryn wiped the rain-slicked flare gun against the leg of her jumpsuit as casually as if she were wiping sweat from her brow. "I found a map."

Rett launched into a fit of coughing, suddenly bothered by the dirt in his lungs, the rotten stench in the air. "A *map*?"

"It was drawn in chalk on the back of the wall," Bryn added.

"What?"

She inspected the flare gun in a way that made Rett relieved it wasn't loaded. "I found it when you shut me in that room."

Rett rubbed the back of his neck. "Sorry about that." *White chalk, on my fingers—I remember that.* "What exactly was on this map?"

"The drawings weren't as detailed as the horror prophesy you sketched in that notebook, but they were labeled: a river and three depots." Bryn tilted her head toward the shelter behind her. "Ours is Number Three."

Scatter 3, Rett thought, remembering the logo on the inside of the door.

"And something else," Bryn said. "Something was marked on the map in between the depots."

"What, like 'X marks the spot'?"

"Sort of. It was a skull and crossbones."

Rett started coughing again. He threw his wet arm over his mouth, trying to block out the stench from the dead creature behind him. "Maybe we should get away from this thing," he said into his sleeve. "It's almost worse dead."

He started back toward the shelter—the depot, Scatter 3—taking a wide path around Bryn for fear of triggering her defensive reflexes. After a long moment during which Rett's heart thumped with equal hope and anxiety, she followed.

"We need the GPS units from your pack," she said behind him.

He turned. "How did you know they were GPS devices?"

"I know all kinds of things I haven't told you."

The ground seemed to tilt beneath Rett's feet. "What?"

She rolled her eyes. "I'm kidding. I *guessed.* There were numbers written on the map. Coordinates."

Rett had to stop himself from launching forward and embracing her. "Coordinates? That's all we need, then. We can use the GPS units and get to . . ." *To what?* The answer brought dread to settle in his stomach: a skull and crossbones. "What exactly do you think they lead to?"

"Something valuable. Isn't that what we decided? Back in the depot?" Bryn held out one hand, ready to receive a GPS unit from Rett's pack.

Rett slowly pulled his pack around, thinking. "Yeah, but a skull and crossbones? Isn't that usually . . . something bad? Not to be too incredibly obvious."

"It's not like whoever drew that map wants to advertise that there's something valuable at those coordinates. They probably figured that symbol would keep away the wrong people."

It actually sounded like a logical conclusion. "But still . . . a skull. And crossbones." Rett dug out a device and handed it to her. A weight dropped into his stomach.

"Remember you said that someone knew we would end up here?" Bryn said, tapping on the device's screen. "Someone sent us out here to find whatever's at that location. I don't think we're going to be able to get home until we get to that spot and find what we're supposed to find."

A voice echoed in Rett's head: *There's only one way left to do this. You'll have to find it . . .* The woman in the lab coat— the one who must have sent them out here.

What did she send us to find?

"What if we get there, find whatever we're supposed to find . . ." Rett couldn't believe he was considering this. "But no one's there to help us get back?"

"We can't just sit here and run out the clock, wait for the game to end."

Rett winced. "You think I'm treating this like a game?"

"I think we must have had a plan. We must have come out

here knowing how to get back. And those coordinates are part of the plan."

"And the coordinates lead to . . ." Rett shook his head. "What?"

"Something valuable, or something we're getting paid to find. Right? I know I'm pretty desperate for a payday. Aren't you?"

A memory flashed through Rett's mind of Times Square at night: towering columns of light and motion, the rush of wind and sound and excitement. "Bigger than I ever thought it would be," he'd said, and reached for his mother's hand, full of an electric fear that he might be swept away at any moment. His mother had crouched next to him so that suddenly, he didn't feel so small. She had pointed at brilliant Times Tower with the black night sky behind it and said, "Brighter than stars."

He looked now at the crumbling spires in the distance, the endless waves of barren rock. *Bigger than I ever thought . . .*

"Yeah," he admitted. "I'm desperate. But who would send *us* out to the middle of a *wasteland* to find something? No water, no trees. Just dirt. It's like a moonscape, completely barren."

"But that's exactly why someone chose us to do this."

"Wait, what?"

"Walling Home isn't holding its breath waiting for us to come back."

Rett's spine tightened.

"No one will care if we never get out of this," Bryn said. "No one's even going to realize we're gone."

"My mother—"

"—will think you gave up on her just like she gave up on you."

Rett clenched his jaw. *That email.* His mother had told him not to worry about her, to make a life for himself instead of trying to take care of her. Even though he'd insisted he'd come help her.

She has to believe I'm coming. She has to know I won't stay away.

But he'd written so many angry emails before that, before she'd gotten sick. *I'm better off without you . . .*

Terrible words that still haunted him. If he looked down he might see evidence of them on his clothes, his skin. Same as he'd seen that bloodstain when he'd awakened this morning.

More than anything else he feared in this place, he feared this: that his mother had believed those words.

"She always planned to come back. She just never could." Rett curled his fists and uncurled them. "She didn't have any money, any place for us to live."

Bryn grimaced at her feet, like she regretted what she'd said.

"What about your boyfriend?" Rett asked. "You're telling me he won't notice if you never show up?"

Bryn's expression went blank. "He's . . . not exactly expecting me."

Rett didn't know what to say to that. He decided it was best not to say anything.

"We can send up a flare if you really believe someone will come save us," Bryn said. "But there's not much good in getting out of here if we've got no money for where we're going."

"Trust me, I know that." Rett looked at Bryn out of the corner of his eye. He'd remembered something about her from

Walling Home, although he wasn't sure when it had come to him. The glint in her eye now made him think of it. "What about . . ." He hesitated. "I heard that you had something saved up for when you graduated."

Bryn tensed. "Saved up?"

"Some things you took. From Walling's staff."

She paled.

"Never mind," Rett said quickly. He shouldn't have brought it up. "Forget I said—"

Bryn started trudging ahead of him. "That's all gone now."

Rett followed her, regret and embarrassment roiling inside of him. *Just drop it. Shouldn't have asked.* "So how far away are these coordinates?"

"I don't know," Bryn said over her shoulder.

"Can't you tell?"

She held up the screen so he could see an icon of an antenna surrounded by moving lines. "It's still searching for signal."

Rett's stomach shrank. "But it'll pick up, right?"

Bryn stopped walking, her eyes fixed on something in the distance. "What's that?"

Something small and black lay in the dirt near the wall of the depot. Rett trudged over to pick it up. "It's a hat." A dirty, rain-soaked cap . . .

. . . marked with a familiar symbol: overlapping, jagged lines.

Rett slowly turned as he sensed something behind him. Lying in the rain-darkened dirt was a man twisted into an odd position. *A body,* Rett thought, and horror washed over him. He scrambled away from it as Bryn let out a gasp and then a tortured moan.

"What happened to him?" Bryn said with a shaking voice.

The man was pale as paper, completely bloodless despite the fact that his torso had been nearly severed. Rett's stomach threatened to empty itself, and he lurched away.

"Let's go," he said to Bryn. "Come on, hurry."

They skidded down a crumbling slope, into the shelter of some scraggly gray junipers twisting out from a cleft in the canyon wall.

"You okay?" Rett asked.

Bryn stood with her face turned away and didn't respond.

Rett tried to rid himself of the images seared into his mind, tried to stop feeling them in his stomach, in his nose, where the smell of death was suffocating. His stomach seized, but nothing came up.

"Bryn?" he said again.

She finally turned back to him, her face pale, lips trembling. "The monster," she said. "It got him."

Rett didn't respond. He wrestled another GPS unit from the plastic packet in the backpack.

"Who is he?"

"He had the symbol on his hat." Rett touched the same collection of jagged lines on his jumpsuit. "I wonder if he was sent to help us."

"Could be he was stuck out here just like we are."

Rett worked the buttons on the device he held and shuttered his mind to all other thoughts.

"That would have been us." Bryn turned away again and leaned over her knees like she might be sick.

"We have the flare. We can defend ourselves."

"He was near the door," Bryn said, still doubled over. "Do you think he was trying to get inside?"

Rett's stomach dropped. That man had been outside the

entire time, just trying to get to safety. As desperate to break into Scatter 3 as they had been to break out. "The door wouldn't have opened. We couldn't have helped him." Rett said it as much to himself as to her.

"If he had come up onto the roof . . ."

"It probably still would have gotten him." *True?* Rett couldn't let himself answer that. His hand shook as he tapped the screen of the device. The antenna icon appeared again, along with the moving lines. "Still no signal."

"Is it broken?" Bryn asked, coming closer to look.

Rett swiped water from his hair, trying to think of what to do. The bloodless corpse kept flashing before his eyes. *Locked out, left outside . . .* Rett's thoughts swirled madly. *If I'd known he was out there . . . if I'd had any idea what would happen . . . What? What could I have done?*

"Rett?"

"Maybe it takes a while to find a signal out here," Rett answered.

"There could be more of those things." Panic edged her voice. "They could come for us at any moment."

The flare gun in her pocket caught Rett's attention. He looked at it, at Bryn. "We could try . . . See if anyone . . ."

Bryn seemed to read his thoughts. "That man was from Scatter. He was in trouble and Scatter didn't come to help him."

The humid air went heavy in Rett's lungs.

"No one's going to come for us. We're on our own." Bryn slid her pack off and yanked angrily at the zipper. "We'll have to make it to where we're going if we're ever going to get out of here." Her hands trembled as she pulled out a compass small enough to wedge into her palm. "The place is northwest from here. I saw on the map. We can head in that direction until the signal picks up."

How accurate was that map? Rett wondered. He glanced back at the depot up on the slope. Even a glimpse of it sent up a flare of horror inside of him. *We can't stay here.* "Okay," he finally said.

"We should consolidate our packs, too. Take turns carrying it."

Rett wasn't sure that made sense, but he didn't have it in him to debate. Bryn unzipped the packs and loaded the contents of one into the other.

"I'll carry it," Rett blurted, suddenly worried by the thought of her having the gun *and* all the supplies.

Bryn reluctantly handed it over. "I'll navigate." Her arm shook as she held the compass out before her. "You keep an eye on the GPS unit and watch for when it picks up a signal."

Her wet boots squelched as she started down the slope. A thought occurred to Rett as he made to follow. "A signal from what?"

"What?"

"How does this thing determine coordinates?" Rett lifted the GPS unit. "It gets a signal from what?"

"A satellite. Does it matter?"

Rett moved his gaze from the barren moonscape to the soup of gray clouds overhead. "Do satellites work when it's cloudy?"

"They should." She started again down the crumbling slope, headed for the canyons. "Just tell me when it picks up a signal," she said, her voice low in the quiet air.

Rett silently added, If *it picks up a signal.*

His thoughts went back to the corpse they were leaving behind. *Locked out, left out.* Rett's stomach turned cold. *We've got the flare,* he reminded himself. *We've got a weapon.*

One flare, he thought while he walked.

8:44 A.M.

Rett stumbled on, his gaze flicking constantly to the antenna icon as he walked. Striated rock walls rose on either side like the window tiers of skyscrapers. A mineral smell hung in the air that reminded Rett too much of the milky water now draining from the depot they'd left behind.

He thought constantly of water as he walked—clean water, the water stashed in his backpack. And of his raw feet inside his damp boots. The mesh uppers had shed most of the water from the depot, but even so, Rett felt like his skin would soon be rubbed right off.

Every once in a while the image of a bloodless corpse would pass through his mind and he would think, *That was almost me.*

If not for Bryn, that would be me.

Just ahead of him, Bryn stopped walking. Her arms hung limply at her side. "Let's stop for a minute." She glanced at the GPS unit in Rett's hand and said, "Signal?"

Rett pushed a button to bring up the antenna display. "Still nothing."

Bryn wilted.

Overhead, the clouds were clearing. The air had turned warm and muggy and was now choked with the dirt they had been kicking up. "Maybe we need to get up to higher ground?" Rett suggested.

"We started on higher ground," Bryn grumbled. "No signal then, either."

Rett dragged his sleeve over the back of his sweaty neck. "Let's have some water."

"You need a new GPS unit, too," Bryn said. "Looks like the battery's about to die."

Rett took one out of the pack and stuck it in his pocket for later.

"And I've been thinking," she said, her voice a dry rasp. "We should have the flare gun ready to go. In case anything surprises us."

Rett nodded, mouth too dry to speak. He retrieved the red case from his pack, and before he realized what was happening, Bryn had taken it from him and opened it. She slid the gun from her pocket, snapped the barrel down, and loaded in the flare. "Okay," she said. "I feel better now."

Rett wanted to agree, but he could only stare, trying to decide if he felt reassured or threatened.

She seemed to notice his hesitancy. "Don't worry. I won't use it on you."

"Right." He cleared his throat. "I guess that'd be a waste after saving my life."

"Especially considering you thanked me so nicely."

"Near-death situations bring out my best manners." He thought about asking if *he* could be the one to hold the flare gun, but she slipped it into her pocket and thrust the case at him. *Guess not.*

They retreated farther into the shade at the side of the canyon and finished two water packets and one maple-flavored ration bar each, then took off their boots and wiped grit from their raw feet.

"I keep hoping for the stupidest things while we're walking," Bryn said. "Like, maybe we'll suddenly come upon a stream by surprise."

"I don't think any surprises we'll find out here will be good ones."

"Once I was backpacking as a kid, and my mom and I stumbled onto this lake, completely unexpectedly. It happens."

"Was your secret lake in the middle of a wasteland?"

She didn't answer. Rett looked over at her. Dirt had settled into the lines in her face so that her worry seemed permanent. Through the opening in the pack, two water pouches showed. The only two left.

"Do you ever worry," Bryn said finally, "that for every good moment in your life, you have to go through the inverse? Like, I swam in a secret lake once, and it was the best day of my life. Now I'm lost in a wasteland, and no one knows I'm stuck out here."

Rett thought of the things he'd done that he regretted. Things he'd said. *I'm better off without you.* Now he was alone. Maybe that was what he deserved.

Not quite alone, he told himself. He looked at Bryn. "After growing up in Walling, we must have a really long vacation coming to us."

She pawed grit out of her boots. "If this is the vacation, I'll pass."

"What are you going to do with your payday when we get out of here?" Rett asked.

"I told you, I'm going to find my boyfriend," she said, her voice tight. "He graduated already."

Why so tense? Rett wondered.

The light had gone out of Bryn's eyes. She hunched over the pack like something deflated.

"You don't know where he is," Rett guessed.

"I have a few ideas. For one thing, we used to talk obsessively about White Castle. Like, we used to pretend to place orders with each other for sliders and fries, and then apologize that the kitchen had *just* closed." Her smile trembled.

"But he hasn't told you where he's gone."

Bryn only hunched lower.

Rett scratched his ear. "You sure he's still your boyfriend?"

Bryn glared at him, then at her boots. *Not exactly a yes*, Rett thought. He tried to figure out what she wasn't saying. Her boyfriend had left Walling without telling her where he was going, and she had left to find him. But desperation had led her here first . . .

"He took your stash, didn't he?" Rett asked her. "All the stuff you stole from Walling's staff. He swiped it from you when he left."

Bryn shifted in the dirt.

"That's why you need money now," Rett said, more quietly. He didn't mean to make her feel bad. He only wanted to understand. "But why do you want to find him? If he stole from you?" Rett considered that she might want revenge. He remembered her standing on the slope above him near the depot, flare gun aimed in his direction.

Bryn finally answered: "Same reason you still want to find your mom, I guess."

"What's that supposed to mean?"

"She left you at Walling."

Rett stifled anger. "She brought me to Walling because she was sick. She couldn't take care of herself and a kid."

"She never came back."

"She couldn't. She didn't have any money."

Bryn squinted at him in the sunlight that was edging its way closer to the cliff wall. "That wouldn't be enough to stop me."

Rett bristled. He worked at pulling his boots back on even while he felt as if he were shriveling in the sun. His mother never came back during all those years, even after he'd begged her to. He would have lived anywhere with her—in a workhouse, *anywhere*. How could she think he was better off at Walling? "She's sick again. The cancer came back." He'd already told Bryn a million times. He stood and brushed dirt off his jumpsuit. "We should get going."

Bryn didn't move. She curled her fingers around the pack's strap. "He didn't steal it."

"What?" Rett twisted back toward her, annoyed.

"My boyfriend. He didn't steal my stuff." Bryn looked up at Rett, but he turned away. "He asked for it. He was supposed to graduate a year earlier than me and he had nothing. He asked for the stuff I'd stolen so he wouldn't have to live on the street."

"And you gave it to him." *Because some people help the ones they love instead of just trying to survive,* Rett thought bitterly. *Unlike my mom—is that what you mean?* Bryn hadn't said anything more, so Rett turned to see if she was ready to walk yet. Her boots still lay in the dirt. She sat curled in on herself, her face lined with regret.

"No," she said.

"You didn't give it to him? I thought you said all that stuff was gone."

"It is. But not because I gave it to him. I wouldn't. And then someone on staff found it. So now neither of us has it."

Rett let it sink in: "You wouldn't share it with him?"

"You can't always trust people," she said to the ground.

"You were worried he'd take it and leave you to fend for yourself."

"That's not what I meant."

Rett's heart sank. "You meant *he* shouldn't have trusted *you*."

"I haven't exactly proven myself." Bryn squinted up at him. "Isn't that why you tried to leave me trapped in the depot? You couldn't trust me."

Rett looked away. *Do I trust her?*

She has the pack, the gun. I need her.

But do I trust her?

You choose who to trust. Or do you?

"I shouldn't have trapped you," he said finally. "I'd be dead right now if you hadn't followed me. I owe you for that."

Bryn tugged on her boots. "No, you don't. The only reason I followed you was to get the GPS units in your backpack."

"I don't believe you."

"Why not?"

Because once—I don't know when—you put your hand in mine and let me trace the trail of freckles below your knuckles. Once, you drew close enough that I could see the color of your eyes shift when you smiled. "Because you have the pack now. And the gun. And you haven't ditched me."

Bryn finished lacing her boots. She stood and swung the pack onto her shoulder without looking at Rett. "I'm going to use whatever we find to help him. My boyfriend. As soon as I get out of this place."

The compass glinted in her palm as she turned to find her

way. Rett followed her, clutching the GPS, wishing it weren't so completely useless.

"Do you think that'll make up for what I did?" Bryn asked.

Rett kept his eyes on the path ahead. He wanted to ask if she actually missed her boyfriend or if she just needed relief from her guilt. Instead, he thought of the workhouses that were closing even now, and of his mother waiting for him or not. "If it doesn't, I don't know what will."

9:25 A.M.

A shadow went scuttling over the top of a distant rise.

It wasn't the first one Rett had seen.

He eyed Bryn up ahead, wondering if she had noticed the creatures, too. She plodded on, head down, every step sending chalky sprays of rock falling to either side of the ridge they had climbed.

They'd been forced to leave the shade of the canyon when it had curved away from their northwest route. Rett felt dangerously exposed—to the sun angling through the thinning clouds, to the creatures lurking in dark crevices. "We need to get down from here."

"How?" Bryn croaked, barely lifting her head to get the word out.

The descent on either side of the ridge was steep and loosely blanketed with rock. Rett felt a surge of annoyance toward whoever had included the rope among the depot's survival gear. *What good is rope when you have nothing to anchor it to?* Only one scraggly juniper jutted anywhere in sight, and Rett wasn't confident it would hold their weight.

"What do you think?" Rett asked Bryn, nodding at the stunted tree.

"About what?"

"Climbing down."

Bryn regarded the tree for a moment. "I think the tree would decide to come with us."

Rett had to agree, but he wasn't sure they had a better choice. "Are we even sure we're heading in the right direction?"

"I know how to read a compass."

Rett held up the GPS so Bryn could see the same antenna icon that had taunted him for hours. "I'd feel better if this thing worked. Why won't it grab on to a signal?"

Bryn looked out over the jagged horizon. "Do you remember . . ." She frowned at him. "I keep picturing myself outside at night, maybe early morning. And—a green light in the sky."

Rett's head snapped up. *A green flame, dancing overhead.* "I remember that, too."

"It made a sort of crackling noise. Like electricity."

Rett looked down at the device in his hand. The little light near the corner of the screen had turned red. Almost out of charge.

"Can an aurora interfere with satellites?" Bryn asked.

"An aurora? You think that's what that green light was?"

"Maybe that's why we can't get a signal. Maybe it takes a while for the satellite to get working again." Bryn moved closer to peer down at the screen in Rett's hand. "The date on this thing is wrong."

"It'll fix itself when it connects to the satellite." *If,* Rett corrected himself.

"But why would it be wrong in the first place?"

Who cares? Rett thought. "It's not broken, Bryn. It's just a little off."

Another shadow rippled over the next rise, this one close enough to send lightning through Rett's heart. Rett's hand went out, quick as a whip, reaching for the butt of the flare gun sticking out of Bryn's pocket.

But Bryn was just as quick. She closed her hand around the barrel as Rett drew the gun.

"What are you doing?" she snapped, trying to yank the gun back from him.

"There's a bug," Rett said as she yanked again.

He lost his grip on the gun.

So did Bryn.

The gun flew from their hands and slid down the incline on a waterfall of gravel, skidding over the rocks until it finally came to a stop near the canyon floor, a glint against pale dirt.

Rett gaped in horror.

Their only protection against the creatures—the bug he had seen moments ago—was gone.

"What do we do?" Bryn said, her voice choked with panic.

"Go down after it?"

They both looked at the spindly tree, their only anchor for a rope. Rett swore.

"You couldn't just let me have the gun?" Rett raked his fingers over his skull. It was the worst thing that could have happened. No, the second worst, after being eaten by a monster that might be stalking them even now. "You want me to trust you, but you don't trust me."

Bryn glared back at him. "You want *me* to trust *you*, but you've been waiting hours for an excuse to grab the gun from me."

They considered each other silently. To Rett, the patter of rocks still tumbling after the gun sounded too much like the tap of scythe-like feet.

"Fine." He looked down at the gun glinting far below. "Next time I'll let you shoot it."

Bryn didn't reply. She slipped off the pack and brought out the nylon rope and a carabiner.

"Bryn, wait, I was kidding," Rett said, gaping at her as she wrestled the end of the rope around the carabiner. "We can't go down there. You said yourself that tree won't hold our weight."

"It might hold *my* weight. Alone. You can come down after I reach the bottom."

Rett scanned the slope for signs of movement, for any twitching shadows among the rocks. "I told you, I saw a bug."

"I don't see anything."

Rett had to admit she was right. Had it been a trick of the light? A thirst-induced hallucination?

Or maybe . . .

Maybe she was right: he'd seen a suspicious shadow and had jumped on a reason to grab the gun. "I still don't think we should split up."

"So you think we should forget the gun? Hope we don't run into anything that wants to eat us? Or you think we should go down the rope at the same time and double the odds of the tree breaking?"

"I think we should backtrack and find an easier way down."

Bryn just went on tying another knot. Rett watched her loop the rope in complicated patterns and tried to take comfort in the fact that she seemed to know what she was doing. "You've done something like this before?"

"It's been a while. Used to backpack with my mom, BW. Before Walling." Bryn gave the rope a sharp tug, testing her knot. "And my stepdad. But then my mom died and my stepdad took me on one last camping trip, except it wasn't a camping trip, it was a ride to the front door of Walling."

Rett opened his mouth to say something, but Bryn went on.

"So trust me when I say I know splitting up isn't great." Bryn gave the knot one final tug and looked up from her work. "But I promise I'm not going to abandon you."

Rett's throat went raw. He felt the pull of Bryn's gravity on his bones, as if he were a satellite to her. Then he was somehow nearer to her, his ears full of the sound of his boots scraping over the dirt, of his breath gone uneven.

She had named a fear he didn't know was pressing on him— that she would leave him.

And now that fear sat heavier in his gut.

He thought she might say something more as his arm brushed hers, but before she could, a high-pitched *beep* sounded from his pocket.

"What's happening in your pocket?" she asked.

"It's the GPS unit." Rett fished it out. The screen showed the familiar antenna icon, but in place of the moving lines was a set of concentric rings. Adrenaline quickened his weary muscles. "I think we have a signal."

"Can you enter the coordinates?" Bryn asked, moving behind him to look over his shoulder.

Rett found the field where he could touch-type the numbers she recited for him. A moment later, the screen showed a topographical map with a location pinpointed among sharp rises. "It's not far," he announced. "Less than a thousand feet."

Bryn gripped his hand, and Rett turned without thinking.

His arms went around her thin frame, and he thought about how odd it felt to hold her—not at all like he'd imagined. And then he wondered when he'd imagined it and realized it was every time he'd stood close to her, and every time she'd moved toward him, and whenever her eyes held that wary challenge she liked to aim at him. *All the time*, he realized.

Bryn put her head against his shoulder for a moment, like she might only be resting. And then she pulled away. She didn't look at him. He remembered about her boyfriend and wondered if she did, too.

"Which direction?" Bryn asked.

Rett poised himself over the crest of the ridge. "Down."

"I guess we're really doing this, then. Let's hope the tree holds." She sidestepped down to the tree and looped the rope around its swaybacked trunk. Then she gave the tree a few solid kicks to test its commitment to staying rooted in the loose dirt. It seemed to shrug at her as it swayed under her weight.

"You sure you want to go first?" Rett said.

They both looked down, searching for the shine of metal against the pale slope.

"I'm lighter," Bryn said, already inching downward. "More chance of the rope holding if I go first."

It's fine, Rett told himself. *She'll get the gun, and then she'll be able to watch out for bugs while I climb down.*

She won't leave.

She won't leave me all alone out here with no way to defend myself.

With no way for me *to help* her.

Halfway down the slope, Bryn suddenly stopped. She stared at a distant rise, her body tense and alert. Rett pivoted to find nothing but barren slopes. And then—a darkly gleaming shape scurried over the top of the ridge and out of sight again, not three hundred feet from where they stood. *I wasn't imagining things*, Rett thought darkly.

Bryn stumbled in surprise. Rett thought she would lose her footing, but she caught herself.

"Bryn, go fast!" Rett yelled. "Get the gun!"

But Bryn was caught in a spell, rooted to the spot. She tipped her head toward him, swaying. She seemed lost in a haze of fear or confusion.

Rett swore. *Get moving*, he told himself. He clambered down to the tree and took hold of the taut length of rope. *Don't look, just go.* The dirt slid under his shoes as he backed down the incline, his gaze darting over the ridgeline for some sign of what he knew was coming.

A black form rose over the ridge like a sun in negative.

The creature picked expertly over the rocks on its six clawed legs. Its mandibles opened to reveal a hooked fang. An image flashed through Rett's mind of a man's severed body, pale and bloodless.

"Go!" Rett shouted at Bryn. "Down, now! Try to get to the gun!"

He scrambled down the rocky incline, hands sliding dangerously over the rope. The creature followed with careful steps, its fang still bared.

And then the rope gave way.

Rett fell back, tumbling crazily over jagged ground. His vision went dark and he felt the familiar pull of his mind retreating into blackness. But then he skidded to a stop on level ground, and the brightness of the gray-white canyon returned, along with a feeling like his ankle had snapped. The creature danced madly on the slope, trying to gain purchase on the falling dirt. They would be at its mercy once it made its way down. Rett couldn't run with his ankle like it was. And Bryn— where was Bryn? Rett caught sight of her in the corner of his vision just as the sun flashed on the flare gun now falling down the trickling slope toward him. He lunged for the gun. Pain ripped through his injured ankle. The gun went skidding over the dirt, out of reach. Rett got on his hands and knees and scrabbled over to it, got his fingers around it, and then—

He lifted his head. The creature was a stone's throw away, looming over Bryn on the shifting slope.

But Bryn had yanked the rope down after her, the broken sapling with it. She swung the sapling like a bat.

Crack. Tree met creature. The black form twitched in the dirt. It rose on unsteady legs and retreated over the slope with jerking movements, trailing putrid liquid.

Rett released the gun out of sheer relief, and it tumbled to the ground, the flare unspent.

"Are you okay?" Rett called after Bryn.

Her breath heaved. The broken sapling lay in the dirt, sticky with black bug innards. "I don't know. Ask me after I get the feel of bursting bug out of my mind."

Rett closed his eyes again, relieved but wishing he could escape into darkness, could escape from the pain fizzing over his scraped skin and throbbing in his ankle.

"Are *you* okay?" Bryn stood over him, blood staining a dozen rips in her jumpsuit. She had a hand cupped over one eye but it didn't stop the blood pouring from a gash over her brow.

"Where's the backpack?" Rett asked. He immediately regretted speaking—it only made his ribs, his *everything*, feel worse. He thought vaguely about examining his injuries, but any movement invited blades of pain.

"Up there."

Rett followed Bryn's gaze halfway up the slope, where the pack showed black against the lighter dirt. Rett cursed softly.

"Check my pocket," he told Bryn. "See if the GPS unit is still in there."

Bryn moved carefully toward him so that Rett wondered exactly how terrible he looked. She reached for him as if afraid he'd fall to pieces at her touch.

"Seems okay," she said, examining the device's display. "We're not far from the coordinates. Can you— Are you—?"

Her unspoken question hung in the air while Rett contemplated the horror of moving. He shifted and let out a grunt of pain.

"What hurts?"

"Moving," Rett replied dryly. He tried lifting himself and gave up when pain shot through his ankle, his ribs. "I need a minute."

"We can't stay here long." Bryn turned to gaze at the top of the ridge. Rett prayed she didn't spot anything more sinister than a broken tree and sun-bleached rocks.

At least they were in the shade now, close to the wall of the ravine they had fallen into.

"You're right," Rett said. "We should get out of here, find the nearest walk-in freezer, and refuse to come out until we've eaten all the ice."

Bryn gave him a faint smile. "Can I get some sliders and fries with that ice? And a fish sandwich with cheese—I hear those are really horrible and I need to find out for myself."

Rett's smile faltered.

"Sorry," Bryn said, "I was just doing that weird fake-ordering-from-White-Castle thing . . ."

"That you used to do with your boyfriend." Rett cleared his throat. "No, I get it."

He didn't really want to keep talking about it. "Your eye," he said, as if she didn't know the cut was still bleeding.

Bryn clamped her hand down harder over her wound. She sat in the dirt and tugged at the shredded fabric at the leg of her jumpsuit until a piece ripped away. Then she pressed it to the gash over her eye and leaned back in attempt to staunch the flow of blood. For a moment, there was only the sound of rocks trickling down the slope, the aftermath of Rett's and Bryn's terrible slide. Then Bryn said, "I almost blacked out. I mean, when I saw . . . that thing. Everything got dark. And it felt like—like something was trying to pull me away."

Rett nodded slowly, grateful that the movement brought little pain. "Me too. After we slid down. I thought for a minute I was going to escape." He looked to her to see if she understood. "Like it was all a dream and I was going to wake up."

Bryn probed the dirt with the toe of her boot. *She knows exactly what I mean*, Rett thought. He could see it in her eyes—that faraway look that meant she had remembered something.

"It's happened before," she said quietly. "That feeling."

"What?" Rett took a few breaths through gritted teeth while he willed the pain in his ankle to subside. "When?"

"A few times. I keep trying to follow it, to let myself—I don't know. Get away. It feels like I'm going into a tunnel but I can't get to the end of it."

Rett thought it over. That wasn't exactly what it was like for him. More like he'd gotten into a tunnel and backed out again on his own.

"But there was one time," Bryn said. "Outside the depot, near the river. I saw that creature coming up behind you. I felt like I was going into that tunnel again. But I fought against it because I knew you were in trouble."

Something stirred in Rett's chest. *She cares. At least a little*, he thought. He remembered the feel of her in his arms when he'd embraced her on the ridge, the weight of her head on his shoulder. He wished she would come closer now, pained as he was.

"I got the flare gun out and the feeling went away," Bryn said.

"Good thing."

They sat in silence for a moment. The knowledge that another creature could come over the rise at any moment made Rett hot with panic. They still had one flare.

He stretched his fingers out, grimacing against the pain that stabbed at his ribs, and slid the gun closer.

"Rett," Bryn said.

Rett looked over at her. The rag she held to her forehead had gone red, but at least the blood had stopped dripping.

"I remember something strange," she said. "Something I can't explain."

Rett's stomach tightened. *That's become the theme of my life.*

"I remember that creature coming into the depot," Bryn went on. "Through the skylight. Falling onto the floor."

Pain glazed Rett's thoughts. He couldn't focus. Had the

creature come through the skylight? The image came to mind so easily: a black form blocking the light, struggling through the opening, falling onto the floor.

But had that happened? "Wasn't it near the river? You shot it with the flare."

"I know," Bryn said. "I remember that. But I also remember it coming down through the skylight."

Rett struggled to understand. He had opened the skylight and hit the creature with the backpack. And then it had come back when Bryn had found him near the river. So why did he also remember it coming down through the skylight?

"Do you think we've been in that depot more than once?" Bryn asked.

Rett remembered something else now, something that surfaced in a wash of anxiety. "That man—the one we found dead outside the depot. He was pounding on the door, trying to get in."

Bryn frowned. "Are you sure?" And then, "I think I do remember that. But did it really happen?"

More memories surfaced in the murky confusion flooding Rett's mind: waking up in the depot, finding blood on his jumpsuit. *How did I know it would have blood on it? I knew before I even looked down.*

He thought of the feeling he'd had that there was something waiting on the roof of the depot, even before he'd opened the skylight to it. "Some of the things that have happened to us—I think I knew they would happen before they did."

"Me too," Bryn said.

Rett shook his head, lost. It was too much to think about at once, too much to try to make sense of.

Bryn trailed her fingers over her hair. "Is this why we get that feeling?" Rett realized she meant the scar over her ear. "Because they put something in our heads?"

The idea jolted Rett. Could it be that whenever he started to black out, whenever he felt that tunnel opening to him, it was thanks to some mechanism implanted in his brain?

And if so, did that mean he could control the feeling? Could *use* the mechanism?

He closed his eyes and tried to move away from the pain pressing at every inch of him, the rocks biting into his skin, the heat and dust filling his lungs . . .

And he felt an invisible channel open before him.

It waited to welcome him to a better place. Someplace lit by stars and bathed with cool air . . .

But Rett couldn't reach it. He couldn't get through the channel.

"I can't do it," he said aloud.

Bryn was watching him, her gaze narrowed.

"I can't get away," Rett explained, although he thought she might already understand.

"When was the last time you got that feeling, like you could get away?"

"When we were falling down the slope. And I think when . . . one of those creatures attacked us before, in the depot." *Did that happen?* "When I get scared, I guess. When I think—" He lowered his head and spoke into the dirt. "When I think I'm going to die."

Bryn touched his wrist, and he felt a rush of gratitude that it didn't hurt like every other inch of him did. He turned his palm so that his hand rested in hers. That was as much as he could do. Even breathing sent waves of pain through him.

"Are we ever going to get out of here?" Bryn asked.

Rett fought against the wave of hopelessness threatening to overwhelm him. "Well, see, this has been my plan for a while now: wait until you're desperate, then offer to finally put some effort into escaping if you'll promise to reveal the location of your secret swimming lake when we get out of here."

"If you get us out of here, I'll take you to every secret lake in the country."

The light in the corner of the device she held in her other hand showed red. The battery was running out. In another minute, the location of the coordinates would be lost to them forever. "Bryn. Last chance. You've got to go."

"Could you stand if I helped you?"

Rett pushed his foot against the ground and felt a surge of pain. "Leave me here. It's not far, right? Go check it out and come back.

The gun lay in his other hand, a slight weight that nevertheless reassured him. He didn't want to give it up. But who knew what awaited Bryn at those coordinates? "You should take the gun with you. Just in case."

Bryn looked over Rett's near-shredded jumpsuit. "Maybe you should keep it." She didn't say what they were both thinking: *In case another bug comes along while you're sitting here like a ready-made meal.*

"After all that, you can't just let me keep the gun without a fight," Rett said. He gave her half a smile.

"Rett . . ."

"Honestly, I don't even need it. I prefer hand-to-hand combat. Hand-to-fang." He pressed the gun into her hand. "Seriously, you better hurry before that battery goes out."

Bryn eased herself onto her feet. "I won't be gone long." She fiddled with the GPS unit for a moment. "Wish me luck."

"Stick to the side of the ravine," Rett said. "Stay out of sight of anything that might be hungry." He tried to say it lightly, but it came out sounding strained.

"Hope they find flares tasty." Bryn's voice was small in the wide space of the canyon. She limped off, GPS unit held out before her.

Rett tried to settle into a comfortable position but couldn't find one. *At least if a bug kills me, I'll be out of my misery.* He counted the seconds that passed so he could keep track of how long Bryn was gone. *And if she's gone too long? What then?* He couldn't very well go after her.

The rocks had finally stopped trickling down the slope of the ravine, though dust still hung in the air. Rett's gaze snagged on a rock that stood out against the pale dirt, a rock as black as ink and veined with sun-flamed silver.

He scrambled for it, pulling himself on his knees and trying not to jar his injured ankle. *Is this what we came for?* he wondered as his fingers closed around the smooth rock.

He turned it over in his palm. The streaks of silver caught the sunlight and sent a thrill through Rett's heart. *I found it. I found what we're looking for.*

Maybe there are more. Maybe they're all over this ravine.

His whipped his head around, searching for another glint of silver, another spot of black against the pale dirt. *I'm missing something. There's more to this.*

His hand kept going to his pocket and he couldn't figure out why. *My pocket's empty.*

Something else nagged at the back of his mind, something important . . .

Bryn came hobbling back into view. Rett wanted to get up and meet her, but he still could barely move. "Everything okay?" he called to her, his voice betraying his alarm. "Did you find it?" He knew she hadn't. He could tell from the slump of her shoulders, the defeat written all over her face as she came nearer.

Bryn collapsed into the dirt next to him. "The GPS unit took me to the coordinates," she croaked.

Rett waited for her to say it.

She shook her head. "There's nothing there. Nothing."

The rock dropped out of Rett's hand. *No.* "How are we supposed to get out of here?"

Bryn turned to Rett, an apology in her eyes. "I don't know."

"Are you sure there was nothing there? Could you have missed something?"

"It's just dirt. Nothing else." Bryn's face was lined with pain and panic.

Rett fought against his own pain. It threatened to take up all the space in his thoughts, and he needed desperately to come up with a plan. "We still have the flare. We can try shooting it up into the sky." A nagging thought was still trying to get his attention, but panic smothered it.

"You know why we haven't tried that yet," Bryn said darkly. "No one will come for us. We both know it."

"What else can we do?"

"We're missing something," Bryn murmured. "There's another piece to this puzzle."

Rett tried to clear his mind, to focus on the thought that pulled at him. *Got to fit the pieces together.* "I have this feeling . . . There's something back in Scatter 3. Something we overlooked."

"There were things in there we never made sense of. We should have figured that place out before we headed out into the wasteland."

Guilt pressed at Rett. If he hadn't tried to hide that jumpsuit from Bryn, if he hadn't left Scatter 3 in such a hurry . . .

He wondered if Bryn was thinking the same thing. Did she feel guilty for hiding the gun from him back in the depot?

"Do you think it would have been better if you'd woken up here on your own?" Bryn asked. "All we've done is messed things up for each other."

The creak in her voice worried him. He touched her arm, wishing he could pull her closer. But she didn't respond. "That man outside Scatter 3 was on his own," Rett said. "It didn't turn out so well for him."

Bryn didn't seem to hear him. She rocked in the dirt next to him, humming her strange tune under her breath so that Rett felt half-hypnotized. He picked up the rock and turned it over and over in his hand. Something told him he knew what they needed to do. He knew how to fix this problem. He could get them out of this. He just had to think.

And then—

The thought came to him, the thing he knew they needed to do. *One, change your jumpsuit.* He thought while Bryn went on humming. *Two, find some water. Three, get the—*

"If I could do it over again," Bryn said, interrupting his thoughts, "I would do it differently."

She reached into her pocket but Rett barely registered the movement. He was too busy wondering why she wouldn't look at him.

"Differently?" Rett's heart thumped. "You mean alone?"

"I'm sorry, Rett." Bryn lifted her arm and pointed the gun at his chest.

No, he thought. "Bryn, wait. I have to tell you—"

Too late. He saw her hand flex as she squeezed the trigger. But as she did, she shifted the gun.

She's not aiming for me, Rett realized, as the sound of the gunshot exploded in his head and he fell through a long, dark tunnel.

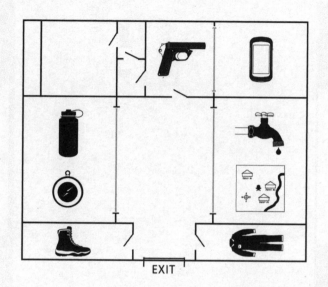

EXIT

Rett emerged in a starlit hollow, panting with shock and confusion. The wrenching pain in his ribs and ankle vanished in
an instant.

Overhead, a green flame rippled across the night sky. Needles
of light piercing the darkness. Rett thought he could feel the
same effect on his skin, but it was only the cold air prickling
his flesh.

The sensation brought with it a sudden realization: he
was outside in the cold and the darkness. Still in the wasteland, but not where he had been a moment ago.

He jerked in alarm—*the gun.*

The *crack* of the gunshot echoed in his head even now. He
brought his hands to his face, to his chest. But he was okay.
No terrible burning wounds, no sign at all that he'd been hit
by a flare.

Bryn—the gun—

He tried to get hold of his thoughts. *She pointed the gun at
me. But she moved it just before she pulled the trigger.*

And then . . .

And then he'd escaped. A tunnel had opened in his mind,

a channel he had slipped through. Like reality had gone soft, and he'd forced his way through it.

But to where?

And to when?

How can it be nighttime?

The sheet of green light overhead flexed like a flag, like the banner of a strange country.

Rett sank to his knees. The gun, the creature, the daggers of pain—all gone. But he was still lost and confused. And now he was alone.

He gazed up at the luminous curtain moving over him. *An aurora?* He wondered if auroras were like shooting stars—if you could wish on them. "I don't want to be alone," he murmured. Not a wish, exactly, but the feeling bled from him and he couldn't help but give voice to it.

"Rett?" Someone called to him from the direction of a lonely boulder.

Rett shot to his feet. "Bryn?"

She and the boulder made a single, shadowy shape until she pushed away from it, her white jumpsuit aglow with starlight. She stepped toward him, and he let out a breath that steamed in the cold air. *"Bryn."* He stumbled forward, flooded with relief, and folded his arms around her, testing the shape of her shoulders, the curve of her back, wondering if she could be real. After a moment, she put her arms around him and pressed her face into his shoulder. Her grip startled him. He leaned into it, grateful for an anchor to stop him from freewheeling into confusion and fear.

She said something into his shoulder, too muffled to make out. He pulled away. "Are you okay?" he asked her.

She only stared back at him, guilt and alarm mingling in her eyes.

"What happened?" he asked her. "How did we get back here?"

"The gun." She looked away.

Rett remembered a surge of fear, an explosion of sound. "You didn't shoot me," he said, his voice wavering along with his conviction.

"No—I wouldn't—that's not what—" Bryn shook her head. "We said every time we got really scared, we felt like we were being pulled away. So I thought maybe we could get away if I used the gun to scare you."

Away would be nice, Rett thought. But they were still in the wasteland.

"I think it's because of whatever they put in our heads," Bryn went on. She brushed her fingers over Rett's scalp. His skin tingled at her touch.

He tried to sort it all out. Fear, pain, the explosion of noise from the flare gun. A quiet hollow, an endless expanse of stars. *This is the place I sensed at the end of the tunnel,* Rett thought. *I reached for safety, for calm . . . and I found my way here.*

And somehow, he'd pulled Bryn with him.

"I think I brought us here," he said. "I think the mechanism in my head helped me find this place, somehow, and I pulled us both through."

He gazed up at the inky sky, the spattering of stars. Like his favorite two-page spread in *Shine Fall,* a boy under a million midnight suns.

"I keep wanting to get home—to get back to my mom," he went on. "But I think this is the closest I can get."

Rett found that he had closed his hand around Bryn's. Her skin was as cold as his. He pressed her hand against his chest to warm it.

Bryn looked up, her eyes full of uncertainty. "I'm sorry."

For what? Rett wondered. *For not knowing how to get us home? For shooting a gun at me? For not wanting your hand against my chest?*

A sound interrupted his thoughts: the crunch of gravel.

"What was that?" Bryn gasped.

Rett turned, searching for the source of the sound. A humped shadow loomed at the top of a rise. "The depot's up there. If we can find a way to get in . . ."

They scrambled up the incline, shedding cardboard slippers Rett hadn't realized he was wearing. *Where did those come from?* he wondered, before fear chased away all thoughts beside, *Get to safety.*

He didn't know how they'd get into Scatter 3, but they could at least climb the rungs up to the roof. And then—

They reached the top of the incline.

The depot's door was ajar.

Rett jerked to a stop, heart hammering. "How can it be open?" It'd been bolted shut, jammed. And the man's body . . .

It was nowhere to be seen now.

He exchanged confused looks with Bryn.

"We've done this before," Bryn said. "Haven't we." It wasn't a question so much as an admission of dread. "We're starting over, somehow."

Rett approached the door warily. The whole structure was battered and weathered. The metal walls, scratched and scarred by sprays of windblown gravel, glowed faintly in the pre-dawn light.

He touched the open door.

How is this happening?

He slipped through the opening. Inside, darkness blinded him. Then, a faint crack, and a green glow filled the narrow space.

"I stepped on something—a light stick," Bryn murmured. She leaned to pick it up, and some of the liquid dripped over her hand. Rett was sure he'd seen this image before—her hands, glowing.

"Hope it's not toxic," Bryn said.

"Probably not unless you drink it. Although we've survived worse in Walling's cafeteria."

Bryn tensed. "Do you hear something?"

Rett tilted his head to one side. Silence muffled everything but his heartbeat in his own ears. "Nothing." Even so, visions of jointed legs and hooked feet flashed through his mind. A long, wet fang . . .

He pulled Bryn into the changing room. They stood close in the narrow space, shoulders pressed against each other.

"If we've been through all of this before," Rett said, "then all of the same things are going to happen again." He tried to take comfort in the weight of Bryn's arm against his, but his mind raced with fearful thoughts.

"We need the flare gun." Bryn looked up at him. Her eyes glowed eerily in the green light. "We found it in the office last time, near the desk."

"And the extra flare." Rett pulled away from her reluctantly and moved toward the doorway.

"Wait," Bryn said, catching his hand. "We know one of the bugs is going to come here to the depot. What if we use the water to kill it instead of a flare? Then we can go up on the roof, shoot the flare up like you said we should do. Hope someone comes to help us. We'd still have one flare left to defend ourselves."

Rett could hardly follow her words for the feel of her palm pressed against his. "You want to lure a bug in here?"

"We'll be safe inside one of the rooms. That's what the water is meant for, right? A defense against bugs?"

Rett wanted to agree, but the tightness in his chest wouldn't let him.

Bryn squeezed his hand, trying to reassure him. It only made his chest constrict more. "We'll go up on the roof and open the skylight," Bryn said. "When the bug comes, we'll hide in an upstairs room, push the button—and drown it."

"What if we get stuck out there again, like last time?" Rett craned his neck to get a look at the heavy door that still stood ajar. He didn't want to move to where he'd have to drop her hand.

"I'll get the rope from the supply room and tie it to the rungs outside the skylight." Bryn dropped his hand and slid past him toward the doorway. "Then we'll have another way in and out of this place in case anything happens to the door again."

Rett followed her, already missing the warmth of her hand in his. "But what exactly happened to the door last time?"

"I don't know, but we have to hurry before that bug comes."

Rett waited, shivering in the cold, while she ducked into the supply room. He thought about her hand in his, her arms around his waist, her head on his shoulder. *We're going to get through this. We're together now.*

Bryn came back with the same rope and carabiner they had last seen tied to the traitorous sapling.

"How is this possible?" Rett mumbled. "That rope . . . everything's back where we first found it?"

"We'll think about it later." Bryn headed for the heavy door, already knotting the rope like she had last time. "Come on." She slipped outside.

Rett started to follow her. But a clatter from the office stopped him in his tracks.

He slowly turned to look through the open doorway. From this new angle, he could now see another green glow coming through an open partition. Fear plunged into his gut.

The clattering stopped. A figure eased into view—a crouching man with deep lines in his green-lit face. Before Rett could react, the man moved his hand into view. It held a gun.

Rett's whole body went numb. His gaze locked onto the green-gleaming metal. Blackness crept along the edges of his vision and then came the familiar pull that promised to take him through a tunnel to someplace safer.

But something rooted him in the moment: the gun—it was identical to the one Bryn had pointed at him so recently. Same tube-shaped barrel, same scratched metal. He started to look toward the heavy door she'd gone through. But the next moment, soft thuds came from the roof, and it was all Rett could do not to look up at the skylight and call to Bryn. *Don't alert him to the fact that she's here.*

The man rose. He kept the gun pointed at Rett's chest. *Flare gun,* Rett reminded himself, but that only made him shake with fear at the memory of the flare burning against the bug's flesh.

"Who are you?" the man asked gruffly, stepping closer so that his blocky frame towered over Rett. His T-shirt was tattered, jeans ripped at the knees, boots coated in dust. The cap pulled over his eyes was limp with sweat, the symbol of over-lapping jagged lines black with grime. Rett imagined him as a corpse sprawled in the dirt outside. *It's the same man*, he realized. *But how . . . ?*

The man thrust out his light stick and looked over Rett's jumpsuit while fear churned in Rett's gut. "You from Scatter?" the man asked. His teeth glowed in the green light.

"Scatter?" Rett croaked, lost in confusion. His gaze flicked from the gun to the logo on the man's hat.

The man pulled on the bill of his cap. "I haven't worked for Scatter in a long time." The barrel of the gun drifted downward. He squinted at Rett as if trying to guess his age. "Someone send you here to collect loot?" The man craned his neck to look out through the doorway. He swiped at a patch of ashy skin under his jaw with a calloused finger. A black talon hanging from a cord around his neck swung like a pendulum. When he looked at Rett again, he peered out from under swollen eyelids. His voice dipped low. "They shouldn't have sent someone so green."

Fear rippled through Rett. The man took slow steps toward him, gun aimed now at Rett's heart.

"Back up," the man barked. "Toward the door. You're gonna tell whoever sent you this place was empty. Will be when I'm finished, anyway."

Overhead, the *click* of a latch sounded. *The skylight,* Rett thought. He coughed, trying to cover the creak of it opening. *Does Bryn see the man?* He prayed she did, prayed she wouldn't call down to Rett and startle the man who held the gun in a shaking hand.

"Go," the man growled.

Rett backed across the main room.

"They sent you here all alone?" The man stopped to look around the depot, pulling at his grimy cap. His gaze lingered on the open closet. "Or is someone else here?"

"No," Rett said quickly.

The man looked him over again. He pulled at Rett's sleeve, and Rett flinched away. "Clothes are so nice and clean," the man said. Rett looked down at the dirt crusted on the cuffs on his pants and sleeves. His jumpsuit was still a lot cleaner than the man's tattered clothes.

"How'd you get out here?" The man frowned at Rett's feet. "What happened to your shoes?"

"I—I lost them." He remembered the cardboard slippers that had fallen off his feet as he climbed the slope to the depot. Where had they come from? And who would wear flimsy slippers in a wasteland?

Gravelly laughter erupted from the man's throat. "You came all the way out here just to get some new shoes? You know, those bugs don't care if you're clean or dirty when they eat you. They ain't picky."

Rett stared at the black talon dangling from the cord around the man's neck and his alarm surged. The man touched the talon. Something like regret flashed in the man's eyes. "You seen them?" he asked in a whisper. "You know?"

Rett recalled the scratch of scythe-like feet on metal, on rock. He shuddered.

The man slowly nodded, vindicated by Rett's reaction. "A man couldn't make up something like that." He was lost in a fog, but the next moment, it cleared. He gripped Rett's shoulders with his calloused fingers and shoved him toward the main door. Rett scrambled for some idea of what to do. He could at least lead the man outside, away from where Bryn crouched near the skylight. What then?

He was within a few feet of the door when the man behind him shuffled to a stop and grunted, "Outside."

Rett hesitated. "You're going to lock me out?"

"What's wrong? Scared of the bugs?" The man chuckled. He scratched at the patchy spot under his jaw and his smile vanished. "I'll let you back inside when I'm finished. What's in this place is mine. Whatever you came here for—you aren't going to get it."

Rett inched forward. He thought about Bryn and her rope. *What good will it be to get back inside the depot from the roof if we don't have a way to defend ourselves against a gun?*

"Hear what I said?" the man growled. "Out!"

Rett moved sideways through the door. He couldn't stop himself from picturing a bloodless corpse sprawled in the dirt. *That's going to be me this time.*

"Wait," the man said.

Rett froze just outside the door. The man stood half in, half out of the depot and squinted at Rett. "Have I seen you before?"

The blue glimmer of coming daybreak revealed nothing to Rett except that the man was even grimier than he'd thought. "I don't think so." *But I've seen you—dead, not ten feet from this spot.*

"I don't believe you're here all alone." His lips were chapped, but a drinking tube dangled over his shoulder from a hydration backpack. Water had dripped from the tube onto his faded T-shirt and the man pressed his free hand to it, as if trying to reclaim the moisture. "No one hikes all the way out here without gear. Someone drove you in."

The man craned his neck to see around Rett. Then he edged out through the opening, gun first.

The next moment, there was a flurry of movement and a heavy *thud*. The man dropped to the dirt. Bryn stood behind him in the doorway, fire extinguisher in hand.

She stared in horror at the fallen man, at the dark blood spreading over his scalp and seeping into his wispy hair. The grimy cap lay in the dirt, a few feet from the gun.

"Is he—?" Bryn's face was pale.

Rett put a shaking hand under the man's jaw, checking for a pulse. "I think he's just unconscious. Get the gun."

Bryn had already picked it up and was now sliding it into the hip pocket of her jumpsuit. "I saw him through the skylight. I used the rope to climb down. I thought he was going to—"

"I'm okay."

"I don't think the door will close, even from the inside."

"It'll have to. Unless you just want to hope he won't wake up angry. Help me move him." The man's legs were blocking the doorway. Rett gripped the man under the arms, trying to ignore the rank smell of sweat and the blood that was now smeared over his own jumpsuit. *He had a gun*, Rett reminded himself as he battled a twinge of guilt. *Bryn had to do it*. He hauled the man a foot or so, grunting with the effort. "Bryn, help me."

Bryn stood frozen, gazing at the distant horizon turning from black to blue. "It's almost morning. We're going to wake up again with no memory. This is when it happens, isn't it? Something's out here, and it's going to make us forget."

Rett stopped to look up at her. Her gaze darted frantically around the landscape. "Just help me and we'll—"

"We should get back inside. We shouldn't be out here." Bryn edged away, slinking back into the narrow opening behind her. Her free hand went to the scar hidden under her hair. "Something bad is going to happen. I can feel it coming."

Rett turned and studied the blue-lit ridges in the distance. A shiver of fear went down his spine. He looked down at the unconscious man. A man he was about to shut out of the depot for whatever dangers were coming this way.

We can't leave him out here, Rett decided.

"We have to get inside," Bryn said again, her voice high with panic.

"Help me with him," Rett said. But Bryn had already vanished into the depot. "Bryn!"

All at once, pain exploded inside Rett's head. He dropped to his knees, arms wrapped around his skull. Hot needles shot down toward his spine. The pressure was unbearable; his head was going to explode any second.

He staggered to his feet. *What's happening?* The pain had come out of nowhere. It was mounting still, and Rett only knew that he had to escape it. He threw himself toward the door of the depot. "Bryn," he groaned. The pressure eased as he stumbled inside. But only a little. His skull still seemed ready to burst.

What's going on?

The thing in his head. Something had gone wrong with it.

"Rett?" Bryn cried.

Rett could barely see her through the spots of light exploding in his vision. He gripped his head, willing the pain to stop.

"What's wrong?" Bryn cried. "What's happening?"

Rett collapsed against a wall. He thought he heard Bryn move to the door, and then there was a heavy squeal of metal. Rett caught sight of her heaving the door shut. Blocking out whatever had prompted Rett's pain.

Rett clawed at his skull, willing the pressure to release. A loud banging echoed through the depot and sent the pain moving through his head in waves: Bryn was slamming the fire extinguisher against the door's rusted bolt.

Rett let out a mangled cry: "Bryn, stop!"

The bolt finally scraped into its housing and Bryn dropped the extinguisher.

Rett slid to the floor and hurtled into oblivion.

5:37 A.M.

Someone is calling to me . . .

But I don't want to wake . . .

I . . .

Rett opened his eyes to blue morning light filtering into a metal room. His skull felt as if it had been put in a vise. He moved his fingers carefully through his hair and found a long scar running along his scalp.

"Rett?"

He rolled his head toward the sound. A girl with short brown hair peered at him, worry etched into her dirt-streaked face.

"Rett?" she said again. "Are you okay?"

His head throbbed. He closed his eyes and opened them again, took in the sight of striped metal walls. "Where am I?"

"Inside the depot." The girl handed him a Mylar pouch. "Drink this. I found it in the medical room with the backpack and everything—right where we first found it."

Rett squinted at the label: DRINKING WATER. But why was it in a pouch? He didn't care—he was so thirsty. He pulled the tab and drained the pouch in one go. "Got any more?" he croaked.

"We should save it." The girl gave him a pitying look. "But the backpack—"

"What happened to my head?" Pain pulsed through Rett's skull.

The girl studied him for a moment. She seemed worried about something. A shock of dark red caught the edge of his vision and he looked down to find blood on his jumpsuit. *Am I bleeding?* He pushed himself upright with a surge of alarm and probed at the stain with careful fingers.

"It's not *your* blood," the girl said.

Rett struggled to his feet. He almost didn't want to know— *Whose blood is it? Did I do something bad?* He looked around for some clue that would tell him where he was. Doorway to the left, corridor to the right. He stepped toward the short corridor and saw a heavy door at the end, bolted shut. He turned back to the girl. "What is this place?"

She hesitated. "You don't remember?"

Rett limped to the heavy door. He tugged at the bolt but it didn't budge. It was bent at one end, jammed into the housing. On the floor lay a fire extinguisher that must have dealt the damage.

"I didn't know what was happening," the girl said behind him. "You were outside and then you came in. I only knew something had hurt you—was hurting you."

Rett tried to make sense of what she was saying. But all he could think was, *The door is jammed.* He turned to face the girl, who was padding down the hallway toward him on dirty bare feet.

"At first I thought that guy was hurting you." The girl pointed at the door. "There's a man out there. He had a gun."

His gaze went to her hip pocket, to a bulge there and a glimpse of metal. Alarm rang through his body. *A gun, she has a gun.*

"But I think it was something else," she went on. "Something to do with an electrical signal or . . . I don't know. Whatever caused that aurora. I think being inside shielded me from the effects of whatever it was. Maybe the walls block signals somehow."

Rett couldn't follow anything she was saying.

"I got the door closed," she said. "I thought that would make it stop."

"You did that? It's *jammed*," Rett said.

"I thought maybe he was hurting you."

Rett's gaze dropped to her pocket again.

"Can you remember anything?" She was frantic now, her words coming out in desperate spurts. She pushed her fists together, as if it took physical effort to get out her jumbled explanation. "We're here because Scatter sent us. They want us to find something. We woke up outside and came up here to the depot for safety. But there was a man here already, and he had a gun. We got him outside and then something happened to your head."

She reached out like she might touch him.

"Don't come closer," Rett barked. At the same time, his hand went to his head, to the scar he had discovered moments ago.

"There's something in your head." The girl held her hands

up as if to calm a spooked animal. "Scatter put it there. I think something went wrong with it a minute ago, and that's why your memory's gone now. It would have happened to me, too, if I had been outside with you."

She slowly lifted her hair with one hand to reveal a shaved swath and a long scar.

"See?" she said. "They put something in my head, too."

Rett gaped in horror. He found he had backed right against the door. To his left was an open closet. He lunged into it and pushed the narrow door shut.

5:41 A.M.

Green light glowed at Rett's feet, where a cracked plastic tube leaked luminous liquid onto the floor. In just a moment, everything would come back to him. Any moment now.

But it didn't.

His breath came fast as panic flared. He dragged a heavy plastic bin to block the door, and then noticed what was inside the bin—more jumpsuits like the one he was wearing. He pulled out one that looked to be his size. He couldn't bear to look again at the blood smeared across the fabric at his torso.

He watched the barricaded door while he stripped off the soiled jumpsuit and zipped up his new one. He'd have to go out there eventually. For one thing, thirst raked at his throat.

But the girl. She had a gun.

He was trapped in this place. That was the worst of it. No getting out if she got violent. He pictured the scar running half the length of her skull and shuddered. He reached to touch his own skull, to feel the scar running through his cropped hair. He jerked his hand away. *What happened what happened what happened?* He tried to squash his panic while he searched his memory for answers. He could find only fragments: a medical lab, a woman with an angular face, a green light in the sky.

The girl said Scatter had sent him here, and something about that rang true. He remembered a woman wearing a lab coat with a logo of jagged lines, her voice edged with frustration: *If you haven't managed it yet, you never will. There's only one way left to do this. You'll have to find it . . .*

Pain sliced through his head. The walls suddenly felt too close. He had to get out of here.

He dragged the plastic bin away from the door. Opened the door and peered into the hallway. No sign of the girl.

He crept out, noticing the grit beneath his bare feet. Dizzying trails of footprints covered the floor of the main area.

Where did the girl go?

From an open doorway ahead—a loud clatter.

Rett's heart lurched. He spotted a handle on the wall to his right and jerked it up. The wall lifted away to reveal a room like a lounge on a spaceship. *I need to find a way out of here.* He turned away from the strange space.

And there it was, right in front of him: a rope, leading up to an opening in the ceiling.

I can't climb a rope, he thought.

But the idea of the girl emerging from an open doorway, gun in hand, sent enough adrenaline through him to make him try. He heaved himself upward.

Adrenaline must be more effective than I ever realized, he thought, marveling at the strength his arms and legs found to climb. Something about the way his muscles strained against his sleeves felt wrong—almost as if he were borrowing someone else's body. *People always feel stronger in emergencies, right?*

At the top, he clambered onto a shelf, and then out through the opening in the roof.

All around was jagged wasteland, spires and buttes like rows of teeth in a gaping maw. No end in sight.

Rett's breath came fast as panic washed over him.

No—there's got to be something.

His gaze roved the metal roof.

Solar panels took up much of the space. A metal contraption sat to one side, its hinged panels like the petals of a closed flower. *Is that an antenna?* Rett wondered. *A way to call for help?* He eased over the rounded metal roof, trying not to advertise his escape, and wrenched the panels outward, confused again by his sudden strength. With a *clunk*, the panels fell open to the sun. But no button, no way to turn the thing on.

The girl had said that something outside had hurt him. Or no, it was something about a man—a man with a gun. *But she's the one with a gun,* Rett thought. *She's the one who jammed the door shut.*

Still—where was the man? Rett peered over the rounded front of the building. Below, a figure lay sprawled in the dirt.

"Hey!" Rett shouted. Doubt seized him immediately. Maybe the girl hadn't been lying—maybe the man really did have a gun. He watched the figure for a few moments more, but the man didn't move. Dead, maybe. Fear swept through Rett. *No, just unconscious,* he told himself, and he tried to believe it. Still, he scrambled back up to the roof's peak, sending down a spray of dust and gravel in his wake.

What now?

He had no water, no shoes. No hope of crossing a treacherous wasteland. He had only two choices: stay outside in the wasteland with a man who might be dead, or go back into the building with the armed girl.

His thirst decided for him. The girl had given him that Mylar pouch of water. There were probably more in the shelter. And maybe a phone, or *some* way to call for help.

He climbed back down the rope, one thought on his mind: he had to keep himself safe from the girl. He needed a weapon. *The fire extinguisher.*

He landed on the metal floor, wincing at the noise his feet made. In a moment, he had the fire extinguisher in his hand.

"Rett?"

The girl's voice came from under a half-lifted wall. Rett shrank against the wall of the corridor and held the extinguisher ready.

"Rett?" she called again, a note of worry in her voice. "We don't have much time. We have to be ready."

Rett lowered the extinguisher. *There's something about the way she says my name.*

The girl ducked into the room. She started when she saw him standing in the corridor, but her surprise quickly turned to concern. "Are you okay?"

Rett wasn't sure what to say. The distress in her eyes unsettled him. *Why does she care?* "You mean, other than being trapped in the middle of a wasteland with a stranger?" he said.

"A wasteland." She frowned at the rope swaying between them. "Did you go up on the roof?"

Rett felt like crumpling. Who cared what he had done? He was caught in a metal trap, and it didn't matter if he escaped because the world outside wasn't any better. "Where *are* we?"

"Rett, I'm sorry, we don't have time for this."

There it was again, that dip in her voice when she said his name. Rett hadn't heard anyone say his name that way in a long time.

"Something's coming," she told him. "We have to work fast, before it gets here."

Rett was lost in confusion. "What's coming?"

"Honestly? You don't want to know."

Rett had a sudden vision of a dark shape eclipsing the morning light. He shook it away and thought, *She's right, I don't want to know.*

"I got together everything we might need," the girl said, her words coming in a rush. "So we can go up on the roof and shoot a flare and see if anyone comes to help us. And if no one does at least we'll have—"

A noise like thunder came from the other side of the heavy door. Someone was banging on the metal.

Rett went cold.

The girl turned to him, accusation in her eyes. "He's awake. Earlier than he should be. What did you do?"

Rett opened his mouth and shut it again. He had no idea what she meant, but it was clear he had done something bad in waking the man. "I thought . . . maybe . . . he could help . . ."

The girl considered, her anger suddenly in check. "He had that logo on his cap. He said he used to work for Scatter. But he didn't know anything about why we're out here." She shook her head. "He had the gun. He's not interested in helping us."

Rett couldn't follow anything she was saying, but she didn't seem to care. She ducked back into the room she'd come from without another word.

Something's coming, Rett thought, shivering alone in the main room.

The man outside is awake. The girl inside has a gun.
What do I do?

He wanted to hide again. Barricade himself in a room where no one could get to him.

She knows my name.

Somehow, she knows me.

He followed her instead.

"We have to get onto the roof to shoot the flare gun," she said as Rett came in. "But if he gets up there, too . . ." She opened a cabinet and pulled out a long metal pole as if sliding a sword from its scabbard.

Rett shrank back.

"Hey," the girl said softly. "I'm not going to hurt *you*. It's for *him*. In case he tries anything."

Rett couldn't take his eyes off the metal pole. He shifted his grip on the extinguisher, trying to decide if he really needed it after all. His gaze traveled to the girl's pocket, where the butt of a gun showed. "Are you going to tell me anything else about what's going on here?"

"Like what?" She turned to eye a button on the wall labeled with odd shapes. "We're kind of in a hurry here."

"Like your name, maybe?"

She stopped, turned to him. He thought he saw pain in her eyes, but the next moment it had vanished. "Bryn." She turned back to her work. "Ward of the state, just like you."

Rett's grip on the extinguisher loosened.

"At Walling Home, just like you," Bryn went on. "We got ourselves signed up for a job and now we're stuck out here in the middle of nowhere. We thought we were supposed to find something but when we got to the coordinates, there was nothing there. So now we're starting over."

Rett reeled at the slew of information.

A job, finding something—that was vaguely familiar. But the rest . . .

"We graduated out," Bryn said. "Workhouses are closing, no place for us to go, so we took a job with a company called Scatter. At least that's what we think. Problem is, the job's impossible to finish. The best we can do now is send up a flare—" She touched the butt of the gun in her pocket, and Rett flinched.

He couldn't help it. He kept envisioning her raising her arm, aiming at his forehead.

She looked at his hand tightening around the fire extinguisher and went rigid. "What's that for?"

"I was going to ask the same thing about the gun in your pocket."

Bryn put a hand over the bulge at her hip. "I told you, I took it from the guy outside."

Rett studied her for a moment. Her hazel eyes glowed with challenge.

"Would you rather I left it with him?" she asked. "He had it trained on you not thirty minutes ago."

Rett shivered.

Bryn pulled the gun out of her pocket and laid it on the cabinet top. "How about we leave it right there? Does that make you feel better?"

It made him feel worse, actually, seeing the scarred grip, the dusty barrel. He moved his hand toward it with the hope that touching it would bring some sense of familiarity.

Bryn's hand shot out to block him. She laid her palm over the gun. For a moment, neither of them spoke. Rett's hand hung in the air, halfway to the gun. He lowered it to his side.

"We need to take it up on the roof," Bryn finally said, and slowly slid the gun back toward herself.

Rett laid his hand on top of hers to stop her. Her face went tight but she didn't move. She watched Rett slide the fire extinguisher onto the cabinet top. "Now neither of us has a weapon," Rett said. "Okay?"

Their hands still rested together on the gun. Rett moved his away. Bryn's fingers were curled loosely around the guard. She hesitated and then turned from the cabinet, leaving the gun.

Her shoulders slumped. She seemed completely lost, for once. "We're screwed, Rett. This isn't going to work. No one's going to come for us. There's no way out of here."

Rett licked his dry lips. "There's . . . There's got to be some way . . ." *There's always something.* Did he really believe that?

"We already tried going out into the wasteland. There's nothing out there for us." When Rett frowned, Bryn added, "Trust me, we did."

Rett touched his throbbing head. "I must have hit my head hard. I don't remember anything."

"Not anything? Here, let's try something." Bryn pointed at a row of devices laid out on the cabinet, trailing power cords. "What are these devices for?"

"GPS?" It came out automatically.

Bryn brightened. "And what's in the room at the top of the ladder?"

Rett squinted at the opening in the ceiling. "I don't know."

"Guess."

"Beds? Some place to sleep?"

She smirked at him the way he did when he beat someone

at checkers back at Walling. Did that mean he was getting this right or wrong?

He hopped up on the ladder and looked into the room overhead. *I was right. It's a dorm room or something.* He grinned down at Bryn.

"I'll give you a whole box of carabiners if you can answer my next question," she said.

"Make it a large Coke and you're on."

"What secret place did I promise to take you to if we ever get out of here?"

Rett searched his mind, watching the corners of Bryn's mouth tremble. He came up blank. "I think I've had my fill of secrets, if I'm being honest."

Bryn's smile fell. "Me too."

She made a show of searching the debris littering the floor, as if she might find something else they needed. But then she swiveled back toward him. "I know I said I'd be better waking up here alone, but—" She reached to touch the edge of his sleeve, and he let her. "Please remember. I need you to remember."

Rett took half a step closer and she wrapped her hand around his arm. Just below her knuckles, a line of freckles trailed. He traced them with a finger. *I remember . . .*

He tensed. He'd just realized—"It's too quiet."

Bryn cocked her head to one side, listening.

No more pounding noises, Rett thought. *Good or bad?*

Bryn ducked under the wall and Rett followed. All was eerily quiet. Then came a sudden pattering on the roof and they looked up to see rain falling through the skylight. Rett reached to catch the cold drops on his palm. *Water,* he thought, and then an image came to him: *The metal contraption on the roof, open like a flower. Open to the rain.*

"There's a rain trap on the roof," he told Bryn. "I opened it earlier."

"What?" Bryn asked breathlessly. She craned her neck as if she'd get a view of the trap through the open skylight.

"We just need to find where the water comes through."

"I already know." Bryn moved to the couch and opened a panel on the wall to reveal a blue spigot. She pushed it with a finger but no water came out.

"Maybe in a few minutes?" Rett said.

Rain drummed harder and harder on the roof. In a minute, the floor beneath the skylight was slippery with it.

"Get the water bottles," Bryn said over the drumming of rain. "In the cabinet on the—"

"—far left. I know."

They locked gazes. *Remember*, Rett urged himself. "And, swimming—that's what we're going to do after this, isn't it?"

He could tell he'd caught her by surprise, but she only said, "Sooner than you think."

He ducked into the supply room and yanked open a cabinet to pull out the box of empty water bottles along with an empty backpack. Then he stopped, pack in hand, when he noticed the GPS units. A tiny yellow light shone on each device, proof that they had gained some charge. Rett probed at the buttons on one until it turned on.

An icon flashed under his fingertip, a stylized question mark. It opened a scrolling image of a hilly landscape.

A game.

Rett tapped on the screen to collect a smooth rock before it passed out of reach. *+1000 points.* He tapped on another rock, this one jagged. *–500 points.*

Not sure what good a game does us, Rett thought. *And it's not even fun.*

Rett looked up from the screen and squinted around at the cabinets, the hiking gear. At the walls of rooms that held jumpsuits and boots and water and beds. All for workers sent to collect some kind of mineral. Could that be what this place was? A shelter of sorts, a depot for miners collecting rocks from the barren landscape outside?

Was that what he and Bryn had been sent to find—rocks?

A memory came to him then: the weight of something in his pocket, the feel of a smooth rock. He'd found it here somewhere—in a little room with boxes and switches. Where was that?

He went out into the main room. Bryn was testing the spigot again. A thin stream of dirty water trickled out.

"Pipes aren't great, I guess," she said, wrinkling her nose.

"Just dusty, probably." Rett licked his dry lips. "It'll clean out."

"Rett." Bryn's eyes darkened. "That guy is out there. If he climbs up on the roof . . ."

"I'll shut the skylight. I can climb up and—"

"And then he'll be trapped out there. But there's something else coming this way. He'll die if we leave him out there."

Rett's stomach lurched. *Die?*

What exactly is coming this way?

"But if we go out there," Bryn went on, "even to help him, I don't think he'll be happy to see us."

"Why not?"

Bryn's gaze went to Rett's abdomen, where blood had stained Rett's old jumpsuit.

"What happened?" Rett asked.

"He had the gun. He was going to hurt you."

Rett's veins filled with ice water. "Okay, bad question. How about, who is he? What does he want?"

"I don't know."

Then an answer popped into Rett's head. "Is he . . . looking for rocks?"

"What?"

"Rocks. I saw one here. In a room with switches."

"The power supply?" Bryn gave him a baffled look.

"Where's that?"

She pointed to the open doorway.

Rett went through and found a bathroom to the left, and beyond that found another door marked with a lightning bolt in a triangle. A ping of familiarity went off in his brain.

Beyond the door was the power supply he remembered: switches and boxes and—

His foot hit something that clattered over the floor: a small, smooth rock.

He picked it up. *Yes, this is it.* He'd found this rock before, somehow. He turned it over in his fingers. Veins of silver flashed in the low light. The effect was mesmerizing.

An eerie song floated through his mind, though he couldn't say where it had come from: *One, change your jumpsuit. Two, find some water. Three, get the—*

Shovels.

Rett had no idea where that last word had come from. *Bryn didn't say anything about shovels, did she?*

And yet the more he stared at the rock in his hand, the more he was sure he needed to find shovels.

Bryn said we're supposed to find something, but when we got to where that something was supposed to be, it wasn't there. Could it have been buried? *Hidden underground and we didn't know it?*

But why had this little rock made him think of that? He could call to mind now a list he must have seen somewhere: *12 feet of rope, 9×9 plastic drop cloth, 6 nylon backpacks, 6 shovels . . .*

There hadn't been any shovels in the supply room, though. That long metal pole had been the largest thing in the cabinets.

A thought surfaced in Rett's mind: *Where there are rocks, there are shovels.*

But there was no room in this small space for hidden shovels. If they were here, they were behind the walls.

He felt along the panels, looking for a handle or a button. All was smooth from ceiling to floor and along every wall. Doubt crept in. *Why would someone want to hide shovels, anyway?*

Rett felt for the rock he had slipped into his pocket. *They don't want to hide the shovels. They want to hide the rocks. And the shovels are with the rocks.*

He ran his hands over the back wall again, but this time he pushed at the panels with sharp thrusts.

Pop. A panel gave way and then clattered to the floor into a compartment beyond the wall.

Rett peered into the compartment, but it was too dark to see anything. He stuck a hand in and groped around. His fingers found a metal basin that he guessed was for storing rocks. And beyond that—a handle.

"Bryn!" he called as he pulled out a heavy shovel. He hefted it and maneuvered back to where Bryn waited. "Look what I—"

He was interrupted by a shout from above: *"Hey!"*

Rett looked up. A figure showed above the open skylight, dark against the gray sky. From the corner of Rett's mind emerged a terrifying memory of a heavy black shape falling through the skylight—

"Hey!" the figure called again in a gruff voice. It was the man Rett had seen sprawled on the ground near the door of the depot. Same hat, same dirty long-sleeved T-shirt and tattered jeans, now soaked with rain. "Stupid kid—you knock me out and leave me for the bugs?" the man called in his parched-throat voice.

Rett looked to Bryn, who stood frozen near the couch, water bottle in hand. Her gaze traveled to the half-lifted wall behind Rett, and he knew what she was thinking: *the gun.*

Another shout from above: "You know what I'm going to do to you when I get down there?" The rope twitched.

Rett shifted his weight on his feet. He tightened his grip on the shovel. *It's not enough. I need the gun.*

Above, the man looked over his shoulder at something and let out a string of curses. *"It's coming."* His voice went high with panic. Rett's scalp prickled at the sound.

"Drop the shovel and back away," the man called. "I'm closing this skylight and climbing down. Unless you want the bug that's headed this direction to come crawling in to meet you?"

Bug? Rett thought. *What's he talking about?* The memory returned of a dark shape falling through the skylight. A high-pitched scream echoed through his mind. Rett's mouth went drier than dry.

"Hey!" the man called again, and the black talon dangling from his necklace swung violently. "You ain't got time to think about this. Drop the shovel."

Rett shifted uneasily, watching the talon swing. He let the shovel *clang* to the floor.

"That's right," the man said, lowering himself through the skylight. "Now back away."

Rett held up his empty hands. "Okay." He gave Bryn a look and then directed his gaze at the spigot. She nodded and went back to filling the water bottle in her hand.

Rett ducked into the supply room. The gun lay where Bryn had left it. Rett eyed it, his nerves buzzing. He slid the gun off the cabinet top and imagined pointing it at the man, ordering him into the closet and shutting the door. And then what? He and Bryn had to get out of this place.

But something was out there.

Rett slid the gun into his pocket. It pulled at his jumpsuit, weighed it down. He wiped his sweaty palm on his sleeves. The man was shouting again when Rett ducked in the main room.

"What are you up to?" the man growled, struggling down the rope in his rain-wet clothes.

"You can have whatever you want from this place," Rett told him, trying to keep his voice steady. "But you're going to let us take what we need and get out of here."

Bryn kicked a pair of boots toward Rett, and he jammed them on, his gaze still locked on the man.

" 'Get out of here'?" the man said, grunting with the effort of climbing down the rope. "You might want to take that up with the bug crawling up the side of the building."

Rett tried to imagine what could be making its way onto

the roof. He saw in his mind a creature sketched on the page of a notebook. A shadowed form baring hooked feet and jagged mandibles . . .

"They're used to hunting down *dogs*, but they'll take anything with blood," the man went on. He dropped to the floor and pressed his red-raw hands together. "Best hope you know what you're doing out there. Doesn't seem anyone has let loose any dogs for them in a while now."

In the light filtering through the skylight, Rett could see the man clearly for the first time. His skin was shrunken and ashy—under his jaw, along his collar. His eyes were dark and frantic beneath swollen eyelids. His hands were chapped, nails broken or missing altogether.

Rett backed away. But the man only tipped his head back to regard Rett through slit eyes.

"You give me this goose egg?" he growled, rubbing a hand over his head and eyeing Rett's shovel. He turned to Bryn. "No . . . it must have been you."

Rett stepped between them. The man's gaze traveled to Rett's hip, where the grip of the gun was barely concealed.

"Never mind," the man growled. "I just want my things. Starting with the backpack I left in the other room. Then I'll have that gun back."

Rett put his hand over the butt of the gun.

"This is no place for junior treasure hunters," the man said. He took a step closer so that he towered over Rett, all gnarled muscle under his rain-soaked clothes. "You've got no claim here."

He clamped a hand on Rett's shoulder and shoved him onto the couch. "Stay there and don't move. Shouldn't take me long to get what I came for. And then we'll figure out what to do about that bug." He gave Rett a grin that was all teeth. "Maybe it'll be satisfied with an offering."

Bryn caught Rett's eye. He knew what she wanted him to do. His fingers twitched on the butt of the gun. *Point it at him,* Rett told himself. *Tell him to get into the changing room.*

He thought of Garrick and his gang hurting him with whatever they could find, coming after him in the yard, trapping him in a box. He tried to use his memories to conjure enough anger to draw the gun and point it at the man.

All he could manage was a sour, weighty dread.

"You can take what you want," he told the man, "but leave us some of the GPS units."

A gravelly sound erupted from the man's throat. "For what?" he snarled. He kicked Rett's discarded shovel so that it clattered against the wall loudly enough to shred Rett's nerves. "Those rocks are all gone. This place is picked clean." The man's gaze darted around the depot, wild and hungry.

Rett pressed his palm against his jumpsuit pocket and felt the round shape of the rock there.

"Don't tell me that's why you came out here," the man said. "For the meteorites?"

Rett's memory flashed back to a cobwebbed firewood box, the lid that closed over him, the meteor shower he never got see—

The man's laughter was like some bit of machinery grinding in his throat. "Those are long gone. Guys like me picked this wasteland clean, so don't think I don't know what I'm talking about. Scatter stripped the rocks of that fancy alloy, gave us next to nothing for it." He sneered at Rett. "Only way Scatter would pay you for meteorites is if you could get a whole *pile* of them."

He backed toward the office and peered inside, didn't seem to see anything he wanted. He vanished into the medical room.

Rett stood, thinking of going for the GPS units. But the man was back a moment later, empty-handed and even more agitated.

"They didn't tell us at the time how much that metal was worth." The man's gaze roved the depot. He found a pack Bryn had left on the floor and jerked it open. "Maybe you've noticed that the countries we just started wars with are all bursting with valuable metals?"

Rett tried to make sense of the man's jumbled ideas. " 'Just started wars'? What are you talking about?"

The man rummaged through the pack. "Don't you listen to the news?" He tossed aside compasses and bandages and foil medicine packets. "When half our farmland has gone sterile, and import taxes are sky-high, it ain't hard to convince people to go to war. You tell them it's someone else's fault they're all sick and hungry and poor . . ."

He stood and kicked aside the empty backpack. "This place is worthless now except for the equipment. And it's *mine*. I worked for Scatter for fourteen months. Long enough to earn more money than I'd ever been paid for a job, but not long enough to pay for my treatment. Scatter *owes* me. So I'm gonna get what I came for."

He lurched toward the supply room. But then he froze. Turned and narrowed his eyes at Rett, then Bryn. Rett felt the man's suspicion like hot oil on his skin.

"Then again," the man said in a low voice that was almost a growl, "maybe you didn't come for rocks. Maybe you came here for something else."

Yes, Rett thought, swiveling to face Bryn, *but for what?* Bryn kept her expression blank, but Rett saw her hands clench on the seat as she waited for the man to say more.

"You think you can find what's buried here?" The man toyed with the black talon that dangled against his chest. He pointed the talon at Rett. "You think I'm too stupid to know it's worth a lot more than what's in these depots?"

Rett slowly shook his head.

The man's face twitched. "I know a guy on the inside. He told me all about it. He *also* says the government keeps tabs on this place. There's a reason they've got it walled off all the way around, keeping people out. And they know when you go digging things up. Only way I got past their walls was because that solar storm knocked their system offline."

Rett exchanged another glance with Bryn. "What's buried out here?" he asked the man.

The man gave a throaty laugh. "If you manage to find it, *you* can tell *me* what it is."

In one quick motion, he turned from them and ducked into the supply room, out of sight.

"The GPS units," Bryn said in a fierce whisper.

Rett looked to the supply room. The man would surely see the devices lined up on the cabinet top and would take them all for himself. "We'll get them."

"How?" Bryn huffed. "He's not going to let us have them."

Rett's fingers twitched over the butt of the gun in his pocket but they refused to pull it out.

"Give it to me," Bryn said.

Rett hesitated. "Are you going to shoot him with a flare for some GPS units?"

"That would be a waste of a flare. I'm just going to point the gun at him."

"That only gets us the GPS units. How are we going to get out of here? He said something was climbing up the side of the building. We can't open the skylight."

"Actually"—Bryn plucked the gun from Rett's pocket and shoved it into her own—"that's exactly what we need to do."

She shrugged off her pack, which was bulging with water bottles, and handed it to him.

Then she grabbed hold of the rope dangling in the center of the room.

"What are you *doing*?" Rett said.

"Getting us the GPS units *and* making a way out of here."

"*Bryn.*"

She kept climbing.

Behind Rett, boots clattered, and then the man ducked into the main room. He took one look at Bryn and shouted, "You open that skylight and we're all dead." He seized Rett's arm in a viselike grip. "Tell her to get down."

But Bryn had already reached the shelf near the ceiling and started turning the crank. "If you don't want to die," she called down, "I suggest you lock yourself in a room with a working door."

The man turned and fled back into the supply room.

"Rett!" Bryn called down. "Push the button!"

"What button?" Rett called hoarsely. But then he remembered odd shapes marking a button in the supply room.

He scrambled under the half-lifted wall and slammed his palm over the button. An alarm blared through the depot, and milky water sprayed over the floor.

"What's happening?" he called, but he heard no reply over the bleating alarm.

A panel overhead banged shut, and Rett realized the man had climbed up into some safer space. Half the GPS units still lay on the cabinet top. If the water that was now over his ankles rose as high as he thought it might, they'd be ruined.

Rett yanked open a cabinet and spotted a plastic sheet. In a minute, he had the devices wrapped and shoved in a nylon backpack. By then, the water had risen over his knees. He shouldered the pack, turned toward the main room—

Bryn screamed.

Water buffeted the stuck wall and surged underneath it. "Bryn!" Rett called. *What's happening?*

Before he could think, he dove under the wall.

The water was too milky to let him see anything. He felt his way under the wall . . .

Only to graze a twitching form.

He scrambled to his feet in waist-high water. A shadow showed beneath the water's nearly opaque surface: a dark bulb dancing madly in the current. It swung a jagged mandible toward him, and he flung himself back.

What is that thing?

It skittered toward him. Its erratic movements brought to mind a flipbook of scribbled drawings, a flickering of mangled stills.

The shovel. Rett twisted in the water, trying to catch sight of his only weapon under the opaque surface. No good—he couldn't see a thing through the white churn of minerals. He dove under, scrabbling at the floor for a handle. A hooked foot lashed through the water and drew a juddering path down his arm. Rett jerked back.

The next moment his hand hit metal. He grabbed for the handle. Rose out of the water, shovel ready.

The creature was a tangle of clenched talons and nothing more.

"Rett!"

Bryn still lay on the shelf up near the ceiling, under the open skylight.

"Are you okay?" he called up.

"Are *you*?"

The mass of talons next to him twitched and then went still again. *Dead*, Rett thought. *Drowned. Isn't that what the water was for?* But he didn't wait around to see if it would come to life again. He swam toward the rope, trailing the shovel.

"The GPS units?" Bryn called.

"I got them. Three GPS units, four limbs, half my sanity." He panted. "And a shovel."

7:03 A.M.

From the outside, the depot was a huge metal canister, scarred by windblown grit. Long scratches showed where the creature had clawed its way up to the skylight.

Rett and Bryn moved around to the front of the depot, rainwater running past their boots in rivulets. *The man's still inside*, Rett thought. Here was the spot in the rain-darkened dirt where he had seen the man sprawled half an hour ago. *Dead.*

No—only unconscious.

So why do I keep seeing him in my mind as a mangled corpse?

"He was dead." Rett turned to Bryn, who was pulling the packet of plastic-wrapped GPS units out of the backpack.

"No, he's probably okay if he went up into the upper room. I don't think the water level went up that high. The other wall was open, remember?" She stuck a GPS unit in each pocket and then dug around in the pack for something else. "He's probably still sitting up in that room, waiting for the water to drain. We should get out of here before he follows us."

Rett couldn't tear his gaze from the wet dirt. A terrible vision kept appearing before him. "But he was dead. Before. Cut in half." He shuddered.

Bryn stopped digging in the pack. Rett looked up to find that she had gone ghostly white. Rainwater ran down the sides of her face.

"Why do I remember him dead?" Rett asked.

Bryn turned away from the depot. She busied herself with the pack again. "It'd be better to forget," she said over her shoulder. "We have to head northwest. That'll take us close to the coordinates of whatever we're supposed to find."

Rett tried to push the haunting images out of his head. *The man's okay. He's alive.*

"Nice job finding the shovel, by the way," Bryn said. "It makes sense now why I didn't see anything at the coordinates before. Hope you're up for digging. At least I didn't cut my hand in the depot this time."

She turned and handed him a GPS unit and then palmed a compass. "Keep an eye on the GPS. Let me know when it picks up a signal."

"Why isn't the signal picking up now?"

"There was an aurora. Or—the guy said a 'solar storm.' I think that's what caused the aurora, and it must also interfere with the satellites. So there's no way to grab on to a signal."

A green flame dancing over jagged spires—so easy to envision. *An aurora*, Rett thought.

"I think that's what happened to you, too." Bryn drew her fingers over his scar, setting all his nerves alight. "An aftereffect of the solar storm. It made the mechanism in your head go haywire. It would've done the same to me if I hadn't been inside the depot. The walls acted like a shield."

"That's—" Rett tried to ignore the tingling left by her touch. "That's what made me forget everything?"

"I don't know, but isn't that what happens with head trauma sometimes? You forget everything surrounding the event that injured you?"

"Forget whole *days*? Forget how I *got here*? I can't even remember how I left Walling."

Bryn studied the compass glinting in her palm. "Maybe when we finish this, things will get clearer."

"When we find what Scatter sent us here to find? And then—how will we get home?"

Bryn shifted her pack. "I'm hoping that'll be clear after we dig up whatever we're supposed to dig up. You ready?"

"Wait. Didn't you hear what he said about the government keeping tabs on this place? How they've got it all walled off and they know if you go digging something up?"

Bryn took a moment to read her compass and orient herself. "Yeah. I heard."

"Aren't you . . . worried?"

"If they catch us digging something up, at least they'll know how to get us out of here. Although . . . I'm not big on the idea of going straight from one kind of prison to another."

"How are they even going to know if we dig something up?"

"He said they would. It sounds like whatever Scatter sent us to find, the government wants to keep buried."

"He said the government has this whole place walled off." Rett wiped rainwater from his face and took in the shining walls of the canyon around them. "Who would want to come here in the first place?"

"They're guarding something. Something they're so desperate to keep secret that they'd bury it in the middle of a wasteland."

"And Scatter wants us to dig it up?" Rett shook his head. "That doesn't make sense. No one would send *us* to do something like that. No one would send—"

"A couple of orphans desperate for a paycheck? Trust me, we've been over this. No one cares if you and I never come back."

Rett started to say something but Bryn interrupted him.

"I know," she said, her voice softening. "Your mom. You told me." She laid a hand on his shoulder. He couldn't help resenting the pity in her eyes.

He shifted away from her. *How much did I tell her?* "Exactly how long have we . . ."

". . . been stuck here together?" Bryn's mouth twisted. "That's something I can't quite figure out."

"What do you mean? How did we get here in the first place?"

"We woke up here," Bryn said. "We *keep* waking up here. Over and over, I think." She must have read the bewilderment on his face because she said, "It doesn't make sense to me, either. But we've done this before. We woke up in that depot and went out to find whatever we're supposed to find. When we got there, we didn't see anything—we didn't know it was buried, and we didn't have shovels anyway. So we . . . started over."

"Started over?"

"There are seven pouches of water in your pack. We already drank all that water the last time we went into this wasteland. But when we showed up back at the depot a couple of hours ago, all that water was back. All of our supplies—everything we left in the wasteland. It was all back inside the depot."

Rett was starting to feel irritated. It didn't make any sense. "But how did we get back to the depot?"

"I . . ." Bryn raked her wet hair back from her face. "I shot the gun at you."

Rett blinked at her. "Sorry?"

"*Near* you, I mean. To scare you. Every time we get really scared, something strange happens. We wake up back at the depot."

Rett struggled to absorb all she was saying. "But . . . how?"

With her hair pushed back, the scar running along the side of Bryn's head was partly visible. Rett tried not to stare, but Bryn didn't seem to mind. She touched a finger to it.

"It has something to do with what they put in our heads," Rett guessed.

"You told me that you felt like the mechanism let you pull yourself back toward the depot, somehow. And you took me with you."

Rett closed his eyes and saw a starry sky, a flicker of green light—just a memory. But he had been there. Could he get there again? "What if I can't do that next time we're in trouble?

Or what if something happens to me—would you be able to wake up and start over on your own?" He clutched her arm. "Bryn, I don't know if I can—"

"We're going to finish the job this time. We're going to end it." Her hazel eyes glowed, full of reassurance.

Rett nodded, released his grasp. Her fingers trailed his palm as he did, leaving him with the dizzying sense that he had felt her gentle touch before, had even held her hand in his. But then she turned and strode ahead, leaving Rett to follow like something tethered by expectation.

7:15 A.M.

Rett's boots rubbed against his feet while he sweated with the effort of climbing another slope.

Bryn let them stop only briefly to drink water and air out their pruned feet. The GPS unit's battery was low, so Rett switched it out for another and checked again to make sure it still hadn't found a signal.

The face of Bryn's compass flashed in the sun while she checked its reading.

"You sure we're heading the right way?" Rett asked.

"We've going to veer a bit. Avoid getting ourselves up where we can't get down." A flicker of doubt passed over her face.

"Is that what happened before?" Rett asked.

Bryn kept her gaze trained on the compass. Fear seeped into Rett's bones. *We've done this over and over. We might never get it right.*

"Last time I insisted we climb down a slope and then you fell and I think you broke your ankle," Bryn said.

Rett drank from his water bottle. "And then?" He wasn't entirely sure he wanted to know.

"And then we realized we didn't have a shovel and we started over back at the depot. Got inside, realized someone else was already in there, and . . . had a bit of an altercation."

"An altercation?" Rett wrapped his arms around his stomach, as if to hide the blood that no longer stained his clothes. "What did I— What happened?"

"It wasn't you, actually."

Rett dropped his arms. "What do you mean?"

"I mean the guy was pointing a gun at you, trying to force you out of the depot and into bug territory, so I came up behind him and . . ."

"And what?" *Why won't she look me in the eye right now?*

"I knocked him out with a fire extinguisher." Bryn squinted into the distance. "Then you tried to help him. Well, first we dragged him outside and *then* you tried to get him back to safety when you thought twice about it. And some of his blood got on your clothes."

So that's where that stain came from, Rett thought, looking down at the spot where he'd seen the blood earlier that morning. *Like something out of a comic book—a stain of guilt, a brand of warning. Except . . .* "I didn't hurt him?"

"Honestly, I . . ." Bryn tipped her head forward so her hair hid her face. "I thought you did hurt someone. I found your jumpsuit last time we went through this. I saw that stain. You told me you hadn't hurt anyone but I didn't know whether to believe you."

Which is worse? Rett wondered. *Not knowing whether you've done something terrible, or not knowing whether the guy you're trapped in a bunker with did something terrible?*

He moved her hair behind her ear so he could see her face. "Hey," he said softly. "That must have been scary."

She looked up, surprised.

"For the record," Rett told her, "I've hurt exactly six people in my life. So it's not like I'm an innocent newborn fawn of a boy."

The corner of her mouth lifted. "Tell me six of them had it coming and I'll restore you to fawn status without further questions."

He shrugged. "Five, maybe." He meant it as a joke, but as soon as he said it, his heart turned to lead. *Those emails, the terrible things I said.* What else could he do but pray his mother didn't believe them? *I'm coming for you. You have to know I'm coming to help you.*

"I'll give you credit for trying to help Mr. Scavenger back there when he was unconscious," Bryn said. Rett's heart lifted a little at her smile. "Now, can we please get moving again?"

He caught her wrist. "Wait. You get what I'm saying, right? I don't blame you for being scared of me. For whatever you did when you thought I could be dangerous. We do all kinds of things to survive."

A question flashed in her eyes.

"What?" Rett asked.

"I said that same thing to you before."

Did she? He couldn't remember. "I'm a good listener. Add that to my credit."

"But you know that doesn't mean you get a pass on attacking someone now? That's not how this credit thing works."

"Disappointing."

Bryn smirked down at her compass and oriented them again.

Rett caught her wrist one more time. "And thanks."

"For what?"

"Sounds like it would have been my own blood on my clothes if you hadn't beaned that guy."

"Actually, I think you were willing to go quietly. So he wouldn't have hurt you at all. You'd just be—" She stopped.

Bug food. Rett shuddered. "Thanks anyway."

They angled down the far side of the slope they had climbed, sometimes skidding over the rocky ground. Rett had to use the shovel to brace himself against the slope so he wouldn't slide all the way down, but Bryn proved nimbler. When they made it to the floor of the ravine, she only quickened her pace.

"Wait." Rett panted.

"It's just ahead," Bryn called over her shoulder. "I recognize this spot."

Rett followed her along the twisting bottom of the ravine, keeping to the shade at the steep wall. Bryn's gaze kept bouncing from the dirt to the cliff tops. *More bugs,* Rett thought, straining his ears for the *clack* of talons. He heard only the scrape of their own boots over dirt.

Soon Bryn veered out to the middle of the ravine and circled the area a few times, head down, eyes trained on the ground.

Finally, she stopped in her tracks, electric with discovery. "I remember these rocks! See how this one is darker than the others? This is the spot."

Rett knelt to examine the rock. Silver glints showed through its dark surface. *Just like the one in my pocket,* he marveled.

She jabbed the toe of her boot into the dirt. "Ready to dig?"

"I need some water first."

Bryn fished a water bottle out of the pack. "We'll take turns." She fished the gun out next. "I'll dig first. You keep watch for bugs."

9:14 A.M.

The dust from Bryn's digging hung in the humid air like a thin cloud of smoke. It made Rett's nausea worse. *Just dehydrated,* he told himself. *Or, you know, could be my steady diet of fear and confusion.*

He watched Bryn dig. *At least I'm not alone.*

"Are we even sure there's something buried here?" Rett called from where he sat in the shade.

"He said there was." Bryn's shovel chucked into the soft dirt.

"He also seemed kind of . . . high-int, low-sanity."

"What?"

"He said the U.S. *just* started a bunch of wars. But I haven't heard anything about that. And he said the government's got this whole place walled off. Why would anyone need to wall off a wasteland?"

Bryn leaned on the handle of the shovel. "Maybe . . ." She took in the crumbling ridges that crowned the canyon. "Maybe they walled this place off because this is where it all started."

"Where what all started?"

"There's a theory floating around the internet about a government experiment gone wrong. This site called Dark Window says the experiment is to blame for the failing crops, the cancer clusters—all of it."

"What kind of experiment are we talking about?"

"Some ecological experiment. That's why people find two-headed frogs in their garden, why farmers can't keep their crops from shriveling."

"Why the trees in the park turned black," Rett mumbled, thinking of home.

"So maybe the government walled this place off because the wasteland is proof that they're to blame."

"It's not just the wasteland they're hiding. They buried something out here where they know nobody can get to it. But what did they bury?"

"You're asking me what people bury in wastelands? And then mark with a skull and crossbones?"

"Pirate treasure?"

Bryn gave him a look like, *Really?*

He grimaced. "Okay, obviously not. Unless I'm making clever commentary on corporate greed? I mean, are we assuming Scatter sent us out here to *steal* something for them?"

"From the government, no less. Any problem with that?"

"I'm pretty sure the *government* would have a problem with it. So there's that to think about."

Bryn stabbed her shovel into the dirt, continuing her work. "It's not like the powers that run this country have ever done anything but screw us both over. Am I right? Ecological disaster, shoddy health care, underfunded facilities—"

"Do you think it might be meteorites?"

"What?"

"The guy in the depot said Scatter had him hunting for meteorites. Maybe the government confiscated them all and buried them."

"Why would they do that?"

"I don't know. But maybe that means Scatter actually *is* the rightful owner of what we're about to dig up."

"Honestly, all I care about is getting this job finished."

"Yeah. I just wish I knew what I signed up for."

"Something tells me *you* wouldn't have signed up to do this if you thought it was *shady*."

"Why do you say that?"

She paused to take a drink from her water bottle. "You sure you're okay using that thing?" She nodded at the flare gun resting in Rett's lap and took a drink from her water bottle.

"Can't be that hard." Rett coughed against the dirt irritating his throat.

Bryn tossed him the water bottle. "You couldn't do it in the depot."

Rett glowered at the distant ridge of the ravine as he took a drink. "That was different."

"That guy would have hurt you, same as a bug would."

"Good to know you don't have qualms about shooting people. Thanks for the warning. By the way, I think I'll hold on to the gun from now on."

"You're not upset that he pointed that same gun at you?"

"I hope you see the irony in what you just said."

Bryn went back to shoveling, head down. "You told me before that you would defend yourself if you had to."

"Don't you ever wonder what kind of person you might be if there was no '*had to*'?"

Bryn paused, leaned on her handle. "You don't remember anything about me. Do you?"

Nausea and anxiety roiled in Rett's stomach. He tried to shift his attention to the images surfacing in his mind. "I remember—" How it felt to be close to her, to hear her say his name. What it was like when she looked at him, angry or scared or otherwise.

"You remember *what*?"

"I remember . . ." It came to him suddenly: ". . . that you have a boyfriend."

Bryn plucked the shovel out of the dirt. "That's right." Sliced into the soft ground. "I've been waiting for that to come back to you."

Rett didn't know why she seemed so annoyed by it. He was the one who should be bothered.

"Any signal yet?" Bryn asked.

Rett checked the display. "Not yet." He coughed into his sleeve, trying to clear his lungs of dust. The scrape of the shovel accompanied the sound, along with the patter of rocks falling down a steep slope.

The sound came again—rocks tumbling. Rett looked up to find a shadow haunting the ridge.

A bug.

He raised the gun, his heart beating wildly.

Just as he fired, Bryn pulled his arm down and the shot went low. A sputter of sparks and a cloud of blue smoke filled a curve of the ravine, sending the bug scuttling back over the ridge.

"What're you doing?" Rett cried.

"Don't shoot up there!" Bryn answered. "That man said the government is keeping tabs on this place. They'll see the flare and know we're here."

"I thought you *wanted* to get found."

"Not until we find what we're looking for."

Rett scanned the ridge again. The creature had gone.

"I think you scared it," Bryn said.

"Or proved to it that I can't aim."

"If someone sees that flare and comes after us, we can't finish this job."

"I get it." Rett grabbed the pack from the dirt and searched inside for another flare. "But if that *thing* comes after us, we're not finishing the job, either." He snapped open the barrel and slid the cartridge inside. "I don't much feel like starting over again. Or, you know, *dying*."

The shovel rang against dirt and gravel. "Just watch my back," Bryn said. "If it comes *down* here, then shoot it."

"I have your permission?" Rett asked.

"Do you want to get paid for this job or don't you?" Bryn snapped.

"Yes, I want to get paid," Rett snapped back.

"So you remember that at least."

Rett dragged his sleeve across the back of his sweaty neck. He thought of his mother, the workhouse. "Yeah, I remember." His mother had always worked so hard to convince him that he'd be better off on his own, that he shouldn't worry about her.

He scrubbed his hands over his face. *How could she think that?*

For a minute there was only the *chuck* of the shovel and the sound of Bryn's labored breathing as she worked.

Rett kept his gaze trained on the ridge where he'd seen the bug. "What're you going to do with the money?"

A scoop of dirt hit the pile. "Going to meet up with my boyfriend. Share it with him."

"He's waiting for you somewhere?"

Bryn frowned at the dirt. "I figure, if you get enough money, people will find *you*."

Rett swallowed. His throat was choked with the dust Bryn was making. He wasn't so sure what she said was true.

Bryn used her sleeve to wipe sweat from her face. "Do you remember *any* of the conversations we had before?"

"Why don't you just tell me what it is you keep waiting for me to remember?"

"I'm just trying to point out that you barely know me. Barely remember me, whatever." She went back to digging.

"If you're trying to tell me not to trust you, too late. Although, thanks for letting me hold the gun, then."

Thunk. The shovel hit something hard.

Bryn looked up at Rett, her gaze electric.

Rett scrambled toward the hole to see what she'd found. Bryn fell to her knees and used the shovel blade to pry a small black box out of the dirt.

"What is it?" Rett asked.

"Some electronic thing."

"Is that what we're supposed to find?"

Bryn jabbed at a small bulb at the corner of the box. "Whatever it is, it's not turned on." She turned it over to examine it, and then ran her fingers all over it. "No power switch." She bent lower over it. "Wait. It says something near this little bulb."

She held it up for Rett to see the tiny white letters: SIGNAL. "Light's not on—no signal," he said. "Just like the GPS units."

Bryn frowned, turning the box over and over in her hands. " '*They know when you go digging things up.*' "

"What?"

"That's what the man said. That the government would know if we tried to dig up something they buried. But how would they know?"

"Cameras?" Rett glanced around, but he already knew they'd have seen any cameras.

"I don't think this is the thing we're supposed to find. I think this is the thing that tells them we're about to find what we've been looking for." She tapped her shovel in the dirt. "I think there's something else down here."

"So this box is what—some kind of alarm? But it's not working?"

"How would it work? It'd have to send out a signal, right? So, the minute we dig it up, it picks up signal, and that's what alerts the government that we're digging where they don't want us to dig."

"Good thing the satellite's not working then. No signal."

In response, Bryn dropped the box at her feet and brought the shovel down on it, over and over. The metal housing cracked and flew apart to reveal wire innards and circuit boards.

"*Bryn.*"

Bryn went on hammering. *Bam bam bam*, until the pieces flew apart.

Rett stared at her while her breath heaved. "Bryn. I think it's dead."

Bryn gave him a brief glance. "The satellites are going to come back online any second. We got here a little faster than last time, but not by much." She looked down at the splintered device and seemed to register its destruction for the first time.

Rett gaped at it in horror. "I hope that wasn't the thing we were supposed to come find."

"Trust me, I have a feeling about this." Bryn held out the shovel. "Here."

Rett was about to trade the gun for it when a loud beep sounded from the GPS unit in his other hand.

Bryn tensed. "Was that—?"

The display showed the antenna icon, this time with a set of concentric rings. "Signal," Rett said.

They both looked down at the electronic components strewn in the dirt. A tiny red light blinked in a nest of wires.

Bryn hacked at it with the shovel. The light went out.

Rett chewed his lip. "Think it sent out a signal?"

"Don't know." Bryn stared at it, almost daring it to turn on again while she stood guard with the shovel. "Hope not."

"Guess we'd better hurry either way." Rett scanned the ravine for signs of hungry bugs.

Bryn was red-faced and sweating. She glared at the busted metal casing with an anger that Rett thought might really be fear. It unnerved him, the way she could bring out that intensity and then lock it away again. *Is it locked inside of me somewhere, too?* he wondered.

He handed Bryn the gun and took the shovel. "Go sit in the shade. I'll keep an eye out for bugs while I dig."

Bryn plodded over to the wall of the ravine and sat. Just as Rett took up digging, she said, "He trusted me and I screwed him over. My boyfriend. I told you but I guess you don't remember."

Rett's muscles locked.

"No one's waiting for me when I get out of here," Bryn went on. "He doesn't want me to find him."

Her words found some hollow place inside of Rett and made it ring.

He wanted to tell her that she shouldn't think like that. That things would seem better once they got out of here.

But he couldn't.

What if my mother isn't waiting for me?

He waited a moment for his frozen muscles to thaw and then lost himself in his work.

10:27 A.M.

Every time Rett stopped digging to rest, doubt crept over him.

Only a little water was left in the bottle waiting at the edge of the hole he and Bryn had dug. It was the last bottle, too. Nothing left after this except what was in the Mylar pouches, and that would be his last defense against thirst and nausea.

He snatched up the water bottle and held it to his lips. Bryn watched him from the shaded edge of the ravine. The gun rested on her knee. Her gaze lingered for a moment while Rett drank, and then she looked away. *Worried about the water?* Rett wondered. *Or maybe—* He thought of all the glances he'd taken at her when she wasn't paying attention. *Maybe she just likes looking at me.*

He shivered at the thought. Then his gaze went back to the gun. *She pointed it at me,* he told himself, trying to gauge how he felt about it. *She tried to scare me with it.*

But his doubts were eclipsed by the memory of Bryn standing close, her hand brushing his hip as she took the gun from his pocket.

He shook the thought away. They were dead if they didn't finish this job. They were almost out of water. Exhausted, alone.

He tipped the water bottle to drink the last of what was inside. But then he stopped, lowered the bottle. A sound floated to him from the shaded edge of the ravine: Bryn was humming. Rett stood frozen, hypnotized by the tune. It seemed to reach deep into his fractured memory. "What's that song?" he asked.

Bryn had her hand draped over one knee now, dangling the flare gun. Rett's question seemed to snap her out of a dream. "What?"

"The song you were humming just now."

The lyrics floated out from some recess in his mind:

> *One lonely lighthouse*
> *Two in a boat*
> *Three gulls circle*
> *Four clouds float.*

"About a lighthouse," he said to Bryn, "and a boat."

Bryn frowned. She started the tune over again, this time mumbling the lyrics. "I think *they* taught it to us. Scatter."

"What for?"

"Don't know."

Rett probed the dirt with his shovel. He stopped. The tune needled at him. "They taught it to us?" he echoed.

"Doesn't make much sense, though," Bryn said. "A lighthouse and a boat."

No, it doesn't, Rett thought as he went back to digging. *Unless it isn't really meant to be about this place.*

Just then he remembered something Scatter had told him. He froze with the shovel still sticking out of the dirt. "It signals the mechanism," he said. "The mechanism in our heads."

"You said that before. What does it mean?"

Rett pulled the shovel free and started digging again, trying to remember more. Bryn came over to squint down at him, but she couldn't seem to remember, either.

And then—*thunk*. The shovel hit something.

Bryn looked at Rett, looked down at the dirt where a gleam of silver showed through. Rett scraped away a swath of dirt with the shovel blade. More silver.

Rett dropped to his knees and swiped at the dirt with his hands. Bryn knelt next to him and did the same until they had uncovered a metal panel, two feet square. "What is it?" Bryn said.

"Are those words?" Rett used his fingers to wipe dirt from the grooves in the metal—letters stamped onto the panel's face.

"It's the song." Bryn gasped. "And there's more to it."

Rett read them aloud:

> *"One lonely lighthouse*
> *Two in a boat*
> *Three gulls circle*
> *Four clouds float."*

He took a breath and read the rest:

> *"Five foaming waves fall*
> *Six stars glow*
> *Seven fish follow*
> *Eight steps home."*

The last word echoed in the stillness: *home.*

I want to go home, Rett thought. "The song is supposed to

signal the mechanism in our heads," he said. "We just didn't have the whole song before."

"Is it supposed to—?" Bryn's question hung in the air, unfinished.

"*Eight steps home,*" Rett mumbled. "This song is supposed to help us find our way back."

"But what does it mean? Eight steps—what does that mean?"

Rett ran a finger down the lines of stamped letters. "It's a numbered list." He'd used the list himself to remember what to do: *One, change your jumpsuit. Two, find some water.* "I think the song is a memory device, something to help us remember how to signal the mechanism."

"We signal the mechanism by singing the song—the whole song."

Rett shook his head. "By saying the words. Eight words, one right after the other. One from each line—like a passphrase."

Rett forgot his thirst, forgot the blisters on his hands and feet, forgot the nausea in his lurching stomach. They could get home. Somehow, eight words from this song would send out a signal, and they would escape this wasteland.

"We can't go back yet. We have to know what this thing is first." Bryn tapped on the metal panel. It loosened in the dirt.

Rett shuffled his tired feet in the dirt. He wanted to get out of this place, before any more hungry bugs came along, before he collapsed in the dirt from exhaustion. He wanted to make sure the words would really work.

But if they really were here to do a job, Bryn was right—they had to finish it.

And then—home. Payday. Money for his mother's treatment.

If she still waited for him.

Bryn pried at an edge of the metal and the whole panel came up like a lid. Underneath lay another metal face inset with a digital display. A list of names took up most of the screen, each followed by a string of numbers and then a tiny icon of an antenna emitting concentric rings.

Cay, Vanessa 118173558

Duvall, Tamara 781778128

Torrez, Andy 817842374

Ward, Bryn 812419393

Ward, Rett 123779243

Stein, Erik 931211466

Michel, Gwynne 617741717

Hotchkiss, Charles 648127353

Reeder, Gayle 968473143

Loyd, Jason 143785017

Nguyen, James 873563755

. . .

Bryn traced the list with a trembling finger. Her hand stopped at WARD, BRYN. "Rett . . ."

All the blood drained from Rett's head. "Our names."

Bryn moved her finger to the antenna icons next to their names. Theirs each had more concentric rings than any other name.

"What does it mean?" Rett wondered aloud.

"We're giving out some kind of signal," Bryn breathed. "And this thing is picking it up."

"Or the other way around."

Bryn trailed her fingers over the display. The gesture

brushed away the dirt along one corner of the screen, and Rett noticed a small logo emblazoned there. Something cold and hard dropped into his stomach. "Bryn, look."

She followed his gaze to the graph of overlapping lines accompanied by a single word. "Scatter," Bryn read. "This device belongs to Scatter."

The silver of the box gleamed in the angled light. Rett reached into his pocket and brought out the rock he'd found in the depot. The bright veins flashed silver.

"Where did you get that?" Bryn asked.

"From the depot."

Bryn took the rock from him. "That man said Scatter was collecting meteorites. So they could strip an alloy from them."

"So they could build this thing," Rett agreed, surveying the box. "But what *is* it?"

Bryn examined the display again—the list of names, the antenna icons. "The mechanisms they put in our heads . . ."

"They're communicating with this box. Why?"

Bryn mumbled something to herself. Rett strained to make out the words. "Every time we get scared, we start over," Bryn said. "The mechanisms in our head know when we need to get away. They send a signal . . . and this box sends a signal back . . ."

"Why? What does it do?"

Bryn turned to him, a faraway look in her eyes. "The GPS unit. The date—what's the date on the display?"

Why does it matter? But Rett took the unit out of his pocket and handed it to Bryn.

"Still wrong," Bryn said. "Six years in the future."

"It's broken."

"No. It can't be wrong. It's connected to a satellite."

Rett let out an impatient huff. "The satellite's wrong." *Who cares?*

"It's not wrong." Bryn pocketed the unit with a trembling hand. "We woke up in the depot—no, *outside* the depot. We just showed up there. That's how we first got to this place. We showed up six years in the future."

"What?" Rett shook his head again. "That doesn't make any sense." But the images swimming in his head said otherwise: dates printed on foil and scratched into the metal of a wall in the depot. All future dates.

"And every time we get scared, we go back to that original point," Bryn said. "Because of the mechanisms in our heads. Because of this box."

"Are you saying—?" Rett couldn't quite make the words come out.

"We've been traveling in time," Bryn said. "And this box is how we've been doing it."

Rett's fingers went to the scar on his scalp before he realized what he was doing. *They put something in our heads . . .* An urgent voice came to him: *There's only one way left to do this. You'll have to find it.*

They'd sent him to do a job. In the future. Some experiment they weren't willing to try on themselves. Only on orphans no one would miss if they never came back.

"Why did Scatter send us to dig up their own device?" Rett wondered aloud.

Bryn touched the silvery metal. "The government's guarding this thing."

"Maybe they know Scatter is using it and they're trying to catch them." Rett fought against the panic needling its way under his skin. "Maybe they don't *want* Scatter to use it."

"But why?"

"Maybe the government wants to use it for themselves."

Bryn lifted her gaze to Rett's, her eyes wide. "They could use this device to go back in time. Reverse the experiment that turned this place into a wasteland. That made everyone sick."

Rett took in the sandy crawl surrounding them. "It doesn't look like they're doing that." *Why not? If we can go to the future, why not to the past?* His nerves went electric at the thought. *We could go to the past and prevent this disaster from ever starting. My mother would never have gotten sick, we'd never have gone hungry. And all those other people—*

"They don't want to," Bryn said. "They don't want to change what they did. The man in the depot said all the government *really* cares about is getting more rare metals. They need to use this crisis as an excuse to go to war."

Rett felt as if he were sinking into the soft dirt. "Scatter could use this device to go back in time and make everything better, but the government's trying to stop them."

Bryn's voice shook when she next spoke. "Which means we walked right into the government's trap."

A distant hum that had been building in Rett's ears now grew too loud to ignore. He looked up. Far off, a black smudge moved across the sky. "The signal from the alarm box," Rett said, rigid with fear. "The government knows we're here."

Bryn followed his gaze. "A helicopter. They're coming for us."

"They know we found the device. They don't want it dug up."

The buzz of the helicopter was loud enough now that Bryn had to raise her voice. "Why did Scatter send us here in the first place? Are we supposed to bring this back with us?"

Rett looked from the device to the helicopter, his heart beating to match the thrum of the blades. Wind from the blades whipped up the dirt around them so that Rett had to cover his face with his arm. "We have to go *now*."

The helicopter descended. Rett gripped the sides of the box, hoping it would go with him wherever he was transported to. After a moment, Bryn did the same, her hands touching his. "Lighthouse," Rett said, and Bryn joined in. "Boat, gulls, clouds." The wind from the helicopter's rotors tore the sound from their throats. "Waves, stars, fish, home—"

2:07 P.M.

The drum of the helicopter gave way to the low hum of an air vent. The whip of wind and dirt vanished. Rett sat in a stuffed armchair, facing a window that looked out on a garden where green vines tumbled down to meet a thicket of green leaves. His mouth watered at the sight.

He eased himself out of the chair and found cool wood under his bare feet. Pain and thirst no longer knocked a steady beat against the inside of his skull. Air from a vent ruffled the sleeves of his clean white jumpsuit.

A crumbling canyon. Then—a cool, clean room.

The shock of it made his legs tremble so that he almost had to sit back down. *Where am I?*

A narrow bed lay along one wall of the small room, a bookcase along another. The window shared space with a nicked wooden desk. A pair of cardboard slippers stuck out from under the armchair. Rett moved to a record player on a little table and set the needle in the groove of the record waiting there. A tinkling melody filled the room, so familiar he stumbled back. *The song. The one Bryn sang in the depot.*

Bryn.

Where is she?

What is this place?

He yanked open a desk drawer. Inside lay a single sheet of thick stationery marked with a logo of jagged lines. Familiar words were printed on it.

. . .

One lonely lighthouse
Two in a boat
Three gulls circle
Four clouds float.
Five foaming waves fall
Six stars glow
Seven fish follow
Eight steps home.

. . .

The song. The passphrase that had initiated their return home.

I'm home, Rett thought, testing the idea. *Is this home?*

He looked around the room. No metal walls, no buttons or levers. No dust or mysterious gouges. Only a bed, a desk, a table, a bookshelf.

A window showing the green world outside.

He opened another drawer in the desk and found a sheaf of papers inside. Sketches of strange artifacts: amulets and staffs and a battered treasure chest. *I drew these.* He recognized them from the comics he'd created at Walling, except these sketches were smoother, the shading better. *I sat at this desk and drew these.*

He touched the drawing of the treasure chest and conjured an image of a metal box unearthed from a wasteland. Unease settled over him. *I was just in a wasteland, and now . . .*

He turned to take in the room again: the bookshelf too nice to belong in Walling, the narrow bed awash with sunlight.

The keypad over the door handle.

He scrabbled at the handle, punched the keypad. "Hey!" The door shuddered under his fists. *"Hey!"*

He landed a kick on the door, and then, to his surprise, it opened.

A woman in a white lab coat stood on the other side, holding the door handle.

I know her. Flushed cheeks, shatterproof expression. He knew what her voice would sound like before she spoke: calm, careful.

"Rett?" She peered at him, eyes wide with concern. "Is everything okay?"

He gaped at her, picturing her standing over a hospital bed, listening to her urgent warning in his ear. *You'll have to find it . . .*

Two men in white scrubs stepped into the room with her, and then Rett found himself sitting on the narrow bed while a penlight shone in his eyes. One of the medics held his wrist, checking his pulse.

"He seems disoriented. Rett, how do you feel?" The woman's musical lilt worked like a spell to calm Rett's nerves.

But something was happening to him while he sat trembling under her concerned gaze. The room around him seemed to gather closer, or at least, it was losing its strangeness. He felt he had sat in this place before, had spent nights sleeping in this bed, days gazing out that single window into the bright garden. He knew this woman, Dr. Wells. In fact, he'd lived in this room for weeks—months, maybe. Ever since he'd left Walling Home.

But how could that be true?

"Rett?" Wells's voice cut through his tangled thoughts. "You know it will take some time. You can't expect to learn how to use the mechanism right away."

Rett stared at the logo on her shirt, the overlapping jagged lines. *Reality splintering to pieces,* he thought. *I was lost in a wasteland, I'm safe in this room.* It didn't make any sense.

"The mechanism," he mumbled, touching the scar on his scalp.

Wells lowered herself into the armchair facing the bed and gave him a sympathetic smile. "It may be years before you're able to use it. These bursts of frustration, pounding on the door—"

"Years?" Rett didn't understand. "But I've used it already."

Wells's gaze snapped to the medics standing now to one side of the bed. One of them entered a number on the keypad, and then they both slipped out and closed the door behind them. Rett felt the *click* of the lock down to his bones.

"Rett." The woman's voice trembled with what Rett thought might be surprise. She leaned forward to claim his attention and settled her featherlight fingers on his arm. "Rett, can you tell me the coordinates?"

"The coordinates?" Rett echoed, unnerved by her sudden fascination.

Uncertainly shadowed her gaze.

"I didn't get the device," Rett admitted. "I found it, but I didn't bring it back here."

A flicker of confusion crossed Wells's face. "Do you know the coordinates?"

Rett closed his eyes, recalling the coordinates he'd entered into the GPS unit in the wasteland. He recited them.

When he opened his eyes, she was fumbling with her tablet, pecking at the screen with a shaking finger. She read something in the display and then looked up at Rett, mouth agape.

The next moment, she straightened, her face blank.

What was that about? Rett wondered.

"Tell me what happened—how you got the coordinates," Wells said in her careful voice.

The air coming through the vent chilled Rett's neck. But his skin still remembered the heat of the wasteland, the itch of sweat mingling with dirt. "I was in a wasteland." *Out in the wasteland, digging in the sun—and then here, in the cool air.* "It was terrible—nothing alive for miles around. Like an ocean, a poisoned ocean."

Wells's hand settled on his arm again, and he calmed.

"Bryn was there, too," he said. "Good thing—I don't know if I would have survived on my own."

Wells gave his arm a reassuring squeeze. "Your mechanisms are synced."

"Synced?"

"So that if you should find yourself in the future, she will find herself in the future, too."

A thousand needles pricked Rett's skin. "You sent us to the future." *Six years into the future. How can that be possible?*

"We activated the mechanism." Wells gave him a surprised smile. "We didn't realize you would try to use it so soon."

Rett touched his scar again. His fingers curled away almost instantly. *We were right. They put something in our heads. It sent us to the future.* "You sent us to find something: the device in the wasteland."

"You found the device?"

"Yes, we had to dig it up. We hiked for miles, we had hardly any water."

Her gaze flicked from Rett to the tablet she still held, as if she didn't know which of them to consult. "That wasn't part of the plan. If you were ever able to get the mechanism to work, if you were able to reach the future, you were supposed to get the coordinates from representatives in Scatter Labs."

Scatter Labs—the phrase rang like a bell in his head. *That's where I am: Scatter Labs, six years before the nightmare in Scatter 3.*

And I was supposed to stay in these labs when I traveled to the future. But somehow I ended up in that depot in the wasteland.

"That sounds like a lovely plan," Rett said with a frustrated sigh. "Much nicer than almost dying of thirst in a metal canister. Or of injuries in a wasteland."

Wells studied him for a moment, head tipped to one side as if he were a puzzle to solve. "You dug up the device." Her brow furrowed. "Did you see the ID codes? The string of numbers that would have been next to your name?" Her fingers tightened around the edge of her tablet so that Rett thought the screen might shatter.

"I don't remember. Was I supposed to remember those, too?"

"No, you've done fine." She patted his arm, and Rett was embarrassed to find himself happy to gain her approval. She waited for him to say something, her gaze probing. "What else can you tell me?"

What does she want me to say? "You only wanted the coordinates? Because . . . someone stole the device from Scatter? And you're trying to find it?" Helicopter blades thrummed in his head. *The government was guarding it.* "They put it in the middle of that wasteland."

"You're confused. You weren't supposed to find the device."

Frustration clawed at Rett. "Can't you just explain it from the beginning?"

Wells took a long breath that seemed meant to prove her patience. "We successfully implanted the mechanism in your head ten weeks ago."

"Ten weeks?"

"We turned it on and synced it with Bryn's. You were told that if you were able to get the mechanism to work—if you ever reached the future—you should ask someone at Scatter Labs for the coordinates of the device. Then you would return to your origin time—here, to this time—and report the coordinates. That would prove that you had visited the future."

Rett shook his head, trying to clear away the static behind his eyes. "How would that prove it?"

"Because the device doesn't exist now, in our time."

Now Rett was really confused. "How do you know it exists in the future?"

"Because it's sending a signal all the way here to the past. When our team first discovered that signal, we founded Scatter Labs to investigate it. All of our research and development has gone into finding ways to engage with the signal. This was a test run, meant to prove that you could successfully employ the mechanism in your head—that you could travel to the future."

"The device is sending a signal from the future? And that signal is what allowed me and Bryn to time travel?"

"It interacts with the mechanisms in your head." Her gaze went to his scar. "The mechanism opens your consciousness and the signal guides it to other moments in time, moments in your own future."

Rett shook his head. "What does that mean?"

Wells thought for a moment, her gaze roving the room. "Normally, your consciousness is tied to the present." She spotted the sheet of stationery on the desk and picked it up. "Your life is like a list of moments that you read in order."

She held the paper before him so that the blank side faced him, and ran her finger down it like she would down a list.

Except Rett's side of the paper wasn't actually blank.

A message was scrawled there that made Rett's heart speed up.

Wells continued, oblivious to Rett's anxiety: "But what if you could skip down the list? Skim over some of those moments and read the ones toward the bottom of the paper?"

Rett wanted to nod, to show he was following and not thinking about the words scrawled just next to the woman's fingers wrapped around the paper. But his muscles wouldn't obey.

"That's what the mechanism in your head does," Wells went on. "It allows you to . . . skip ahead." She laid the paper on the bed, message-side down, and Rett could breathe again. "We've been over this before. Do you understand now?"

"So you're saying I . . ." Rett tore his eyes from the paper on the bed and struggled to process what she'd told him. "I somehow moved forward to a time in my life when . . ." His stomach lurched as he realized— "You're saying that the wasteland—being trapped there—that's my future? That's where I'll be six years from now? I skipped ahead in my own life, and that's where I end up?"

No. That can't be.

Please say it's not true.

Wells smoothed Rett's sleeve. "I'm saying—"

He jerked away. "I'm supposed to find my mom. She's sick, she needs me—"

"Of course. We can help you with that." Her voice was smooth, placating. "Whatever you experienced in your future, it's not set in stone."

"Other people have changed their futures, then?"

Wells hesitated. "No one's ever done this before."

"No one . . ." Rett gripped the edge of the bed. "You're saying Bryn and I are the first people you've tried this on?"

Wells pressed her lips together. She seemed to be trying to come up with something to say.

Rett shot to his feet. "Where's Bryn?"

"She's fine." Wells held up her hands, as if Rett were a spooked animal she needed to corral. "She's resting now. Everything's fine. Please calm down."

"I want out of here." Rett jerked toward the door. "I want to see Bryn and then we're leaving."

Wells stood, smiling at him as she smoothed her lab coat. "That's fine. But you need to rest first. You've been through a lot." She tapped at her tablet. "I'll have a medic come back and run some tests to make sure everything's checking out okay. And then you can go."

Rett raked his fingers through his short hair. He didn't want to wait. He wanted to go now.

Wells put a hand on his shoulder. "You've done a huge thing for this program, for this country."

The country?

She must mean the wasteland—now Scatter can go back in time and make sure the government never carries out its terrible experiment. Is that it? Could they really undo all of that?

"The government was guarding your device," he told Wells. "In the future—six years from now, in the wasteland."

The doctor's face went as pale as her lab coat. "The government?"

"I don't think they want Scatter to use it to go back in time and prevent them from carrying out their experiment."

For a moment there was only the sigh of the air in the vent, the rustle of leaves outside the window. Wells turned toward the door. "You should rest. You're back in your own time now, back where you started." She brushed her hand over Rett's head, like his mother used to do ages ago, before he'd gone to Walling, before he'd left Walling and come to Scatter Labs. Rett's lead-heavy heart lightened a little. "None of those things has happened yet. That's all in the future and you don't need to worry about it anymore."

Everything will get better. Rett could hear his mother promising it in his head.

His mother—

"The money?" he asked.

"Fifty thousand, as promised," Wells said over her shoulder as she slid a keycard through a slot over the door handle.

Rett went numb with disbelief.

"If there's anything you need, I'll make sure you have it," Dr. Wells said, smiling at Rett as she opened the door. "You're safe here." Her face glowed in the sunlight coming through the window, and for a moment, she could have been his mother singing over him to wake him from a dream.

Then she closed the door, and Rett sank onto the bed, weary to his bones. *You're safe here,* he told himself, basking in the soft light filtering through the leaves, the quiet hum of the air vent. *You'll have your money, you'll have everything you need.*

His hand brushed a crumpled paper.

He froze, wishing he could forget what was written on the other side. *Maybe I imagined it, maybe it wasn't real.*

He turned the paper over.

They're lying. Don't trust them.—Bryn

4:39 P.M.

Rett woke to sunlight and stirring leaves. Late afternoon, by the slant of the light. He must have slept for hours.

A plate of food waited on the desk. Rett devoured cheese and crusty rolls and the largest plums he'd ever laid eyes on. An entire pitcher of chilled water vanished next. He was unwrapping a Hershey bar when his gaze fell on Bryn's note. *They're lying. Don't trust them.*

The food in Rett's stomach shifted. *What does Bryn know that I don't?*

Or . . .

Wasn't the truth that Bryn had a hard time trusting *any-one*? Hadn't she told him that she felt better off on her own?

Annoyance hummed underneath Rett's thoughts. *What's so bad about waking up in a nice place with real food and someone to take care of you?*

Was he wrong for wanting to be here rather than in Walling's cold dormitories? Scatter's nightmare depot?

He plucked the note from the desktop. He needed to put it out of sight. Not for his own peace of mind, but because he worried what Dr. Wells might think if she saw it. Rett would ask her to take him to Bryn, and then he'd find out why Bryn had written the note. The two of them would figure this out together.

He went to the bookshelf, rows of gleaming leather spines that seemed to prove Scatter thought better of him than Walling ever had. He could tuck the note into one of the books, keep it secret.

He tugged on one of the spines to pull the book from the shelf, but it didn't budge.

He tried another book, but it didn't budge, either. Tried reaching to the back of the shelf. His fingers jammed against wood.

Fake. They're all fake. The spines were only thick foam glued to the back of a too-shallow bookcase.

Just then the door clicked open. Rett stuffed Bryn's note into his pocket as Dr. Wells entered the room.

"Rett? How are you feeling?"

"I'm fine." Rett wasn't sure why he felt guilty, but he turned away from the strange bookshelf. "Where's Bryn?"

Wells's smile seemed to say that she was pleased Rett had thought of his partner. "She's fine. She's in her room. She said she needed some time to rest. I thought you two wanted to leave together, so I assumed you would stay until she's ready."

Rett noticed for the first time a pouch Dr. Wells held at her side. She held it out to him. "As promised."

Rett took the bulging pouch and slowly unzipped it. His heart stopped.

Inside lay a thick wad of bills.

"You know . . ." Wells went to the armchair and sat, this time leaning on one chair arm like she wanted to divulge a secret. "There's more where that came from."

Rett pressed the pouch of money between his palms, reassured by how solid it felt.

"You and Bryn have achieved something incredible," Wells said. "There's so much more you could do for us."

Rett zipped the pouch shut. "You want us to go back and stop the government from carrying out whatever experiment created that wasteland. Gave my mother cancer."

"I would like to do that very much. But it isn't possible."

Rett's heart was a stone dropping into deep water.

"Of course we've thought about how we could do that, but it wouldn't work." Wells folded her hands in her lap and bowed her head to show her regret. "You couldn't travel back any farther than the time at which the mechanism was implanted in your brain. So our only option at the moment is to look to the future."

"Then what kind of job do you want me to do?" Rett cradled the pouch of money against his stomach.

Wells leaned toward him, her eyes shining. "With your ability, we can know about disasters before they happen. Prevent the kinds of horrible things that made your mother and all those other people sick. All you would have to do is get the information from the future and then give it to us now."

"I don't exactly know how to do that. Last time I ended up in the middle of a wasteland."

"We need to perfect your technique, that's all." She gave him a patient smile. "We could start with something very simple. And if you complete the job, we could give you, say, another fifty thousand."

Rett's fingers went numb. He almost dropped the pouch of money.

"Scatter could make sure your mother is well taken care of, you know."

Rett looked down at the brick of cash in the pouch he held. It really was his after all, enough to make his mother well again. "And if I don't want to do it?"

Wells gave him a small, sad smile. "Then I give you a code, you say it aloud, and that's it—your mechanism dies and your work with us is finished."

"Simple as that?"

She nodded. "You don't have to decide right now." She stood and gave her lab coat a brisk tug. "I just came in here because I thought you might want to go to the common room. There are a few new operatives there, and I remember you play a mean game of checkers."

Rett flushed, and then felt stupid for caring that she knew about his one and only skill in life. Well, maybe not only. His drawing was improving, if the sketches in the desk were any proof.

"Why don't I remember more about this place?" he asked her.

"It's understandable, considering you've been jumping around in time. It'll come back to you as you get your bearings."

Rett felt she must be right. Already, he knew to expect the

click of the cooling system turning on, and to avoid the nicks in the desktop if he was going to sketch. Other memories were starting to surface, too, mundane visions of tiled hallways, wooden checkers sets, padded chairs.

And then, as if those few memories had opened a gate in his mind, more rushed through: The director of Walling calling him into his office, telling him about an "exciting opportunity with a company named Scatter." The surgery he'd undergone—the hospital bed, the bank of lights, the smell of antiseptic. Coming to live at Scatter Labs. Recovering in this very room, waiting for the day Scatter would call on him to use the mechanism in his head to force his consciousness into a time in his own future. *Time travel*, Rett thought, awestruck.

Wells held the door open, waiting for Rett to walk through. He shut the pouch of money in a desk drawer and then gave Wells an uncertain look.

"No one else will come in here," she assured him. "It's safe."

He followed her into a tiled hallway. White walls and heavy doors guarded by keypads. *Is Bryn behind one of these doors?*

A single poster interrupted the white expanse of a long wall. It showed proposals for three identical, humped buildings.

Scatter 3. Rett stared at the label, startled by its familiarity. Three different depots, planned for construction. Three shelters to house the workers Scatter planned to send to the wasteland to collect meteorites so they could use the alloy to build their device.

A device that doesn't exist yet, that will exist in the future, just like these depots.

He fought a wave of dizziness.

"Rett?" Wells put a steadying hand on his arm.

"That's where I was," Rett said, pointing at the depot in the poster. "It's some kind of shelter for workers collecting meteorites. For Scatter."

He watched her reaction, wondering if she would lie to him about the danger Scatter had put its workers in.

But she only nodded, her face smooth and calm as ever. "The meteorites have been there for some time, but we recently discovered that they're traced with a rare alloy that's hard to re-create in a lab. We're still experimenting with making our own version of the alloy, but so far it's proven unstable. We hope there are enough meteorites to provide us with the metals we need to create the device you found in the future."

"If you find a way to make the alloy in your labs, you won't need the meteorites? No one would have go into the wasteland?" *And I won't end up in your depot in six years.*

Wells pursed her lips. Her gaze flicked toward the end of the hallway. "The truth is, the future echoes into the past. If we were going to find a way to replicate this alloy in the future, you wouldn't have seen the depot six years from now. There wouldn't *be* a depot."

"So . . . that proves that the meteorites are the only source for the metal you need?"

The look in her eyes changed from intrigue to pity as she realized why he wanted to know. "I said before that the future isn't set in stone. We can't be sure exactly what will happen, can we? If you decide to stay here, I can promise you that I'll do everything I can to make sure nothing bad happens to you."

She waited until Rett gave her a reluctant smile and then steered him down the hallway. At the last door, she said, "I'll be back to check on you."

The common room was like Walling's rec room but without the holes in the walls or stains on the furniture or busted lights sending the place into gloom. Basically, nothing at all like Walling. Gleaming leather couches clustered around a television, where a couple of teens in jumpsuits watched a show with a roaring laugh track. Arcade games lined another wall, and a pool table hunkered in a corner. Rett realized he already knew where he could find the checkers set (underneath the table along the far wall) and which movies he could play on the TV (mostly comedies and patriotic thrillers). He felt he'd spent hours slumped on the couches and scratching up the pool table. He even remembered that he could get snacks delivered if he asked—

—the guard standing next to the door.

It's not going to be easy to duck out of here to find Bryn.

Dr. Wells had already left, so at least Rett only had one person to shake off. "I have to use the bathroom," he tried.

"Over there." The guard pointed to a door next to the pool table.

Rett had been hoping he'd need to go out of the common room to get to the bathroom, but it looked like he wasn't allowed anywhere without a guard.

When he came out of the bathroom a few minutes later, he didn't even notice the guard still blocking the door to the hallway—his attention was locked on the girl sitting in an armchair facing the TV.

"Bryn?" He lurched toward her, but when the girl turned, Rett realized he didn't know her.

"Who are you?" she asked, her dark eyes full of uncertainty. "I'm new." She gestured at the line of stitches showing through her cropped hair, then shrank down in her chair as if embarrassed by the wound.

"I'm Rett." He turned his head so she could see his scar. "Don't worry, it gets better. Mine's actually kind of cool. I swear it plays music when no one's around."

The girl's mouth quirked. "They did say the mechanism they put in my brain is like an antenna."

"I just wish I could switch channels. There's only so much country music one guy can take."

Another form stirred on the couch nearby, a boy not much younger than Rett who angled to shoot him a sharp look for interrupting the TV show.

"Do either of you know a girl named Bryn?" Rett asked as the boy slumped back down on the couch.

"We're new," the boy mumbled, sipping from a can of root beer, "like she said."

"Who's Bryn?" the girl asked.

"She's . . ." Rett wasn't sure how to explain it. *The girl I was trapped in a wasteland with. The girl who helped me escape.* But if he were going to give her the full picture, he'd have to tell her that ever since he had woken up in this place, something had lodged itself in his chest, something that blossomed into pain whenever he thought about Bryn locked away somewhere he couldn't get to her. He settled for, "She's my partner."

The girl gave him a pitying look. "I heard they keep synced pairs separate after the first week or so."

The boy on the couch stuck his head up to say, "I wouldn't mind that. Maybe I could watch my show in peace."

"Why would they do that?" Rett asked the girl. A familiar pain throbbed behind his eyes.

"You're supposed to report on each other. So Scatter knows you're completing the jobs they give you, the right way."

The throb turned into a drumbeat.

The girl pulled her knees to her chest. "But don't you think it'd be better if they let you be friends? If you had a connection to each other, maybe you could help each other more."

"They only need one person to do the job," the boy said from the couch. "The other person's just a backup in case something happens to the first." He gulped root beer while Rett tried to ignore the sinking feeling in his own stomach.

I need to find Bryn.

He glanced at the guard, whose gaze was fixed on the TV. Rett moved to where the guard wouldn't see him, and then shot a hand out and knocked the can of root beer from the boy's grasp.

"Hey!" The boy sprang up from the couch. "What the—"

Rett kicked the boy's ankle. The boy tumbled to the floor. Rett hesitated, horrified by what he had done. *I have to get out of here.* "Something's wrong," Rett shouted to the guard. "I think he's having a seizure."

The guard spoke into his radio as he hurried to the boy's side. Rett didn't wait for whatever was coming next—he bolted into the hallway.

He ran past locked doors until he found an opening to duck into. Three men in black uniforms and matching black caps sat at the desk, glancing between monitors and a television tuned to a news channel.

Great, I found the security office.

The men had their attention focused on the screens, but if they turned around, they'd see Rett standing there. He inched backward, grateful for the blaring news program.

"The president-elect has promised to honor the treaty that his former opponent argued placed too many limits on imports of rare earths, or metals, into the country. The announcement comes as the treaty falls under new scrutiny . . ."

A blast of radio static made Rett jump back. One of the uniformed men turned from the monitors to speak into his radio, and Rett scurried around a corner, out of sight.

"Nothing on the monitors," the man said into his radio. "I'll do a visual now."

Another door opened and Rett ducked, trapped in the hallway with nowhere to hide. But the man who came through the door was in too much of a hurry to notice him. He went running down the hallway in the other direction, lab coat flying behind him. Rett shot toward the door he'd just exited before the latch could close, and pushed it open to slip through.

Electrical components lay strewn over every surface of the room. Rett hunted through wires and metal casings, searching for a stray keycard that would let him into the rooms that lined the hallway. *Bryn's got to be in one of those rooms.*

His hand bumped a terrarium on the cabinet top. Inside, fat black beetles lumbered over strips of bark, their jagged mandibles no longer than paper clips. Rett edged away from the glass. He had a feeling he'd dread the sight of bugs for the rest of his life.

He moved to another table, where his gaze lit on a small, familiar box in a nest of wires and screws—a half-finished device, with a tiny bulb in one corner under the word *signal*. For a moment, the heat of the wasteland beat down on the top of Rett's head, and dust choked his lungs as he examined the tiny box. *It's the alarm box. The one the government was using to guard Scatter's time travel device.*

But what's it doing here?

He shoved it in his pocket, going hot all over, needled by a fear he couldn't explain. He turned back to the door, eager to move on. *Bryn, where are you? I need you.*

He stepped out into the hall. The door clicked shut behind him just as he realized someone stood there in the hallway.

A man in a khaki uniform looked up from the broom he'd been pushing over the tiles.

No, not a man. Someone just a couple of years older than Rett. Someone who gripped the broom with crooked, overlapping fingers.

"Garrick?"

A slow grin spread over the older boy's face. "Oh, look. It's the box boy."

Rett cringed at the nickname. He tried not to recall the feeling of rough wood against his fists, of air going stale, of darkness pressing against his eyes—

"So it's true." Garrick looked over Rett's jumpsuit, his bare feet. "Scatter *did* make you one of their test subjects. Out of the box and into the echo room, huh?"

Rett pushed on the door at his back, but it had already closed, and he couldn't open it without a keycard or a code. "The what?"

"They stick you in a room with no one to talk to but yourself. Day after day. Just you and the echo of your own voice. I hear it when I walk down the hallways: people talking to themselves, bored out of their minds."

"What're you doing here?"

"What does it look like?" Garrick nodded at his broom. "You think you're the only orphan Scatter picked up from Walling? At least I didn't get the science project treatment."

A burst of radio static told Rett that a security guard loomed just around the corner. "I did a visual check," came the guard's voice. "He's not in the south hallway."

He means me, Rett thought, heart racing.

Garrick frowned in the direction of the security guard. He looked back at Rett, and realization widened his eyes.

"Don't say anything," Rett mouthed. "Please. Don't tell him I'm here."

"Tell me one reason I should help you," Garrick said in a low voice. "I'll tell you one reason I *shouldn't*." He held up a hand in front of Rett's face, showing him the broken fingers that had never healed properly.

Rett winced at the sound that went through his mind: the *crack* of knuckles breaking against a wrench.

But then Bryn's words came back to him: *We do all kinds of things to survive.*

I did what I had to do to survive, he told himself.

But how am I going to survive now? Cornered again. He glanced down the hallway and prayed the security guard would go into his office, wouldn't come this way. "You can have some of the money," he whispered to Garrick. "When Scatter pays me."

"You think they're going to pay you for this?" Garrick scoffed.

"They already did. Fifty thousand dollars. They said I was the first person to—"

"Shut up, you think I believe that?" Garrick crowded him

close to the locked door. "Think I don't know your game?" He jabbed Rett's chest with his fist. "You always acted like you were better than the rest of us. Always saying someone was going to come take you home. But no one did. We both ended up *here*, didn't we?"

Rett glanced down the hall again. The security guard must have heard them by now. He'd come around the corner any minute, find Rett in his obvious white jumpsuit. Take him back to his room before Rett had the chance to find Bryn.

Garrick grabbed the front of Rett's suit. "Both of us landed here, but you'll be stuck here like a rat in a lab while Scatter sends me out to one of their depots. I finish my job, go home, never need to sweep another floor in my life."

Rett could hardly breathe with Garrick's fist pressing into his chest, with the thought of the security guard rounding the corner at any moment. "You're going to collect meteorites for Scatter?"

Rett pictured the poster of Scatter's depot, and then the sun gleaming on the metal shell of Scatter 3. He imagined the hammer of fists on the jammed door, the sight of a corpse sprawled in the dirt . . .

"Garrick, listen, six years from now, if you hear of someone planning to go back to Scatter's depots to scavenge their equipment—"

Garrick shoved his fist harder into Rett's chest. "Are you calling me a thief?"

Rett struggled to breathe. He recalled an image of the man in the depot, the one who had come to scavenge Scatter's equipment. *The one I saw dead, drained by a bug-monster.*

Could that have been Garrick? Six years in the future?

He studied Garrick's face. Easy to do with it scowling just inches from his own.

But no, Garrick didn't look anything like the man from the depot, even if Rett imagined six years added onto Garrick's age.

Even so, if Garrick were going to work in the wasteland, he'd be working alongside whoever the scavenger was. He could warn him about what would happen if the man came back on that day—could warn him about the bugs that would hunt him down. "Listen—six years from now, there's going to be a solar storm. It's going to take down Scatter's security system."

Garrick took his hand from Rett's chest and turned away, uninterested in what must sound to him like ranting.

Rett pressed on. "Someone who works for Scatter is going to break into their depots—"

"He's over here," Garrick called.

A man in a black uniform swung around the corner. He locked eyes on Rett and spoke into his radio.

Rett didn't even hear what the man said. He grabbed at Garrick's sleeve. "Garrick, listen, you need to know, six years from today—"

He doubled over as Garrick sank an elbow into his stomach. The next moment, a hand locked around his upper arm, and then Rett was scrambling down the hallway, pulled along by not one but two security guards in black Scatter uniforms.

"Check his pockets—what is that?" one of them said at the door to his room. "You go on a little shoplifting spree in the utility room, kid?"

He ripped from Rett's pocket the small black box, the alarm. A keycard zipped through a slot, and then Rett went stumbling back into his room. But not before he saw what was printed on the inside of the half-finished alarm box in the security guard's hand, the box that the government would use six years from now . . .

Scatter's logo.

The door clicked shut and Rett sank onto the bed, shaking.

Six years from now, Scatter is the government.

8:01 P.M.

> *They're lying. Don't trust them.—Bryn*

Rett clutched the paper in his hand, reading the words over and over while he lay on his bed.

More memories had surfaced in the time he'd sat alone on his bed while the light from the window died: Dr. Wells telling him that she'd switched on his mechanism, then explaining she had synced it with that of a girl named Bryn. He remembered spotting the girl in the hallways, in waiting areas, in the garden during exercise hours. Rett had recognized her from Walling, but he didn't really start paying attention to her at Scatter Labs until the day he'd seen her leaning over a bed of daisies in the garden, struggling to conceal something in her pocket. "Hey," he'd said, because he wanted to know what she was hiding. Something from the one of the medical rooms maybe—he'd been warned not to try to smuggle extra pain pills, and he could really use them for nights when the pain in his head wouldn't let him sleep. Maybe she'd share.

The girl had straightened, her expression sharp as glass.

And Rett saw what was spilling out of her pockets: a fringe of daisy petals. She had picked flowers and stuffed them into her pockets to take back to her room. "Did you get bored of staring at books you can't open?" he asked her.

"They won't give me real books," she'd replied. "They said reading is too much of a strain for—" She flattened her hair over the spot where Rett thought her scar must be.

"They said it's too dangerous after, you know, brain surgery."

"Not to mention every other day," Rett said, thinking about the comics that went around Walling: zombies and mutant soldiers and, most dangerous of all, ordinary kids rebelling against their captors.

He turned so she could see the scar running along the side of his own head, so she'd stop being self-conscious about her own scar.

"You look like you could use something to read, too," she said. She pulled a stub of a pencil out of her pocket, along with a piece of paper, and scribbled something.

Rett held out his hand for the paper, but she reached and stuffed it into his pocket just as someone in a uniform came to show her back to her room. Then she was gone, and Rett wondered if he'd ever see her again, or if the mysterious note she'd shoved into his pocket would be all he had to remember her by.

The zip of a keycard called Rett back to the present. He sat up and jammed Bryn's note into his pocket just as Dr. Wells stepped into the room.

"I heard you were upset," she said, using her best no-need-to-try-to-escape-again voice.

Rett shifted his gaze to the wall behind her. "No one would agree to play checkers with me."

She ignored his joke and lowered herself into the armchair. "Rett, I need to tell you something. Bryn decided to leave."

Rett's gaze snapped back to Wells. "She left?"

"This job is more than some people can handle—"

"She wouldn't have left without saying good-bye." Rett clenched his fists. *Would she?* Heat rushed to his head.

"She said it was too painful." Wells mouth twisted with pity. "She wanted me to tell you that she's grateful for everything you did for her in the wasteland. But she felt she didn't have it in her to do any more assignments for Scatter. We gave her the code to stop her mechanism from working and let her leave."

Rett's head swam. He didn't know what to believe, but a twisting in his gut told him that Bryn wouldn't have wanted to stay in Scatter Labs. She wouldn't risk another trip to that wasteland.

"I know this is hard," Wells went on. "I don't want you to feel like Bryn didn't care about you."

Rett sank against the wall.

"I promised Scatter Labs would take good care of you." Wells clasped her hands together. "The truth is, you're the one with the unique talent, Rett. Bryn told us that it was thanks to you that both of you were able to find your way into the future." She beamed at him so that he almost felt proud of himself.

All he really wanted was to see Bryn again.

"I promised you that if you did another assignment for us, I'd make sure both you and your mother were taken care of," Well continued. "And they won't be difficult assignments— nothing that puts you in danger. I'll only ask you to gather information. We'll start with something simple: You wake up four years from now and find out who the next president will be, then find your way back to this time and tell us."

An alarm went off in Rett's head. *Is that how Scatter comes into power in the future? They align themselves with the candidate they know will win the next election?*

Or do they use time travel to make sure their preferred candidate wins?

He looked down at the floor, trying to hide his feelings. "I could find out if the next president will get rid of the treaty the current guy won't fight against. The one about the rare metals." He waited to see if she'd fall into his trap, if she'd prove Scatter's greed after all.

The garden beyond the window turned to a bank of shadows while the sun set. The leaves were jagged black shapes.

Wells said, "We're getting ahead of ourselves."

Maybe I've got it wrong, Rett thought. *Maybe Scatter really does want to make things better.*

Bryn's note crinkled in his pocket every time he shifted.

"Rett." Wells sighed. "I know it's hard to think about Bryn leaving you here. I know you've been left behind before."

Rett felt like he'd been kicked in the chest.

"You've had to do a lot of things you didn't want to do," Wells said, "because no one ever took care of you like you needed them to."

Something stirred deep within Rett: a ghost born of bitterness and anger.

"You deserve to be taken care of," Wells said. "You shouldn't have to take care of yourself any more. Let us take care of you."

Rett's bitterness melted into exhaustion and relief. *Would it be so bad to stay here?* He wouldn't have to worry any more about his mother. Scatter would take care of her, would take care of them both.

"You need sleep." Wells stood and moved to the door. "In the morning, we can talk more. Some of our team want you to debrief them on how you managed the incredible feat you pulled off."

Rett slumped back against his pillow.

Wells swiped her card, and the door clicked open. She turned back to Rett. "I know this has been hard. But everything's going to be better now."

Then the door clicked shut, and Rett was alone.

The light outside the window had gotten so low as to leave Rett in near darkness. The *click* of the door echoed in his head, loud as the slamming of a box lid.

I'm safe here, he told himself.

So why didn't he feel that way?

His gaze fell on the bookshelf. The rows of false books. *They're lying. Don't trust them.*

He shot up from the bed. *I have to see for myself if Bryn is gone.*

How am I supposed to find her?

He tried the door handle, but he knew there was no point. Why did he always seem to come back to this situation? *I'm ten years old, trapped in a box, lid shut tight.*

He'd waited so long that night, while Garrick held the lid shut, while the stars rushed past somewhere high above. He'd stopped banging on the lid and only prayed for Garrick to get bored and leave.

And then he'd finally remembered the trading cards in his pocket. *There's always something that can help.*

The trading cards were only cheap bits of paper printed with historical facts, but they were rare currency in a place where you had little to call your own. He'd forced them out under the lid of the firewood box, one by one, until Garrick had hauled himself off the lid of the box to snatch them, and Rett was able to break free . . .

Rett pressed his ear against the door. Waited.

Finally: footsteps passing. A security guard, or a medic, or *who knows.*

Rett pulled hundred dollar bills from the zippered pouch and shoved them underneath the door, hard enough to send them zooming into the hallway.

The footsteps stopped.

Then quickened.

A keycard slowly passed through the slot on the other side of the door. *Click.* The door opened.

A man in a khaki uniform stood there, and Rett suddenly knew he'd been right: the man he met six years in the future, in the depot, wasn't Garrick.

It was this man.

The man standing in the doorway, eyes wide with surprise under the brim of his black cap.

"You," Rett said.

Confusion lined the man's face. Rett imagined him lit by the green glow of a light stick, by muted sunlight coming through Scatter 3's skylight. "Do I know you?" the man grunted.

"No. But you will." Rett looked down at the bills in the

man's hand. "Or maybe you won't." Maybe the money would be enough to allow the man to leave Scatter's employ. To avoid the wasteland altogether.

Rett had been hoping for anyone at all to open his door for him, but he was glad this man was the one who had found the money. Much as he recoiled from his memories of the man, he didn't want him to end up as a bloodless corpse, sprawled in dirt.

"Here." Rett thrust more bills at him and took the keycard from his hand. "I'm sorry for what happened to you. I hope it doesn't happen again."

The man frowned at him, at the money Rett had shoved into his hands. "You're not trying to get me in trouble, are you?"

"No trouble. I think we've both had enough of that." He scrambled out of the room before the man could change his mind. *I'm coming, Bryn.*

He slid the keycard through the slot on the next door over, hoping it was Bryn's room. Yanked the door open.

The room was larger than his own. Two beds lay along separate walls. Rett crept toward one. A figure lay under the blankets, just visible in the light of the monitor next to the bed. An IV line trailed from the monitor to an arm.

"Bryn?" Rett whispered. He crept closer to the bed, letting the door shut behind him.

But the figure wasn't Bryn. Propped on pillows lay a boy his age, gray-skinned and unconscious. Wires trailed out from under the blankets to connect to another monitor hooked onto the wall.

Rett recognized the boy from Walling—someone who used

to kick soccer balls with him in the yard, who used to scrawl tilted zombies in the pages of *Epidemic X*—but he almost couldn't believe this thin wraith was the same boy. He ran a hand over the boy's forehead, over the sunken cheeks, but the figure didn't stir.

Rett backed toward the door, stomach twisting. His hand shook so hard, it took three tries to get the keycard through the slot. Then he was in the hallway, fumbling to unlock the next door over.

When he opened the door, a slumped figure looked up at him from the bed.

Bryn.

The next moment, his arms were around her, his heartbeat thundering against hers. "Are you okay?"

She pressed her forehead into his cheek. "They told me you left. They said you took your money and . . ."

"No way I'd leave without you." He fought against the image that rose in his mind: the wraithlike boy withering in the room next door. *That's not Bryn—she's okay.*

"They were trying their usual game on us," Bryn said, "making us think no one else can take care of us but them."

Rett's heart sank. *How could I have believed that Bryn left?* He let go of Bryn so he could sit on the bed next to her and pull the paper out of his pocket. "I got your note."

"What note?"

He held it out to her. Her fingers brushed his as she took it, and it was all he could do not to pull her to him again. *She's okay. She's not sick, she's okay . . .* He couldn't get the image of the too-thin boy out of his head. He looked Bryn over in the pale light, trying to memorize her profile, to burn it into his mind in place of the terrible visions he'd imagined he'd find when he'd opened her door—

"I must have written it before," Bryn said. "Before we ended up in the wasteland."

Bryn's hair looked different. Shorter, Rett realized. Not even long enough to hook around her ears. It hid her eyes while she looked down at the note in her hands.

"Did Dr. Wells tell you why we ended up in the wasteland?" Bryn asked. "She said it was a test run. But I don't think that's right. I don't think we were supposed to end up out there."

"She told me we were supposed to be here in Scatter Labs in the future. Something must have gone wrong."

"I remember . . ."

Rett moved her hair out of her eyes so he could study her face. She looked different from how she'd looked in the wasteland, younger. *The wasteland is six years in the future*, Rett realized. *I was older then, too.*

A line appeared between Bryn's eyes while she thought. At least *that* was the same as Rett remembered. "You remember what?" he asked her.

"Thinking something wasn't right around here."

Rett thought of the boy in the other room and his stomach dropped. "I saw . . . in the other room . . ." He did his best to describe it to her.

"Dr. Wells told me we were the only ones," she said when he'd finished, her voice choked with horror. "She said—"

"I think we were the first ones to get to the future," Rett said. "But we weren't the first ones to try, were we? We're not just the first ones, Bryn. We're the *only* ones."

Bryn found his hand and gripped it in hers, and he felt how

hard she trembled. "Scatter's never going to let us leave. If we're the only ones who can do what they want, they can't afford to let us go."

"We have to get out of here." Rett pulled her up from the bed and passed her the zippered pouch so he could use the key-card.

"Where did you get this?" she asked, breathless.

Rett glanced back at her. She was gaping at the cash in the pouch. "I think we've earned it."

Bryn zipped the pouch shut. "Same here."

She followed him into the hall. The thud of boots echoed nearby. Rett pulled Bryn in the opposite direction.

They ran, without any idea how to get out, with Rett strain-ing to listen for the *clack* of more boots on tile. He thought of the girl in the garden—Bryn—with stolen daisies stuffed in her pockets, and he wanted so badly to get her someplace where no one could keep her locked away from anything again.

"Rett." Bryn pulled him to a stop. The shadows at the end of the hallway grew, and then three security guards rounded the corner.

Rett turned back the way they'd come, but at the other end of the hallway, a familiar white lab coat stood out against two more black-clad guards. "Rett. Bryn," Dr. Wells called. "You're disoriented. You're not thinking straight. Whatever you're feeling, we can work through it."

Rett ignored her. He reached out and clutched Bryn's hand. "Bryn, I'm sorry I wasn't always honest with you. I'm sorry I've screwed things up over and over."

Bryn shook her head, but Rett didn't have time to explain more. "Do you trust me?" he asked her.

She looked up, confusion in her eyes. Rett took her other hand and pulled her close.

Her eyes lit up. She understood.

She leaned in and pressed her lips against his.

Rett's heart jolted and they spiraled into the ether.

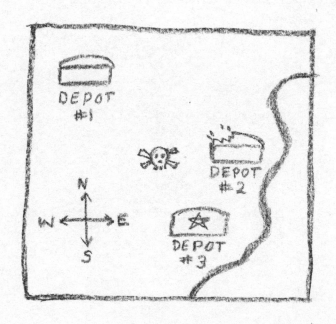

4:38 A.M.

So many stars hung over Rett that the sky seemed to press down on him. He felt its chill through his jumpsuit. Heard nothing but the sound of his own breathing.

He knew this hollow well, knew a curtain of green light would unfurl overhead even before it did so.

I've come to the future.

Six years in the future.

He turned, searching the hollow for Bryn. *Did I come here alone?*

"Bryn." He whispered it, reluctant to break the spell cast by starlight and silence. The weight pressing on him made breathing a struggle. *Please be here, Bryn. Please don't leave me alone . . .* "Bryn?"

The muffled scrape of shifting dirt answered him. He turned to see a shadowed mass split in two—Bryn stepping out from behind a boulder.

She slid her arms around his waist and he pulled her shoulders close to him. *I'm not alone,* he thought, and the weight lifted from his chest.

He looked up at the light dancing in the sky. *Something about this moment . . .* The quiet, the calm, the endless stars and flexing sheet of light. He felt like anything he wished might come true. Like he might close his eyes and find himself lying on his stomach in the middle of his living room, marveling over the comic book panels of a boy who wished his way to magical adventures and home again. The one his mother had read aloud to him, her voice pushing away all thoughts of darker days.

Under these stars, under this magical dance of green light, that one wish might come true: *come back.*

And now he finally understood: this moment was the heavy stone pulling down the fabric of his reality, so that every moment in his life circled this one.

"Rett?" Bryn spoke into his shoulder. "What are we going to do?"

They'd left Scatter Labs behind—left locked doors and secrets and isolation and lies.

But they'd also left everything else. Rett ached at the thought of the money he'd held in his hands, enough money to finally help his mother.

He lifted his face to the stars, to the shimmering fall of green light. *Time will fold like a curtain, and we'll be back together.*

He eased out of Bryn's arms and turned to where he knew he'd find the shadow of Scatter 3 rising over them. "We have to go back in there."

Bryn shook her head. "That guy's going to be in there. He had the gun last time. He pointed it at you."

Rett saw the scarred barrel in his mind, green in the light of a glow stick, and wondered where the image had come from. *He pointed the gun at me,* Rett thought. *I remember.* The spiky feeling of panic came back to him.

But I gave him that money. He recalled the surprise on the man's face back in Scatter Labs when Rett had stuffed hundred dollar bills into his hand. "I don't think he'll be here this time around. I think he might have left Scatter Labs. I gave him some of the money they paid me, which means he probably wasn't desperate enough to come out to the wasteland this time."

Bryn didn't respond. Rett turned to find her marveling at him like he had at the curtain of light hanging over them. He ducked her gaze.

"Six years older," he said. "Is that why you're staring? All that 'wisdom' showing on my face?"

"Wisdom and stubble." She drew her fingers over his jaw and he could have sworn he felt his skin sizzle.

"I thought it was grit before." He rubbed his own hand over his face and startled at the unfamiliar rasp. And where his sleeves had been baggy six years ago, his arms now strained against the fabric. "Guess I ate pretty well in Scatter Labs."

"And wasted all your time on push-ups when you could have been working on more nightmare comics," Bryn said, squeezing his shoulders.

"Actually, I think I did both." Rett thought of the sheaves of paper in his desk drawer at Scatter Labs. "A *lot* of both. Come on, it's cold out here."

"Wait." Bryn caught his hand. "We know how to get back to the time we started in: the passphrase, plus a little adrenaline."

Rett recalled the kiss she'd given him in the hallway of Scatter Labs and thought, *More than a little.* "But that'll only take us back to Scatter Labs. We'll be stuck there again."

"You found someone to help you sneak out of your room.

Do you think he'd help us sneak out of the Labs altogether? If we paid him?"

Rett nodded, thinking. "We can go back, try it all again. Pretend like we don't suspect anything, ask for the money like I did last time. Wells will pay us, she'll ask us to stick around, we'll pretend to agree. And then—we find the guy who helped me last time, pay him to help us get out of there."

Bryn was frowning. She moved her fingers through her hair. "But our mechanisms. Scatter could find a way to use them against us, maybe use them to hurt us until we agree to come back to them and do what they want us to do."

A twinge of remembered pain went through Rett's head. Last time he'd been in this wasteland, he'd suffered through the worst headache of his life.

"I saw you when your mechanism went haywire." Bryn smoothed her fingers over the side of Rett's head, and he leaned into her touch. "It was terrible—the pain made you lose consciousness."

Rett didn't want to think about that. He'd rather focus on the warmth of her hand moving over his head.

"We can't get away from Scatter." Bryn let her hand fall back to her side. "We're tied to them as long as we have these mechanisms in our heads."

"Wait. Wells said . . . When I asked her whether we'd be allowed to leave, she said she'd give us a code to say aloud that would turn off our mechanisms for good."

"She was probably lying."

"No. I don't think she was." Rett's mind raced. "When I first told her that we'd found Scatter's device, she asked me if I'd seen some ID codes on the display. She said they'd be a string of numbers next to our names. Do you think those could be the codes we need? We say them out loud, and our mechanisms will die?"

Bryn gripped Rett's hands in hers. "I remember seeing those on the screen."

"You don't happen to remember what they were, do you?"

"If I told you that yes, I'd memorized two random strings of numbers whose significance I didn't understand at the time, how much would you love me?"

Rett's heart thudded. His hands suddenly felt heavy in Bryn's, like he'd never noticed that his hands existed before she'd held them. "I . . ."

"You know that's not possible, right?" Bryn tugged his wrists. "Although it's nice to know you didn't immediately doubt that I could hold that level of genius." She gave him a wry smile that he couldn't return.

"Bryn . . ." He brushed his thumbs over her palms. "I . . ." He didn't know how to say it.

But Bryn seemed to understand. She looked down. "When we first showed up here, I didn't know if you were here. I was confused, and . . . I'm glad I'm not alone."

But it's not just that, Rett thought. *It's not just that I'm glad I'm not alone.* He tried to find a way to say it—

"It's cold out here," Bryn said. "And you and I both know there will be a creature heading this way soon. We better go inside."

Rett nodded. "We need to get the supplies together and get out of here as fast as we can if we want to avoid the bug."

"We'll dig up the device one last time, get those codes." Bryn started up the slope, leaving Rett to feel the cold and darkness in a way he hadn't before. She stopped to look back at him, a little unsteady on the incline. "And then we go back to our time for the money Scatter owes us. Say the codes out loud. And we're free."

Free. The word drummed in Rett's head.

He wanted to be free of Scatter.

But not of Bryn.

She has someone to go back to, he told himself. *Just like you do.*

She had said her boyfriend wouldn't be waiting for her, but would she go look for him? To give him the money she felt she owed him?

"Rett?" She had noticed his hesitation. She stepped back down the incline to take his hand. "At least we'll be working together this time."

The weight of cold and darkness lifted a little.

She pulled him up the incline after her.

At the top of the slope, the door to the depot stood cracked open. "Are we sure no one's here?" Bryn whispered.

"Maybe it's been open like this for a long time," Rett answered.

He peered in through the opening. Only darkness.

The edge of the door raked his jumpsuit as he slipped inside. *No way a big guy like the one in Scatter Labs could get through an opening this narrow,* he thought. *If he were here, he'd have opened the door wider than this.*

Even so, Rett ducked into the changing room first thing. Bryn crept in after him, and then they were breathing in the dark, waiting for their nerves to calm.

"There's a fire extinguisher here somewhere," Bryn whispered. "I can't see it in the dark."

Rett furrowed his brow. "Why—"

"It's our only weapon."

"Against a possible *gun*?"

"We need those GPS units," Bryn said. "And water, and a compass."

Rett leaned out of the room, straining to hear any sign that they weren't alone. He took a few timid steps into the corridor. The grit underneath his boots made his footsteps crackle.

"Rett, what are you doing?" Bryn whispered.

Rett could just make out an empty room under a skylight, and an open doorway yawning black at the other end of the depot. "I don't think anyone's here," he said over his shoulder.

Muffled sounds from the closet told him Bryn was putting on boots, and a moment later, she appeared in the corridor with another pair for him.

"Last time, the guy who was here didn't exactly announce himself," Bryn said in a low voice.

"What exactly happened last time?" Rett asked.

Bryn fidgeted next to him. "I think he came out of the room at the back of the depot. He pointed the gun at you, made you walk to the depot's main door."

She trembled and Rett pressed his shoulder against hers in the dark. "Walking doesn't sound so bad," he said. "What else?"

"You both went outside. I grabbed the fire extinguisher, hit him on the head."

"I thought it would have been more exciting. You sure I didn't kick him or anything?"

"You felt bad for him after I knocked him out and you tried to pull him back inside."

Rett shook his head with mock skepticism. "Doesn't sound like me." He took a few more steps down the corridor and peered around at the empty space. "I'm pretty sure he's not here this time."

Bryn came up and pressed a plastic tube into Rett's hand. "Then I guess it's okay if we use this."

A glow stick. Rett cracked it. "I feel like a superhero with this thing glowing." He held it out in front of him like a wand. "The Time Master."

"Great name," Bryn said flatly.

"How about Clock Breaker?"

"Okay. But the jumpsuit is ruining the effect."

"Scatter doesn't issue capes." Rett swiped the glow stick through the air, illuminating dust and metal. He came to the dark doorway, and his pulse pounded. *No one's here,* he told himself. *I'd have heard them by now.*

The glow stick shook as he held it out in a trembling hand and inched forward.

Its light fell on a familiar desk. And atop the desk, a dark lump.

What is that?

He held his breath, as if that might make him invisible to whatever lurked there.

Inched forward.

The backpack! He let out his breath and scooped up the pack.

"Bryn, I found the pack."

He turned back to where she waited and passed the pack to her. He couldn't figure out why she moved so stiffly to take it, why she wasn't happy to see that the devices and the water pouches were now safely in their possession.

"It wasn't in the supply room," she said.

"Why would it be the supply room?"

"Why would it be in the office unless someone—"

The lights came on.

Rett threw his arm over his eyes to shield them from the sudden brightness.

Someone's here. His heart all but burst from his chest. "He's in the power supply. We need to seal the doors!"

He wrenched up the wall over the lounge and reached to slap the button on the wall, to set off the chain reaction that would shut all the doors and seal them when the place flooded— seal the power supply where someone must lurk even now.

But Bryn moved to block him from the button. "The GPS units aren't in the backpack!" She had jerked open the pack and now held it out so he could see: only the water pouches lay inside. "We need them to find Scatter's device. We can't flood the place unless we know they're safe."

Rett shot to the supply room and stomped on the wall. It lifted and he dove underneath. The sight that greeted him made him pause. No mess of strewn supplies, like last time. Instead, neat rows of equipment sat in organized sets.

Someone came through here. Someone who knows exactly what he's doing.

One glance told Rett that the GPS units weren't here. He ducked out of the room.

And lightning went through his heart.

In the dark doorway to the office stood a man in a white jumpsuit with a black Scatter cap, pointing the flare gun at Rett's chest.

"Wait," Rett said, as the man lifted the gun. "Wait, don't shoot." He was numb all over with fear.

"I wondered if I'd see you here," the man said.

Rett couldn't take his eyes off the gun. The man tightened his grip on it, and that's when Rett noticed something odd: the man's crooked fingers overlapped. As if his hand had once been broken and never properly healed.

Rett peered at the face under the grimy cap, a leathery face more lined than Rett remembered, but still unmistakable. "Garrick?"

"You shouldn't be surprised to see me," Garrick replied, one corner of his mouth lifting in a smug smile. "You told me six years ago that Scatter's security systems would go offline today. The day of the solar storm."

Bryn shifted in surprise, and Garrick gave her a fleeting glance. "Figured you'd be here too," he said.

Rett caught Bryn's eye. *I only told him about the solar storm to warn him away—I didn't mean to invite him out here.* He tried to say it with a look. Bryn seemed more concerned with the flare gun pointing at Rett's chest. Her gaze darted between it and Garrick's shadowed face.

"The solar storm was all over the news," Garrick went on. "They said it'd be the biggest one in decades. And I remembered what you'd told me that day in Scatter Labs. All I had to do was get close to this place and wait for the light show to start. I guess I should thank you."

I'm not so sure about that, Rett thought, as visions of a bloodless corpse flashed through his head. "You shouldn't have come here, Garrick. It's dangerous—"

"I know about the bugs," Garrick cut in, his hand shaking so that the flare gun trembled. "I worked for Scatter for years collecting meteorites. I lived in this depot." He gestured with the gun at the wall over the supply room. Rett remembered what he'd found scratched on the wall: *G. W. was here.*

G. W.

Garrick Ward.

"Can't say I'm glad to be back," Garrick said. "I'll take what I came for and get out of here. In the meantime, I know how to drown any bugs that might wander in. Oh yeah, and I've got this." He twitched the gun upward and then aimed it at Rett's chest again.

Rett tried to remember to breathe. The flare gun was like a black hole sucking all his attention. He forced himself to think, to look around.

He realized Garrick held a nylon backpack in his other hand, identical to the one Bryn clutched. Rett made a guess about what it held. "You can have whatever you want from this place. Just leave a GPS unit for me and Bryn."

Garrick lurched forward, and Rett pressed himself back against the wall. "I'm not giving up *anything*," Garrick growled. "Scatter *owes* me. They ruined my life when they hired me to collect those rocks for them. They said it'd be better than enlisting, said the army wouldn't take me anyway with my hand like it is." He held the gun up to show his crooked fingers curled around the guard. "It never did heal quite right. I have *you* to thank for that."

Rett swallowed. *Get him to think about something else.* "Scatter ruined your life?"

"I got so sick working out in this wasteland I almost died. Scatter paid me just enough to get treatment. But in the meantime, my sister—" Garrick tightened his grip on the pack. "Everything in this place belongs to *me*. Got that?" He shook with agitation.

Rett eyed the pack in Garrick's hand. *The GPS units are in there. They must be.* "Please, Garrick. My mom's sick. If I don't get back to her, she'll—"

"She'll what? Die?" Garrick's gaze turned cold. "And then you'll be no different from the rest of us who grew up in Walling. Shame."

Rett felt sick. He needed those devices. And Garrick was going to do everything he could to make sure Rett didn't get them.

I could start over, try this again. Reach back in time, find that cool, calm place under the stars . . .

But Garrick would still have the backpack with him in the power supply. If Rett couldn't get it from him now, he wouldn't be able to get it from him on another attempt.

He started to shake. *I can't do this.* "One GPS unit from your pack. What do you want for one GPS?"

"I want my life back," Garrick spat. "I want to forget about the things I saw when I was working in this hellscape. I want my sister to . . ." He dropped his gaze for a moment and Rett almost lunged for the pack, but then Garrick broke free of whatever emotion had seized him. "You think you have anything I want?"

Think. The rock in the power supply, the dark round one veined with silver—"There's a meteorite here, I can show you where it is."

"You mean this one?" Garrick dropped the pack to dig a rock out of his pocket. "I found it myself, thanks."

Rett eyed the pack.

"It's got some of that alloy," Garrick went on. "Not enough to be worth much."

"How about water?" Bryn said from where she stood in the lounge area. "I've got eight pouches of it in this pack. You're gonna need it since there's no rainwater to come through the *trap*."

Rett looked up at the last word. Bryn shot him a meaning-ful look. *We've got to trap him so we can get out of here*, Rett thought. *I know that. But how?*

Garrick pulled at the strap of his hydration backpack. "Nice try. Got my own."

Rett's chest might burst with his heart racing the way it was. "What do you want, then?"

Garrick didn't take his gaze off Bryn, but when he next spoke it was clear he spoke to Rett. "I want you to tell Bryn how you got this assignment."

"What?" Rett said. *What's he talking about?*

Garrick smirked. "Tell her why Scatter picked you."

"They picked me because . . . because they knew I was desperate, that I need the money. They knew I'd say yes, no matter what." *Bryn already knows that.*

Garrick slowly turned to regard Rett with cool indifference. "They picked you . . . because no one cares if you never come back."

Rett wiped sweat from his brow. "That's not true." *My mom . . .*

"Then why have you been in Scatter Labs for the past six years?"

"I haven't." Confusion clouded Rett's brain. "Bryn and I left."

Garrick cocked his head. "You mean you jumped forward in time."

"I . . ." Rett braced himself against the wall, suddenly dizzy. *I was in Scatter Labs with Bryn. Now I'm here in the depot. But what happened in between?*

"You jumped into some future point in your life," Garrick said, "but that doesn't mean that you didn't live your life in Scatter Labs in the meantime. You might have hit the fast-forward button on your life, but you still lived it."

A flurry of images went through Rett's brain: Bryn coming close to kiss him in the hallway of Scatter Labs. The black-clad security guards hurtling toward them. The door shutting on Rett's room, where he sat alone in the dark.

And now it all came flooding back to him.

He'd lived in Scatter Labs for six years after that kiss. Spent his days hooked up to machines while Dr. Wells studied the interaction of his brain with his mechanism. Spent his nights thinking of Bryn and what he'd do to get her out of that place. They stole moments together in the garden, in the lab rooms; they shared looks in the hallways when security guards marched them past each other. She managed to teach him Morse code so they could use the light switches in their rooms to shine messages into the garden at night. They had a plan: get back to the wasteland, to that dark hollow beneath a sky of endless stars. And it had worked—

Because here they were.

Bryn had kissed Rett in that hallway six years ago, and they'd both left that moment and arrived at a moment beneath the stars.

But Rett also remembered a life lived in between those moments, even if he'd skimmed over it.

Rett clutched his stomach. The strange paradox of it all made him feel sick.

"Remember now?" Garrick let out a small chuckle. "Is it coming back? Time travel isn't quite what they sold it as, is it? You didn't jump from one point to another—you rushed through your life, skimmed over it like a bird over water." He stepped closer. The gun dangled from his loose fist, forgotten for the moment.

Rett slid along the wall, away from Garrick. "I've been in Scatter Labs for six years?"

"Yes. And then you left the Labs the same day I did. Dr. Wells drove you out here and dumped you. Got sick of trying to convince you to play the game her way and decided it'd be easier to get rid of you."

No, that's not what I remember. Maybe that was the way it had happened before—maybe that's how he and Bryn had ended up in the wasteland last time.

But this time had been different.

This time, Dr. Wells had started having second thoughts. She'd asked Rett again and again about the future he had visited—the spreading wasteland, the unchecked ruin. *Scatter's mission is to make the future better,* she told Rett. *We're going to make things better.* But guilt hung like a weight around her neck, bowing her frame, slowing her steps.

Finally, late one night, she'd taken Rett and Bryn from their rooms, smuggled them into her car. *I wish I could give you the codes that would turn off your mechanisms forever,* she'd told them as the car had hurtled down the interstate in the dark of early morning. *But I don't have access to them. There's no way Scatter will just let me cut you free after you've proven you can visit the future.*

They'd reached the wasteland just in time for the solar storm. Rett could still hear the last urgent words she'd said to him before she'd left him and Bryn alone in the starry hollow: *I can't help you. There's only one way left to do this. You'll have to find it . . .*

Rett pushed himself away from the wall, though he still felt he might collapse. "It doesn't matter," he told Garrick. "When this is over, Bryn and I are going back to when this all started. We'll leave Scatter Labs for good. Go back to living our own lives."

Rett looked to Bryn, but she wasn't standing in the lounge anymore. She had circled behind Garrick, who had forgotten the pack he'd dropped on the floor.

"When *what's* all over?" Garrick's sharp laughter echoed off the walls. "Scatter's got no use for you anymore. They dumped you out here because they don't want you. They're *done* with you."

Rett inched back along the wall, drawing Garrick with him.

"They've got a hundred other operatives now who can do what you can do," Garrick said. *"Scatter owns Walling Home now.* They own all of the boarding facilities. Direct recruitment."

Rett wavered for a moment, caught in the thought that Scatter was now doing to hundreds of orphans the same thing they'd done to him.

But he couldn't think about that now.

"We're not here to do Scatter's work." Rett tensed, readying himself.

Garrick smirked at him. "You don't believe me. So tell me— what are you doing out here?"

"We've got our own plans."

Rett launched himself at Garrick, sending him sprawling back into the lounge area. They fell together onto the metal floor. Rett scrambled to his feet, but Garrick landed a kick on Rett's ankle. Rett just managed to grab the ladder mounted to the wall to keep himself from going down. He lashed a foot at Garrick and got only air as Garrick recoiled.

The button, Rett thought wildly. He slammed his hand over it. The alarm screamed at Rett to get out before the wall closed, and he found himself tumbling forward, his bones jarring as he hit the metal floor again. Garrick scrambled to follow him, but Rett put his boot to Garrick's chest and shoved him back.

The wall sealed shut, with Garrick behind it.

Rett lay on the floor a moment, panting, and then the shock of cold water sent him to his feet. Bryn grabbed his arm to help him up. In her other hand, she held the pack Garrick had left on the floor. Mineral-laced water poured past their boots to run out through the cracked-open front door.

"We don't have long," Bryn shouted over the noise of the alarm. "Once the water stops, we'll have maybe ten minutes before that wall opens and lets him out. We need to get the rest of the supplies."

"What else do we need?" Rett shouted.

"More water, a compass." Bryn's face fell. "The shovel! It's in the power supply room."

Rett turned to face the door that had shut them out of the back rooms.

Bryn looked from the door to the wall closed over the lounge, which shuddered as if Garrick were pounding on it from the inside. "If we wait for the door to open . . ."

"Then he'll get out, too. And he still has the gun."

"What do we do?"

Rett raked a hand over the back of his neck. "I don't know."

"We need to charge the GPS units, too," Bryn said, nodding at the backpack. "And there are only eight pouches of water in the other backpack. The water spigot's locked away in the lounge, and anyway we can't get more water from it until it rains."

This isn't going to work, Rett thought.

Bryn looked at him and he knew exactly what she was thinking: *We have to start over.*

"No." He shook his head as misery welled up inside him. "I can't do this again. I can't—" *I can't face the gun again.* He'd barely been able to do it *this* time.

Bryn slid her arms under his and pulled him close. The feel of her against him dampened his panic. He thought, *Have we been missing each other for six years, locked away in separate rooms in Scatter Labs?*

Before we found ourselves in that starry hollow, had it been years since I held you?

And when she let go, he thought, *It's always years, always ages. Time always slows when we're apart.*

"Rett," Bryn said, wonder in her voice. She strode to the front door and traced the logo of overlapping jagged lines on the metal and then the number three inside the circle. "This is Scatter 3—there are other depots."

A hazy image came to Rett's mind, a poster of the three depots he'd seen in Scatter Labs.

"There's another depot along the river—I saw it on a map," Bryn said. "And it's closer to the spot where Scatter's device is buried. We'll go there, get some more supplies, and head out."

Rett tried to remember the map she was talking about. But he could only think about how it had felt to have her so close to him. How much he wanted to make sure they could do things right this time. *I can't spend another six years locked away from you.*

The lounge wall shuddered again, and Garrick's muffled shouts followed.

"We have to go. Before that wall unlocks." Rett hitched the backpack's strap over his shoulder. *Garrick's going to be angry. He might even come after us.*

He slipped the backpack off again.

"What're you doing?" Bryn asked.

"I'm going to leave him some of the GPS units. I need to put them in a dry spot." He couldn't look at her when he said it. Garrick had held a gun on him not moments ago, but Rett needed to do this. "It's my fault he came out here. It's because I told him about the solar storm taking out Scatter's security." *And I don't know what's going to happen to him. I don't know if he'll even make it out of here alive to sell these GPS units or do whatever he planned to do with the gear in this place.*

He went into the supply room and jerked open the pack to dump four of the six GPS units onto the dry counter.

Bryn came in behind him, but she didn't try to argue. "Let me plug one of these in," she said, ripping a power cord out of a cabinet. "Just for a minute, just in case."

Rett started to say that they didn't have time, but Bryn spoke first.

"Your ankle's hurt," she said. "Stop trying to pretend it's not. You need to wrap it."

The pain throbbing in Rett's ankle finally claimed his

attention. He'd hardly registered it when Garrick had kicked him, but now he realized his other leg bore all his weight.

He grabbed a first-aid kit from the neat rows on the floor, which were now drenched with water, and sat on the cabinet top to pull off his boot. A minute later, he eased himself back down, ankle wrapped, mind shut to the fear that he wouldn't be able to get far with his ankle throbbing the way it was.

Bryn transferred the water pouches into the pack they'd taken from Garrick. Then she unplugged two GPS units and slid them in alongside the water. "Is your ankle going to be okay?"

Rett ignored the question. "We need to get out of here."

They ducked into the main room, where water still poured over the floor. Rett followed the stream to the door.

"Bryn?" Rett turned to see why she hadn't followed him.

"When he made you go outside last time, something bad happened," Bryn said, plodding toward him. "Something that erased your memory." She cupped her hand over his scar in a way that made his heart leap. "What if it happens again?"

"I don't understand. What happened?"

"I don't know. Whatever they put in your head went haywire. I think it was because of the solar storm that caused the aurora."

Rett put his hand over hers. "We were just outside a minute ago. I saw the aurora. Nothing bad happened."

Bryn shook her head, her face lined with confusion. She pulled her hand away. "But last time . . . I don't know. We were scared, is that it? The man had just pointed a gun at you and we were scared."

"So the solar storm stressed the mechanism in our heads, and then we made it worse with adrenaline. Overloaded it."

"I guess. I don't know."

"Well, we can't stay here. We'll go out one at a time. Okay?"

Bryn nodded, her face blank but shoulders pulled in tight.

Rett slipped out the front door. The rocks and dirt were blue in the predawn light, the towering buttes cold and distant. *A poisoned sea*, Rett thought, remembering what he'd told Dr. Wells.

He touched his fingers to his scalp, where he thought he felt a tingle of electricity. "I'm okay," he called back. "No brain trauma, promise."

Bryn slid out through the door and stood just outside it, poised for danger.

"You okay?"

She let out a breath and nodded. "Let's go." She led the way around to the back of the depot. Here the slope dropped away more steeply, and a wide swath of white water churned at the bottom, catching the brightening light.

"We'll follow the river north to the second depot," Bryn said. "Scatter 2."

Rett settled the pack over his shoulders. "You said you saw the depot on a map?"

Bryn froze midstep. Then just as suddenly, she picked up her pace again.

"What is it?" Rett asked, struggling to keep up, hobbling on his sore ankle.

"Nothing. Just . . . we need to go fast."

"Bryn, what's wrong?"

She didn't answer. Rett caught her arm. Her face was a grim mask as she met his gaze. "Garrick said he came here to scavenge Scatter's equipment."

"So?"

"So now he knows where the device is buried. We locked him in the room with the map."

8:48 A.M.

Rett's left boot was a vise for his swollen ankle. Every step brought a flash of pain. He leaned on Bryn for support as he limped along, conscious of the dirt and sweat that covered him.

"We should stop for a minute," Bryn said, easing out from under Rett's arm. She rummaged in the pack and brought out a tube of painkillers they'd discovered during their last break.

Rett swallowed two of them dry while his gaze flicked toward the top of the ridge where he'd last spotted a scuttling shadow. "We've stopped too many times already."

He didn't think Bryn had seen what he had. She seemed to believe they'd be okay if she just kept her voice low.

"There's no water left," Rett went on. "We need to get to the depot." The air hung heavy with dust and warmth. The rain had long ago stopped falling. The rush of the river below was maddening. *Someone might have left the rain trap open at Scatter 2*, Rett told himself. *There'll be more pouches of water anyway.* He'd told himself that so many times that the words came automatically now.

He scanned the horizon again.

"You see something I don't?" Bryn turned to peer in the direction he was looking.

"I'll feel better when we get inside the depot and close the door behind us." He kept walking, even though Bryn had stopped, even though his left boot squeezed his swollen ankle.

"You can hardly walk," Bryn said. "We should rest, just for a minute."

A shadow moved at the edge of Rett's vision, but it was gone before he could turn to look. "Maybe you don't remember what those bugs can do." The image was sharp in Rett's mind: a mangled corpse with white, bloodless flesh. And another scene: a dark form lunging for Bryn with serrated mandibles.

"It's not just the bugs, is it?" Bryn said behind him. "They're not the only reason we have to hurry."

Rett turned back to find her worrying at her sleeves, which were still damp from the rain.

"We have to get to Scatter's device before Garrick does," she said. "He's probably heading for it right now. He won't even bother looting the rest of the depots. Scatter's device is a thousand times more valuable than GPS units and meteorites."

"You're sure it was marked on that map?"

She frowned.

"What?" Rett prompted.

"It's not exactly *labeled* on the map. It's marked with a skull and crossbones. Not what you'd call tempting."

"Why a skull and crossbones?"

Bryn shook her head. "I don't know. But he might realize that it marks the spot where Scatter's device is buried. The guy we met in the depot last time knew Scatter had buried something valuable in the wasteland, so Garrick probably knows, too."

"So he could already be out there digging it up." Rett's stomach twisted.

"The alloy it's made of is worth a fortune. Garrick will probably break the device apart and sell the metal to the highest bidder."

"And then we'll be stuck here."

The sound of the churning river floated to them from the ravine below. The noise of it mixed with the roar of anxious thoughts in Rett's head.

"He had only his hydration backpack for water," Rett said. "Maybe he waited for the rain so he could collect water from the rain trap. He might not even have started out yet. If we get to the other depot, we can get our supplies and beat him out there."

Bryn glanced at his ankle, and Rett bristled.

"My ankle's fine," he lied. "We can do this. We just have to hurry."

Bryn pulled his arm over her shoulders again and they started off in silence. Rett was happy to concentrate on the dust in his throat, the pain in his ankle. It kept him from darker thoughts.

Then another question came to mind, one that hardly seemed important, almost not worth asking. "Who drew the map in the depot?"

Bryn squinted against the light reflecting on the pale dirt. "It must have been . . ." Her voice trailed off and Rett could feel her confusion in her bunching shoulders.

"Do you think it was Scatter?" Rett said.

Bryn shook her head. "They wouldn't have wanted just anyone to find their device. It must have been one of the people they hired to find meteorites years ago. Those workers are the ones who lived in the depots."

"But how would they have known that Scatter's device would be buried there?"

His question hung in the air with the dust. Neither of them could answer it.

Another shadow flicked at the edge of Rett's vision. He turned his head. A bug hunkered on the nearest rise, not five hundred meters away.

"Let's go faster," he told Bryn, his mouth dry.

And then—

A jagged shape came into view over the edge of the slope: the depot, Scatter 2.

It was all wrong.

Rett's breath came in shuddering gasps. "*No*," he choked out.

The depot before him was a metal carcass. One wall wrenched outward. A ragged hole in the gaping roof. Rust-colored smears along the edge of the open door. *Blood.* Rett's throat constricted.

Bryn scrambled for the door, which hung open at an odd angle. Rett hobbled after her. The smell almost drove him back again. Metal and blood and rotting eggs. It filled Rett's mouth, left a taste like death.

He pushed himself into the cloying space, his heart flooding with dread. Shafts of sunlight showed the dust in the air, the rust-colored stains on the walls. The bones littering the floor.

Rett nudged a broken rib cage with the toe of his boot. Knelt to inspect it, his legs shaking. Clumps of fur clung to the bones, matted with blood. "Dog." His gaze met Bryn's. She trembled.

"They let them loose for the bugs," she croaked.

She helped Rett to his feet. They crept farther down the corridor, picking over broken skeletons. Rett winced at the *snap* of bones under his boots.

"What *is* that?" Rett whispered.

In the main room, a huge papery orb glowed in the sunlight. Not just *one* orb, Rett realized as he stepped out of the tilted hallway. A dozen thin brown paper shells towered, each almost as tall as he was and each cut open with some jagged tool— the mandibles of a bug. "Eggs," he said into the quiet space. Some were dusty and ragged. A few, dark and oily. Fresh.

Bryn made a noise behind him. Rett turned to find her gaping at the orbs in horror.

"Something hatched here," Rett said, nudging aside another dog skeleton with the toe of his boot as lead filled his veins.

"Bugs." It came out in a whisper. Bryn looked around, and Rett suddenly felt that the creatures that had hatched from the eggs might still be lurking. "We're in their nest."

Rett turned and took in the sight of the bloodstained walls, the splintered furniture showing in the open lounge, the cabinets wrenched to pieces in the supply room.

No supplies. No water. The rain trap long ago made useless.

His muscles seemed made of stone. He crept between the eggshells to peer into what had once been the office, his senses alert for any sign of movement. The back wall had been peeled upward and lay curled to the sun. Open to the bugs that were headed their way even now.

He turned back to find Bryn standing frozen in shock. The same thoughts going through her head as through his: *There's nothing here for us. No weapons, no water. And the bugs could be on us at any moment.*

"We have to go back," Rett said. "We have to start over, back at Scatter 3. We have to—"

Bryn fell against him and pressed her lips to his. Heat exploded under Rett's skin, speared his heart. He put his arms around her but she was already pulling away, and his stomach sank with the realization of why—

"It didn't work," she said.

Rett prayed for the pull on his consciousness, the sweep of blackness that meant a return to safety.

It didn't come, even after Bryn's adrenaline-inducing kiss.

Rett touched his scar. *Why isn't the mechanism working?*

"He dug up the device," Bryn said, voice trembling. "He must have figured out a way to turn it off. He knows Scatter's keeping tabs on this place. He doesn't want to risk the device giving off some signal that it's been moved."

Rett's stomach threatened to send up what little water he'd drunk in the last two hours. *Garrick has the device.* "We have to get it from him."

"How? He has what he wants—we'll never see him again."

Rett pictured Garrick trudging through the wasteland, hauling the device with him, heading toward whatever break in the perimeter wall had let him into Scatter's pale desert. Gone forever, the device—and their codes—with him . . .

"No," Rett said. "He needs water. He must not have used the rain trap if he's already hiked to the dig spot. He can't make it all the way out of here without getting more water first."

"Do you think he'll go back to Scatter 3?"

"I don't think we can make it back there to meet him if he does. We're out of water. My ankle's no good. And . . ." Should he tell her he had spotted bugs not far from here, that he was listening for them even now? Every scrape of their boots over the floor set his nerves aflame.

"Then we have to make him come *here*." Bryn fumbled with the backpack and pulled out a GPS unit.

"How?"

Bryn turned on the display and tapped at the screen. "I've used units like this one before. We can ping him with our location. And if we do it just right, we can use it like Morse code. We'll tell him we have water."

Rett looked at the red light on the GPS unit. *Low battery.* His chest went tight. "Does he know Morse code?"

"You didn't hear it? When the other guy banged on the door to get us to let him inside Scatter 3?" She imitated the sound: *"Bam-bam-bam. Bam. Bam. Bam. Bam-bam-bam."*

"SOS." One of the many patterns Bryn had taught him while they'd been locked in Scatter Labs, using the light switches in their rooms to shine messages into the garden at night.

"They probably *all* learned Morse code," Bryn said. "Part of their training for defying death by bug and wasteland."

Rett didn't tell her what he was thinking: *Everybody knows SOS. It doesn't mean the man knew Morse code. And it doesn't mean Garrick knows it at all.*

He looked out through the curled back wall while Bryn tapped away. The sun beat down on the rocky slope, on the ridges that loomed beyond, ragged and sinister. "They're coming. I've seen them—while we were hiking."

Bryn twitched toward the doorway. "There's got to be something here that can help us. Some way to fight off a bug."

Like what? Rett thought. A row of cabinets still hung in the medical room, but nothing lay inside except the shattered glass that had once fronted the doors. *This place is gutted.*

"We have one flare in the pack," he said. "But no gun."

Bryn had gone to the supply room; he could hear her searching through the splintered remains of the cabinets on the floor. Rett turned to follow, gaze darting from the blood on the walls to the hole in the ceiling, watchful for any sign of danger. A glimmer of silver among the broken glass caught his eye: another of Scatter's meteorites. Like a charm among the ruins. He pocketed it.

"I found these, at least." Bryn held up a pair of binoculars. "We can keep lookout."

"We'll hide in one of the upper bedrooms and hope Garrick gets here with the gun before any bugs find us. At least if we can convince him we need to save the flares for the bugs, he won't use the gun on us."

"But how are we going to get the device from him?"

"We'll offer a trade. We'll give him the extra flare if he'll let us turn on the device and get our codes from it. He'll need the flare for the bugs if he's going to get out of here alive." He picked his way over the littered bones, heading for the ladder that led to an upper room.

"Rett."

He turned. Bryn made a ghostly figure in the gloom, shrouded in white, standing amid the boneyard. "Do you remember?" she asked. "Living in Scatter Labs? Did it really happen?"

Rett moved to put an arm around her shoulders.

"Six *years*. We were trapped there for—" Bryn broke off,

face lined with misery. Her gaze roved their shattered shelter. "And now—are we ever going to get out of here?"

"We'll figure it out. We'll get home."

She winced at the word *home*. Neither of them said it: They didn't have a home to go back to.

Rett half closed his eyes, and for a moment, the sun flooding in through the broken back wall was the early morning light flooding the apartment he shared with his mother. He imagined green leaves brushing window glass, leaves that had eventually turned black on withered branches. He heard his mother's chiming laugh, felt her fingers ruffle his hair.

She left me, he thought. *She left me, and now I'm here.*

The papery orbs looming over them gave off a putrid smell that made Rett clamp his sleeve over his mouth and nose.

Bryn had gone for the ladder, and Rett followed her, eager to get away from the smell. Bryn started to climb, but then she turned. "Rett? I remember something. From Scatter Labs." Her gaze traveled to his abdomen.

He looked down, half expecting to find the red-brown stain of someone else's blood.

"Comics in your pocket," Bryn said. "You used to draw them for me."

Rett's hand wandered to the pocket of his jumpsuit. He almost thought he'd find Scatter stationery there, covered in sketches of his adventures with Bryn in a quarantine tank, in a haunted warehouse, in a zombie prison. "I remember, too."

"Is that why you dragged me back out here?" A smile played at the corners of her lips. "Trying to get new material?"

He wondered if when she'd kissed him earlier she'd been thinking only of escape, of triggering the mechanism in his head. "See, that's the problem. You make me want to draw a thousand comics."

She reached down and brushed her fingers over the side of his face.

He thought, *What a strange place to feel at home.*

"Come on," she said. "We better find a spot to hunker down."

9:39 A.M.

In the silence of the dim upper room, Rett listened for the sound of claws picking over rocks. Sunlight angled in through a gap in the damaged roof panels. Rett imagined bugs pouring in through the wide crack, scrabbling over the walls, mindless and bloodthirsty . . .

He huddled farther into the recess of the bunk bed, the only stick of furniture left in the place. The room had been closed off when they'd found it, a panel shut tightly over the ladder. Except for the opening in the ceiling, it seemed a safe place to hide and wait for Garrick.

No place is safe, Rett told himself. *Not once those things realize we're in here.*

The bed frame creaked as Bryn shifted on the top bunk, where she was keeping watch through the gap. "Anything?" Rett asked her, his voice tight.

"No."

Rett pulled his collar away from his throat. "Garrick will come." Secretly he feared that Garrick had encountered more bugs than he had flares for. *We might be stuck here forever,* he thought.

Unless we go out there and find him.

He shuddered.

"I hope he makes it here before the bugs do," Bryn said from above.

Rett shifted, trying to get his injured ankle into a better position on the bed. His hand brushed something half covered by the pillow, and he looked down to find a photo there. He slipped it out and leaned into the light to get a look at it. It showed a woman holding a baby, a family snapshot left behind by one of Scatter's workers.

Rett stared at it without knowing why he should be interested. It was something new to think about, anyway. Something other than the bugs and his thirst. The woman's gaze went off to the side, as if Rett didn't concern her. The baby in her arms was an awkward bundle she seemed ready to shift.

A creak of wood told him Bryn was looking down from the upper bunk. "Where'd you get that?"

Rett flushed, suddenly self-conscious, as if it were his own family photo she was spying on. "It was here."

"Someone's family, looks like. Wonder if the worker who left it behind ever made it back to them."

Rett wondered the same thing. The thought hollowed him out. "I left my mother on her own. Sick, no money, workhouse closing. If I don't get back, I don't know what will happen to her."

He waited for Bryn to say, *You will get back*. But there was only the creak of the bedframe again.

Rett thought about the wasteland that separated him from his mother. And all the *other* things that separated them: sickness and poverty and time.

But maybe even more than that had come between them: Maybe she didn't *want* him. Didn't *need* him the way he needed her. Could that be? Mothers didn't need their children as much children needed their parents.

Is that true? he asked the photo, silently.

Or why else didn't you come back for me?

"Bryn?" he said, because she hadn't spoken in so long. "Do you think there's a way to prevent the awful things that happened to everyone—the crops dying and people getting sick?"

"If there is, Scatter's not interested. It's giving their shadow government a nice excuse to invade other countries for the resources we don't have." Bryn was quiet again, maybe listening for the patter of bugs over rocky soil, like Rett was.

"Wells said it's not possible to go back to a time earlier than when they started implanting mechanisms in people's heads."

After a moment, Bryn said, "But don't you think there must be something Scatter can do to keep it all from getting worse? I bet there are groups out there who could help us come up with something if we shared what we know with them. Dark Window, for one." Bryn's voice dropped low. "*If* we get out of here."

Rett stood and leaned over the edge of the bunk to take Bryn's hands. "We're going to get back. We're not going to be stuck here."

Bryn wouldn't look at him. The light streaming through the broken roof illuminated her face, and still Rett couldn't read her. He let go of her hands. "I shouldn't have left those GPS units for Garrick," he said.

She caught his sleeve. "No, you were right to help him. Scatter hurt him as much as they hurt us. I just wish that helping Garrick didn't mean screwing us over."

"We'll get those codes."

"And then what?"

"And then we go back, pretend like nothing happened. Let Scatter pay us. Then we run. With those codes we'll be free from them. I can go back to my mom and you . . ."

Bryn squinted into the sunlight. "And I don't have anyone to go back to."

"Your boyfriend."

"Don't you remember what I told you?"

The pain in her voice sparked some memory. "About your boyfriend?" Rett looked away. "How you wouldn't give him any of those things you stole."

"I . . ." She made a quiet sound low in her throat. "I was scared to. I thought he might take everything and disappear."

"Maybe he *would* have."

Bryn didn't seem to hear him. "I've been telling myself that I'll find him, and that he'll be happy to see me. But the money won't be enough, will it? He probably feels the same way I do: it's better to be on your own."

"Is that really what you think? That you'd rather be on your own?" Rett reached to touch her arm, but she leaned away.

Bryn dropped her face into her hands. "I keep getting this feeling," she said, voice muffled. "A premonition. That something is going to happen to one of us, and the other won't be able to get back."

Rett started to speak, but Bryn cut him off.

"The mechanisms in our heads are synced." Bryn lifted her face, her eyes dark with worry. "If one of us dies, the other might be trapped here."

"We don't know that." Rett's mouth went dry. "And neither of us is going to—"

"We have to get that device turned on. Before something

happens that gets us stuck here for good. I might not have anyone to go back to, but your mother's waiting for you."

Rett sank away from the bunk. The photo he'd left on the bed caught his eye and his throat went tight.

"Rett?" Bryn slid to the edge of the upper bunk and leaned over him. "She is waiting for you, isn't she?"

Rett flicked his head to the side, brushing off her question. The air in the close space was stifling. Rett imagined he could still smell the putrid debris downstairs, even with the panel closed over the ladder. "She doesn't know I'm trying to meet up with her," he admitted. "She told me I shouldn't come for her, that I should take care of myself and not think of her."

He'd sent her those emails—he'd written terrible things: *I'm better off without you anyway.* Because he'd been angry that she wouldn't come for him. But after that, he'd told her he was sorry. He'd said he would come for her, no matter how many times she told him not to. He'd said it over and over.

But she'd stopped responding.

Rett moved his hand over his chest, tried to will his heart to calm. His bitterness was like a crazy food for it. The smell of the abandoned eggs below was like the smell of rotting corpses. Rett put a hand over his nose. *You're imagining it,* he told himself.

"Rett!" Bryn's sharp voice pulled Rett out of his thoughts. "Garrick's out there!"

Rett pulled himself up onto the bunk with shaking arms to look through the broken roof.

"He's near those boulders," Bryn said, pointing. "He's got the device."

Rett's heart jumped. *He's here—Bryn's plan worked.*

"He's stashing it behind some rocks," Bryn went on. "He's heading for the depot now."

"He's not stupid. He knows we'll try to take it from him if he brings it in here."

Bryn lowered the binoculars. "I'm going to go out and get it." She jumped down from the bunk, and the *thump* of her boots hitting the floor sent another jolt to Rett's fluttering heart.

"Bryn . . ."

Bryn ignored him and kneeled to pull open the trapdoor. "He doesn't know we've seen him hiding it. I'll go around that ridge while he's heading here. Just keep him distracted until I can turn on the device and memorize our codes. Then I'll say the passphrase that will take us out of here."

"*Bryn.*"

She paused. "You have a better plan?"

The open trapdoor gave Rett a keyhole glimpse of the chaos below: littered bones and splintered wood. All he could think was, *What if we don't both make it out of here?*

I don't want to go back alone.

Bryn interpreted his silence her own way. She dropped down through the opening and vanished from sight.

Rett grabbed the box with the flare and followed Bryn down. He'd get the gun from Garrick. Then he'd go after Bryn and make sure nothing hurt her.

The sound of Bryn's boots crunching over bones gave way to scrape of the depot's door as she headed out into the wasteland. Rett flew to the other end of the depot, where the wall was wrenched upward. Garrick was a dark figure in the distance. If he turned as Bryn ran out to the ridge, he'd see her.

"*Garrick!*" Rett screamed.

It worked. Garrick turned all his attention to Rett standing under the wretched awning of misshapen metal. He quickened his pace.

Rett drew back into the ruined depot, searching for something to put between himself and the man with the gun. The tilted floor gave him the feeling he was staggering through a demented funhouse.

"No tricks," Garrick barked as he came close to the opened back of the depot. "I just came for water."

"There isn't any." Rett eased out from behind the rotting orbs, holding the case with the flare out before him. "But I've got another flare."

Garrick stood in the office doorway, gun held out like a talisman more than a threat. His troubled gaze moved over the towering eggs, the debris covering the floor, the smashed furniture. "You can give that flare to me. It's no use to you without the gun."

Rett stood close to the cluster of eggs, even as he doubted they'd provide much protection against a flare. "It'd be dangerous to try to get out of this wasteland with only one flare in your gun."

The gun dipped uncertainly.

"Or maybe you already used a flare," Rett said. "I bet you ran into a bug at the dig site."

Garrick didn't answer, only lowered the gun to his side.

"So that gun's useless to you now." Rett stepped away from the eggs, the case holding the last flare still clutched in front of him like a shield. "Might as well give it to me."

Garrick gave a short laugh. "Why would I do that?"

"Because by now Bryn is at the rocks where you hid the device." *Or anyway, she's close to there.*

Garrick jerked toward the open back of the depot.

"If you want the device back, you better give me the gun," Rett said. "And you better do it before any bugs get close, or we're all screwed."

Garrick swiveled and lunged for Rett. For a moment, Rett was a scrawny kid bracing for a blow he knew he couldn't fend off.

And then he felt the power in his flexing muscles as he swung his fist. His knuckles glanced off Garrick's jaw, sending Garrick reeling out of surprise as much as pain. Garrick steadied himself against the wall, hand to his jaw, testing for injury. The crooked joints of his fingers sent a stab of guilt to Rett's gut.

The distraction was all Garrick needed. He lunged again. Rett stumbled toward the broken cabinets and snatched up a jagged piece of wood for a weapon.

Too late. Garrick had the case, snatched from Rett's hand.

He opened it and took out the flare. Loaded it into the flare gun while he frowned at the wooden stake Rett held out like a weapon. "I need that device," Garrick said.

"You can have it when Bryn's finished with it." Rett tried to judge whether the end of the wooden stake was sharp enough to cause serious injury. "We just need some information from the display. Then you can have it. Take it out of here and sell it, or whatever you're going to do."

"I'm not going to sell it." Garrick seemed to forget the stake. "You think that's why I came out here? I heard rumors Scatter's precious device was buried somewhere in this wasteland. I came to get it. To make a trade."

A trade?

"Your sister," Rett said. "She grew up in Walling, too?"

Garrick glared at him. But then he gave a short nod.

Direct recruitment, Rett thought, remembering what Garrick had told him earlier. "And now she's an operative."

"I need that device to exchange for my sister. I have to get Cassie away from Scatter."

Rett looked at the stake in his hand and suddenly felt sick. The crack of breaking knuckles went through his mind, and he felt even sicker. *We all just want to get away from Scatter.*

Garrick watched Rett drop the stake. He slid the flare gun into his pocket. "We'll go out there together. You'll tell Bryn to give me the device. No one's going to give anyone trouble."

"Fine." *But we're going to get our codes from it first.*

He edged around Garrick, making for the open back of the depot. "Might want to get that gun out, though. In case there are any bugs around." He couldn't believe he was saying it, considering how relieved he'd felt when Garrick had stopped waving the gun at him. But he was more afraid of bugs than of Garrick at this point.

"Wait." Garrick's voice trembled.

Rett turned back to find Garrick's face shadowed with misery. "I saw something on the device's display. My sister's name."

The phrase rang through Rett's head again: *Direct recruitment.* His heart sank. Scatter had put Garrick's sister through the same program he and Bryn had suffered through.

"What does it mean?" Garrick asked. "Why is her name on the screen of Scatter's device?"

"It means she's traveling in time. Just like me and Bryn."

"She . . ." His face twitched. Rett couldn't stand to watch him realize the horror of what Scatter had done to his sister. Garrick must have seen, over the past six years, what Rett and

Bryn had gone through. At the very least, he had a full view of the scar running along the side of Rett's head. "She can't be . . ." Garrick's voice hung in the air for a moment, and then he said, "I have to get her out. I promised her."

His desperation made Rett think of another girl locked in Scatter's grip, the new operative he'd met in the rec room at Scatter Labs. *Bryn and I aren't the only ones who need to get free.*

"I can't take care of her, I'm too sick," Garrick said. "I'm— I'm not going to get better. But she has a mother to go back to. Not my mother—Cassie's my half-sister. It's too late for me, but Cassie could still go home."

Rett wrestled with what Garrick had said—*He's sick? He's not going to get better?* An image flashed through his mind, but he couldn't hold on to it long enough to understand it.

"Some of the names on the screen disappeared while I was looking at it," Garrick said. "That's why I turned off the device. I wasn't sure if—" His face crumpled.

"It doesn't mean they're dead," Rett said quickly. *Not necessarily.* He couldn't help but feel pity for Garrick. "It just means they've returned back to their origin time."

Garrick's eyes flashed. He turned toward the open back of the depot, face lined in thought. "So if I wait until her name disappears from the screen and then destroy the device, she won't be traveling. She won't ever travel again."

Rett jerked forward and grabbed Garrick's arm. "You can't do that. Bryn and I will be trapped here."

Garrick looked at Rett's hand on his arm, moved his shadowed gaze up to Rett's face. "Trapped? Like my sister's trapped now?"

"We can figure out how to—"

"Scatter's taken everything from me," Garrick snarled. "For once, I'm taking something back from them."

Then he yanked free from Rett's grasp and hurtled through the ruined back of the depot.

Rett ran after him.

The sloping landscape was an ocean of dirt, the ridges colliding at angles like storm-tossed waves. The glare of sunlight on the pale rocks blinded him as he staggered for the boulders where Bryn was hiding with the device.

She has to have gotten the codes by now, he thought. *Say the words that'll get us out of here, Bryn!*

Would she even be able to do it? It seemed to them both that Rett had been the one pulling them through time when they did so. He was the one who could grab on to that starry hollow, those thoughts of home, and of wishing things better.

Could Bryn do it? By now, could she figure out how on her own? If so, she only has to say the words and pull us both out of here.

But as he drew close to hiding spot, he saw why she hadn't yet finished the job.

Bryn stood atop the largest boulder, staring down at a monstrous bug picking its way up the side of the rock.

"Garrick, shoot it!" Rett cried.

Garrick stood still as a stone just a few meters ahead of Rett, transfixed by the sight of the bug.

"*Shoot!*" Rett cried again, and this time his voice called Garrick out of his shock.

Garrick aimed the gun—

A second dark mass darted out from behind another boulder and eclipsed Garrick before Rett could call out.

Garrick screamed as giant mandibles locked around him.

His shot went high, the blue flare exploding in the air over their heads.

He screamed again.

Rett scrambled away, searching madly for some rock large enough to fight off the bug that was attacking Garrick. But then Garrick was silent, and Rett knew it was too late to help him.

Bryn! Rett picked up a rock—too small, he knew, but there was nothing else. He hurled it at the bug climbing Bryn's boulder.

But Bryn had done better. He saw that she had pried a piece of the boulder away from its crumbling top, and now she dropped it onto the creature. There was a wet crack, and then the bug lay shuddering in the dirt, a spiky black mass soon veiled by a cloud of dust.

The second bug scuttled away from the reverberations, heavy with the blood it had feasted on, and crept toward the depot in the distance. Garrick lay sprawled in the dirt, dead. Rett scrambled away from the gruesome sight, his stomach lurching, his chest caving under the weight of pity and regret.

"Bryn."

She stumbled toward him, scraped and bloody from climbing down from the rocks, and he wrapped his arms around her.

"The device is over here," she said, and broke away to pull him into the shelter of the towering boulders.

Rett knelt near the bulky block of Scatter's device. The brittle hinges creaked as he opened the lid. The screen underneath was dark, powered off. Rett fumbled for a power button and finally found a slide-away panel covering a switch. "Here goes." He flipped the switch and the box seemed to hum under his fingers as the screen glowed to life.

Bryn, crouching in the dirt next to him, put a hand over her stomach.

"You okay?" Rett asked her, but he realized that underneath the shock and pain and adrenaline, he also felt a pang of nausea that hadn't been there a moment ago. "It's the device—I felt this way last time, when we were digging it up."

"I did, too. Maybe it's the signal this thing is giving out?" The list of names and numbers on the screen claimed all of Rett's attention now. "So many Wards." He ran his finger over the list. "All kids who went straight from Walling to working on assignments for Scatter."

A fresh wave of nausea seized Rett. "Because of *us*," he realized. "Because I gave Scatter the coordinates that proved I could travel through time. And then they had six years to study my brain and work out how I'd done it."

Bryn touched his shoulder. "It's not your fault. You didn't know what you were doing when you gave them those coordinates."

Rett scanned the list again. "One of these is Garrick's sister. That's why he came out here—to try to use this device to bargain with Scatter. Scatter's using her for an assignment."

"I think I'm going to be sick," Bryn said, and her hand on Rett's shoulder trembled.

Rett put his arm around her waist. "Let's move away from the device for a minute."

"We need our codes. We have to memorize them."

Rett found his and Bryn's names on the list and read the codes silently, trying to score them into his mind. The nausea made it hard to concentrate. "I wish we had some water."

Bryn turned and lifted something from the dirt: Garrick's hydration backpack. "There's a little in here. Not much."

Rett reached for the pack—and then stopped with his hand halfway to it.

Garrick had used a chalky rock to draw a map on the pack, complete with the skull and crossbones marking the former location of the device.

"Skull and crossbones," Rett murmured to himself. "Poison."

"Rett?"

Rett's hand shook as he traced the symbol. *This is what I thought of back there in Scatter 2 and couldn't quite grasp.* "What if the workers Scatter hired to find the meteorites drew that map in the Scatter 3 depot after all? They drew this symbol because they realized that this certain spot in the wasteland was making them sick. They didn't know about Scatter's device; they didn't know it was sending signals through time. They only knew *something* was making them sick, and they wanted to warn each other."

Bryn was silent. She leaned against the side of a boulder as if she needed to steady herself.

Rett turned to her, his head full of lightning-hot ideas. "Garrick said he got sick working out here."

"But that was from whatever went wrong with government's experiment. Whatever made this wasteland. Not from the device's signals."

The lightning spread through Rett's veins. "Bryn . . ." The whole of the surrounding wasteland seemed to press in on him, the weight of crumbling canyons, the stench of poisoned rivers. *Is it true . . . ? Is it possible it wasn't some experiment that caused all of this after all?*

Rett finally managed to say the words: "The signals from the device created the wasteland."

Now he felt sicker than ever. He touched the device. The strange silvery metal was safe enough—he'd handled the meteorites without a twinge of sickness. But the signal the device gave off—that was a different story. He imagined it pulsing through him, and it was all he could do not to empty his stomach into the dirt.

"Scatter didn't bury their device in a wasteland to keep it safe," he said. "Their device *caused* the wasteland. Or at least the signals from it did. Scatter said the signal can reach into the past, to a time even before the device was created. To a time even before the meteor shower that provided the metal this thing is made from. It spread and spread, poisoned our food, made everyone sick. It wasn't some ecological experiment that did that. The signals from this device started it all, and it's getting worse."

He expected Bryn to argue with him. *Tell me I'm wrong,* he thought. And he couldn't even figure out why he *wanted* to be wrong, until—

"Then we have to destroy the device," Bryn said, her voice hollow.

Rett turned sharply. "We'd never be able to go back. We'd be stuck here."

"You can go back," Bryn said, her gaze trained on the dirt. "I'll stay and destroy the device."

Her words were a vise tightening around his lungs. "No. I'm not going to do that." Rett gripped her hand and tried to fight off the horrible hot feeling smothering him.

"I told you already," Bryn said, pulling free and kneeling at the device. "I have no one to go back to. You do. If only one of us gets out of this, I want it to be you."

"I'm not leaving you." Rett scanned the boulders, the rocky crawl of dirt, the distant horizon, searching for some way out of this. *There's always something.* The static-and-boil sound of the distant river called to him. "The river—we'll throw the device in just as we say the passphrase. We'll both get home, and Scatter's device will be destroyed. They won't even know exactly what we've done. They won't know pieces of their device are being eaten away by corrosive water until it's too late to get all those pieces back."

Bryn trailed her fingers over the device's display, her expression uncertain.

"We're both going back, Bryn."

In the silence that followed, Rett thought he could hear a faint echo from the flare Garrick had shot still reverberating in the hollows of the wasteland.

Then he realized it was the sound of a helicopter's blades cutting the heavy air. He looked up. A dark smudge showed against the bright sky.

"They saw the flare," Rett said. "They're coming for us."

Bryn followed his gaze, her face lined with dread.

Rett lifted the device from the dirt. The lid fell away, its brittle hinges finally breaking.

"Rett, what're you doing?"

"We're going back," he said, his voice grating against his ragged throat. "I'm going to say the passphrase right as I smash the device, and you and I are going back."

He ran.

The broken-glass sound of the rushing river met him. Rett stopped at the edge of the cliff, the device cradled in his tired arms, and looked down at the white water running in a wide swath below. He lifted the device, ready to smash it on the rocky side of the ravine, ready to make Scatter's invention disappear forever in the wild currents of the river.

But something stopped him: a cold, trickling realization.

He slowly lowered the device. Dropped to his knees with it in his hands.

"Rett?" Bryn said breathlessly behind him.

"It won't work," he said, so exhausted with the weight of disappointment that he felt he might tumble forward, into the river. "If either of us goes back to the past, it'll be like rewinding time. The device won't be destroyed anymore."

Bryn sank down next to him.

"Haven't we come to this wasteland over and over again?" Rett said. "And every time, don't we find a different future? Not *completely* different. We find the same depot, same supplies. And a scavenger, someone who always shows up to take what we most need. Someone who . . ." A lurch of deep regret. "Someone who—no matter how we try to help—always ends up dead."

Bryn trailed her fingers down his arm and slipped her hand into his.

"But still," Rett went on, "every time we go to the past, we reset the future. If we destroy the device now and go back to the past, the device will still be built, will still send out its poisonous signals. We won't have destroyed it."

The distant beat of helicopter blades grew louder now, competing with the churn of the river for Rett's attention. "It won't work."

Bryn squeezed his hand and then slipped her fingers free. "So we'll both go back," she said. "We'll go back to Scatter Labs, six years in the past. And you'll get out, like we talked about. Go back to your mom. Say the code that'll kill the mechanism in your head—"

What is she saying? "Bryn—"

"And I'll come here alone. After you're safe in the past, I'll come here and destroy the device."

"No. You can't do that." Rett gripped her wrist like she might vanish right before him. "You don't know if you'd even be able to get here to the wasteland on your own to destroy the device."

Bryn lifted her eyebrows. "You don't think I can manage it? How about we put some money on that bet?" She nudged his shoulder, but he didn't much feel like joking around. He leaned closer, pressing his arm against hers.

"There has to be another way," Rett said.

"There is no other way." Bryn leaned her forehead against his. "I have to come back here on my own. You have to stay in the past. You have someone to go back to—I don't."

"You have me."

Bryn brushed her lips against his, and it was all he could do to stay rooted in the moment.

"You'll go back to your mom," Bryn said. "Then, six years later, you'll come find me. You'll help me get out of this place. Okay? Hey, maybe that's you in the helicopter." She put her hand on the side of his face. "I can picture you stealing a helicopter."

The device's display flickered at the corner of Rett's vision. He pulled back to look at the names blinking on and off the screen—operatives moving into and out of the field. Time traveling, and returning home to their own times.

His gaze snagged on a name: *Cassie Ward.*

Garrick's sister.

"I have to get her out," Garrick had said. *"I promised her."*

Rett sank. Sank like the dirt could turn into lightless ocean depths and let him go on sinking forever. *She promised, but she never came back for me. My mother never came back.*

He curled his fingers underneath the device. Anger and grief roiled in his veins, churning like the water below.

"She never came," he said to the hot, nerveless air. "She took everything from me when she left me." His anger crested like a wave and he shuddered with the pain of it. "Took everything I needed, because I just needed *her.*"

Bryn wrapped an arm around his shoulders but he shrugged her off.

"I want to go back," he said. "Just once, I want to have what I need."

"We'll go back. You can go back."

The blinking display called Rett's attention. Flashing names—appearing, disappearing.

So many Wards.

Scatter took everything from them, too.

And I was going to smash the device and leave them stranded. They would never have gotten home to their own times.

They'd be like me, no home to go to. No one to care for them. No one to care for.

He thought of Garrick's sister, and the mother who waited for her. The brother who had died trying to save her.

He thought of his own mother, who had never come for him. Who wouldn't even answer his frantic messages. Who had been silent for . . .

Years.

Not just since he'd gone to Scatter Labs. Before.

Before he'd ever gotten the offer to leave Walling. Before he'd asked if he could leave the facility early.

Before any of this had started, he hadn't heard from his mother in . . .

Three years.

The putrid smell of the rotting eggs came back to him, pushed on the wind whipped up by the helicopter blades.

No, he was imagining it.

Because he knew.

He knew why his mother had gone silent. Knew why she had never come for him.

He knew what had happened to her. And he knew that it had happened a long time ago.

The names flickered. Blinked onto the screen, blinked off. Suddenly there was a moment when all the Wards, except for Rett and Bryn, vanished from the screen. When all the children Scatter had taken from Walling were home in their own times.

Rett flipped the power off.

Ensuring that all those Wards were safe.

Safe *until* the device turned back on.

But it never *would* turn back on—

Rett swung the device, smashing it down onto the cliff's edge. Splinters of silvery metal exploded outward, flashing in the sun. A mass of sun-brightened wires erupted from the metal casing. The box hit the rocks again, tumbled and spun, a bundle unraveling. A moment later, all vanished beneath the churning surface of the river, lost forever in the currents.

Rett felt Bryn at his back. He turned and fell wearily against her, almost surprised to find her in his arms. His voice came out ragged in the wind that buffeted them: "We can't go back." And then, with a sob, "She's dead. My mother's dead."

10:12 A.M.

The square building that made up Scatter's outpost seemed mostly to be an excuse for the helipad on the roof. The helicopter pilot and a man in another Scatter uniform led Rett and Bryn down into the dust-muted building and ordered them into a pair of folding chairs facing a metal desk. The pilot pushed paper cups of water into their hands and leaned against the desk to inspect her guests (—*prisoners?* Rett wondered). The pilot's face was brown with dirt and sun, eyes puckered as if with surprise at this sudden break from boredom. Her partner, the one who had earlier directed them into the helicopter, stood swaying in the doorway as if he might run back up to the roof the moment another flare went up. Both wore black uniforms with Scatter's logo showing in white.

Sunlight struggled in through the dust-coated windows. Beyond, the wasteland fell away in every direction, so that Rett felt as if he were still riding in the sky above it. His cup was empty already. The pilot took it and Bryn's empty cup and refilled them at a cooler.

"You said you shot that flare? Just the two of you?" She held the cups out of their reach. Her uniform was rumpled, the cuffs frayed—a change from the pressed uniforms and starched lab coats of Scatter's past.

"Just the two of us," Rett agreed, glancing at Bryn. The pilot and her uniformed friend hadn't seen Garrick's body. The less they knew, the better.

The pilot handed over the cups of water. Rett drained his immediately and the woman refilled it again while Rett tried to figure out why her first question hadn't been, *What the hell were you doing in the middle of our wasteland and how did you get past our walls?*

The other uniformed man fidgeted in the doorway, biting his nails.

"Found the flare gun in the depot?" the pilot asked.

Rett nodded. Bryn tried to shake the last drops of water from her cup into her mouth.

The pilot settled against the desk but her feet wouldn't stop moving, scraping over the gritty floor with nervous energy. "People try to sneak in here from time to time. See what we've gotten hidden away." She gestured toward the windows. "Lots of dirt."

The pilot's eyes flicked from Rett to Bryn, waiting for some cue. "Against the law to get anywhere near this place. Serious business."

She's not angry, Rett thought. *She knows we wouldn't break into this wasteland without more supplies than we've got on us. She knows something's up.*

"Got those clothes from the depot?" the pilot asked Bryn.

"Flare gun, too," added the man in the doorway, earning a glare from the pilot.

"We've established that," the pilot said.

But did *the flare gun come from the depot?* Rett wondered. They'd gotten it from Garrick. He stole a quick glance at the man in the doorway, whose nervousness was written all over his face. *What's he so nervous about?*

"Take off your boot and Sanders will have a look at your ankle," the pilot told Rett. "Nasty limp you got."

"I already wrapped it," Rett said.

"All right. We got some painkillers here—Sanders, go get those."

Sanders disappeared from the doorway and then reappeared with two white pills for Rett. Rett swallowed them without hesitation, draining the last of the water in his cup.

"How about you?" the pilot asked Bryn. "Could swear I saw you limping, too."

Bryn tucked her feet under her chair. "I'm fine."

The pilot studied her for a moment, then Rett. "I've seen my share of strange things around here. Never thought I'd see Scatter's own operatives."

Rett felt the hard pills stick somewhere in his chest. He stopped breathing.

"You get lost somewhere along the way?" the pilot asked. "Don't think you're supposed to be out here, are you?"

Bryn lowered her head to look at Rett from out of the corner of her eye. Rett glanced at her, tried to breathe.

"You got stuck here?" the pilot asked. "Had to shoot off a flare for us to get you? What happened?"

Rett stared into his empty cup.

"The mechanisms in our heads malfunctioned," Bryn said.

It wasn't exactly a lie, even if it wasn't the reason they couldn't get back. They'd never get back now, with Scatter's device smashed and swirling in the river currents. These two didn't seem to know what Rett had done to the device, though.

The pilot moved her tongue along her teeth, thinking. "That kind of thing happened a lot in the early days. When they were still working out the bugs."

Rett flinched at the last word. The pilot didn't notice.

"Hell if I'll ever let them try to put one of those things in my head." The pilot looked to Sanders for confirmation, but the man only stared out the window, his face pinched.

"Lucky you've never been desperate enough to *have* to," Bryn said under her breath. Rett reached for her hand and squeezed it.

"Network's been down all day," the pilot said, oblivious to Bryn's annoyance. "Solar storm. The sun's been pushing huge flares our way, scrambling signals and putting satellites offline. Never thought you could see an aurora this far south, but it was showing half the night. I'll try again to connect to the system, ask HQ what to do with the two of you."

She straightened. Rett studied the floor so his nerves wouldn't show.

"If your"—The pilot gestured at her head—*mechanism*—"isn't working, looks like you might be stuck here. Won't be able to send you back to your own time. Can't guess it matters much, though. Isn't that why they use orphans? Won't matter to you which place you're stuck in."

Rett's anger flared, but he kept his mouth shut. The pilot waited a moment for an answer she realized she wouldn't get, and then she went out through the doorway opposite Sanders.

Sanders jumped to refill Rett's and Bryn's cups again, then hovered as if expecting something in exchange. Rett thought he knew what Sanders wanted.

"He's dead," Rett told him.

"What?"

"The man you were waiting for," Rett said. "The one who shot the flare. Garrick. The bugs got him." Rett's stomach twisted. *As much as I hated Garrick, he didn't deserve that.*

Sanders froze, alarm showing on his face.

"He told us he had a contact," Rett explained. "Someone who helped him get in here? Someone who was going to help him get out?"

Sanders shot across to the other doorway and peered through it, anxious to make sure the pilot hadn't overheard them. Bryn caught Rett's eye, and he could see that he'd surprised her.

Sanders turned back. "He was just a scavenger," he said in a strained voice that made Rett wonder if he were lying or just nervous. "Just wanted some of Scatter's old stuff. I didn't see any harm in letting him take it."

"You mean, for a price." Rett dug something out of his pocket and held it out on his palm: a small, dark rock, marbled with more silver than any of the other meteorites Rett had seen in the wasteland. He thought it must be worth a fortune. "Did he promise to give you some of his loot? Any rocks like these that he might find? He said the alloy inside it is worth a lot of money. What will you do for us if I give it to you?"

Sanders glanced through the doorway again, then darted toward Rett like he meant to snatch the rock. "What were you doing at the depot?" he said in a low tone, ignoring the rock.

"I told you, our mechanisms—"

"Did Wells send you here?"

Rett blinked at him in surprise.

"She did, didn't she?" Sanders bit a thumbnail. "Some of us, we've seen what Scatter can do, and we don't like it." His gaze shifted to the wasteland outside the window. "But you can't take down a goliath like Scatter without first finding a chink in its armor."

Rett's thoughts buzzed. A distant memory floated to mind:

Wells, sorry at last for the part she had played in their misery. She'd driven them to wasteland, left them in the starry hollow. *There's only one way left to do this. You'll have to find it . . .*

"Scatter's armor is gone," Rett told Sanders, and pictured silver shards swirling in river currents.

Sanders stared at him for a long moment. He pushed away the hand that held the rock out to him. "There's a boat. Half a mile south. You can ride the river out, the wall doesn't go across it. Cameras might be out, too, because of the solar storm. So you don't even have to wait for nightfall." He glanced at the door the pilot had gone through, and then smiled at Rett and Bryn as if they were sharing a joke. "Better go now. Won't it be a surprise that you two have vanished? Like those mechanisms in your heads just decided to send you off to who knows where?"

That's not how it works, Rett thought. But if he and the pilot didn't know, Rett wasn't going to tell them. It was as good a story as they were going to get, and it might just be enough to keep the pilot from looking for them.

Rett jammed the rock back into his pocket and pulled Bryn up as Sanders slid a window open for them. "There's water and ration bars in the boat," Saunders told them. He grabbed Rett's arm. "Don't tell anyone I did this."

Rett nodded. He and Bryn climbed out into the sunlight, sending up dust when they landed. They skidded down the embankment toward the wet dirt along the river.

"Stay close to the embankment," Bryn said. "Maybe it'll cut off the view from the windows, and the pilot won't see us."

She pulled his arm around her shoulders so he could lean on her while they walked. They turned along the bend of a river, and the boat came into view in the distance, humped with the supplies Sanders had mentioned. Drinking water, food. Rett felt properly hungry. The churn of nausea and dread had finally calmed.

"Scatter will find out, sooner or later, what we did," Bryn said. "Let's hope that by then, everyone who's working against Scatter is ready to deal the final blow."

The clouds moving behind the distant ridges left streaks like white flags, like banners. Rett stopped to admire the sight. "It's over. The wasteland, its poison. It won't spread anymore."

He pulled the rock out of his pocket. The sun flashed on veins of silver. "I bet I know a conspiracy theory website that will want a look at this."

"Dark Window?" Bryn stopped in surprise. "Nice of you to join in my hobbies."

"We've got enough people taking Scatter down from the inside. Maybe this will take them down from the outside."

"The rock that kills Goliath? I like it. But right now I just want to get down that river, find the interstate, and get as far from this place as possible."

"Maybe if we write to Walling they'll send us a bus ticket," Rett joked.

In answer, Bryn leaned down to reach into her boot. When she straightened, she had in her hand a thick shard of silvery metal. "It came off the device when you smashed it on the rocks. I hid it in my boot when they were coming for us."

Rett stared, transfixed by the shine of the metal. "It's got to be worth thousands."

She held it out to him. "We'll find out."

He slipped it out of her hand to marvel at it, bright against the dirt of his palm.

"I want to share it with you," Bryn said. Her eyes were gray, shadowed with uncertainty.

Uncertain about what? Rett wondered. *That we'll be okay? Or that I want to be with her?*

He leaned close and kissed her. She kissed him back. It came with the same jolt of electricity it had last time, but this time Rett knew for sure she didn't do it for any reason other than that she wanted to.

He broke away, shot through with a feeling too close to the panic he had felt at Scatter 2. When those two dark hungry shapes had loomed. When he had held that device over the sharp canyon rocks and had forever destroyed his chance of going home.

"All those kids are safe now," he said, as much to himself as to Bryn. "Scatter can't make them time travel anymore. They can go back to their families."

His voice caught on the last word.

Bryn circled his waist with her arm. "That's all thanks to you."

"Thanks to both of us." Rett managed a smile that must have looked awful on his weary, dirt-streaked face. "Anyway, it felt good to smash something."

Bryn smiled back, and Rett's heart fluttered. *So rare, that smile.*

He leaned on Bryn and they made for the boat, the sky overhead stretching endlessly in every direction, bright ocean blue.

ACKNOWLEDGMENTS

Thanks to Ammi-Joan Paquette for championing this story and finding it a great home.

Thanks to Ali Fisher, Tom Doherty, Kathleen Doherty, Seth Lerner, Rafal Gibek, Jim Kapp, Heather Saunders, the Macmillan sales force, the Tor/Forge marketing and publicity team, the Macmillan Audio team, and the rest of the Tor team for working to bring this book to life.

Thanks to Katie Silvensky and Charles Hotchkiss for answering my questions about all kinds of unlikely scenarios. (Any mistakes are mine.)

Thanks to Emily Henry, Jo Whittemore, Traci Chee, Regan Kirk, Heather Bouwman, and Gwynne Breidenstein for reading and helping with early drafts.

Thanks to Jennifer Noble for helping me get unstuck.

Thanks to all my Bay Area writer friends for their encouragement and support (and sandwiches and board games).

Thanks to all the amazing Bay Area booksellers who have cheered me on and promoted my work.

And thanks to Jason Peevyhouse and the rest of my family for being awesome.